Mike is in his seventy-third year, with writing among many first loves. Born in Isleworth, west London during the Blitz, and now living a few miles further east along the A4 in Chiswick, Mike's career was in PR and marketing, leaving school aged fifteen in 1958. Marriage and fatherhood in the 1970s followed a dissolute 1960s comprising mainly rock and roll with, very occasionally, sex and drugs.

Mike's career highlights are few but in the mid-1990s he was fortunate to be working as PR manager for the American computer company that gave life to the World Wide Web. Before that, he was in charge of PR for Sam Wanamaker's Shakespeare Globe on Bankside, joining when the project was a £6m hole in the ground. By the time Mike left, his global editorial successes had created an income tsunami, accelerating completion of the timber-framed theatre.

Today, Mike is a grandfather, indulging his love of writing while listening to his collection of 1960s rock and roll, regretfully unable to summon the sex and the drugs.

I Got You Babe

Mike Abbott

I Got You Babe

Vanguard Press

ISBN 978 178465 106 0

Vanguard Press is an imprint of
Pegasus Elliot MacKenzie Publishers Ltd.
www.pegasuspublishers.com

First Published in 2016

Vanguard Press
Sheraton House Castle Park
Cambridge England

Printed & Bound in Great Britain

For my children

CHAPTER ONE

Mark Dean caught his reflection in the window of a shop in Kingsway as he crossed the busy road that took traffic north to Bloomsbury, south to Fleet Street. He enjoyed, appreciated, his stick-thin look, carefully cultivated, after absorbing the fashion pages of *Playboy* magazine for some four years, thanks to Transworld importing it to the UK at 2/6 a copy, a 'Mod look' that was to gain wider currency beyond London a few years later following Steve McQueen's *Bullitt* 'cop caper' movie.

Now blond, but once ginger, his hair was short, manicured and carefully textured around a right-hand parting, the white, non-iron Rael Brook poplin shirt, the Burtons charcoal grey suit, the Dolcis penny loafers, buffed to a shiny black, Mark felt very good about himself despite the inner concerns, if not demons, that asked too many questions about his failure in securing a successful relationship with a girl.

That wasn't of course, why he was weaving his way in the late September, cooling sun towards Holborn's Red Lion Square and Princeton College to begin his very first night school class in six years or so. No, he was en route to study for and pass his 'O Levels' in English language and literature, having been told as a boy in the late 1950s by his teachers that he had no hope of gaining any academic qualification.

But also on her way to Princeton College was Lynda Fowler. Little did she – and Mark – know they were destined to become boyfriend and girlfriend, form a very intense, if short, relationship, one that for Mark was to have far greater meaning, falling in love with Lynda as he did, a depth of feeling he was to eventually discover not reciprocated by her – *One Way Love* as Cliff Bennett was later to put to song.

Lynda was slim but with more covering than Mark's beanpole, her brown hair bouncing off shoulders, looks that said *Barbra Streisand*, an attractive figure, a broad, confident smile framed by lips invariably presented in a muted pearl pink.

Intellectually she was to become his equal but, at first meeting in a class room, then during the break in the Princeton College canteen, he couldn't exercise control over his arrogance, presuming no-one around him knew as much as he did about everything. Clearly Lynda could take him or leave him and in the approaching darkening winter nights Mark's interest in her was piqued by not just her quiet disdain but her intellectual prowess when they did occasionally engage in conversation.

While he worked as an account executive for one of the UK's leading PR agencies, Welbeck, Lynda worked for British Railways as a shorthand typist in the offices over Liverpool Street station. He was west London born and bred, living at home with parents while she was from a town on the Cambridgeshire-Norfolk border where her father ran one of the local shops. Now in London, Lynda rented a cell-like room at Warwickshire House, Gower Street, a hostel originally created in the 1920s for the young lady sales assistants employed at Bourne and Hollingsworth.

For Mark, sex was, like out of work actors, 'resting'. The activity with girls he enjoyed in the years immediately following leaving school in 1958 was now in suspension. He'd been sexually active for four years before becoming jaded, easily slipping into celibacy for some two years. It was a state he found welcoming, enjoyable as he monastically drew satisfaction from diverting his time and energies to reading novels, devouring Pan and Penguin paperbacks from Elizabeth Gaskell to Solzhenitsyn, Orwell to Greene, Pinter and Wesker to *This Sporting Life* and *Dr No*, consuming from front page to back, *The Guardian, Observer*, occasionally the *New Statesmen* and tuning into *That Was The Week That Was,* making the odd foray to the theatre to see *Beyond the Fringe, Oliver!* and a small clutch of cerebral films from directors like Joseph Losey and Roman Polanski.

Lynda was a lot less pretentious. Yes, she had read well but didn't pretend to know, or wish to know, the sinewy story of Orwell's days of Spanish republicanism, or his being down and out in Paris. And was careful not to discuss politics, feigning ignorance when, in reality, she was as well versed as anyone, including Mark, but opting for that very British trait of easy silence, fearful of upsetting any or all with cogently presented views.

She slowly, almost insidiously, tackled and unpicked his arrogance. Across two nights, Tuesday and Thursday, English language and English literature classes, in fifteen-minute tea breaks, they began to tenuously engage each other, sparring in low-key intellectual conversation. Lynda matched him with statements, information, facts that had him on the metaphoric ropes, struggling to regain his composure, regain the initiative or, at least, stand on his own two cerebral feet and invent an alternative route for their gentle mental workout.

Then one evening, in their tea-break conversation, came the revelation that Lynda liked Frank Sinatra, as he did. It was the first real area of common ground. His interest in the singer began in the mid-1950s when he would tune into American Forces Network on his parents' old Cossor valve radio. There, amongst the rock and roll music from Bill Haley and Elvis Presley would be regularly played Sinatra tracks, someone he'd never heard before, knew nothing about. Yet in his voice was something anarchic, impish, iconoclastic that appealed to him.

There, he would tell himself some five years later, was the spark that fired his own desire not the follow the herd, not to be too keen to jump on bandwagons, not to follow worn paths, look for those wild and overgrown. It was, he would later admit in his thirties, the moment - aged thirteen - his pathology forged his need to guard his individualism, his desire to value being private, secretive, alone.

"My dad is a big fan, had a lot of his records. I grew up listening to Sinatra, just got to like him." Her voice was lighter, relaxed. They had found something not to over-intellectualise, something to enjoy without need for artifice. "What's your favourite Sinatra LP?"

Mark enjoyed the question. "I haven't got them all but I do play *Come Fly With Me* and *Songs for Swinging Lovers* a lot. What about you?"

"Same as you, as well as *Come Dance With Me.*"

"What about *I Remember Tommy*?"

"Haven't got that one."

"Would you like to borrow it?"

She hesitated. "OK, but I share a room with another girl so I hope she doesn't play it when I'm not there. Wouldn't want it scratched."

By the end of October Mark had difficulty in telling himself he had *not* fallen in love with her. She had stirred his emotions and he now found himself asking what exactly were these warm, positive feelings he felt for her? Yes, he admired her. Yes, he enjoyed her intellectually battling with him, more than matching him in their jousting. Yes, she was attractive. Yes, she was engaging, friendly, occasionally revealing a vein of sexiness.

And he began to increasingly think about her. At the end of Thursday evenings he walked away from Princeton College, and Lynda, with a jaunty "Bye, see you next week!" telling himself he'd not see her for another five evenings. He had to do something about his feelings.

But she gave no hint of interest in him. Lynda said nothing to indicate she was in a relationship. He believed she wasn't since she spoke freely about going home to her parents every fortnight for the weekend. And no mention of a boyfriend, current or past. Perhaps she wasn't interested in men. Perhaps she wanted Platonic relationships.

He was to let October slip to November, then mid-December, before finally generating the necessary courage to ask for a date. The last week of evening school was approaching before shutting down for Christmas. It was going to be the Tuesday but, no, he couldn't muster enough to suppress his fear of being rejected, the embarrassment for him, and her. In the break on Thursday evening he offered to buy her a tea, as he had many times before.

And as he returned to the table where she sat he blurted it out: "Would you like to see a film?" She smiled broadly, clearly welcoming the question. "Yes, I'd like that." Wow! Phew!

His mental processes went into a helter-skelter vortex. "What about this Sunday?" *Sunday*? Why did he say Sunday? Why not Saturday? Because, he told himself, she might be busy, have another date, on Saturday. Her smile dropped. "Sorry. Can't do anything before Christmas. I'm away on Friday, not back until New Year's Eve. What about that weekend, when I get back?"

He dug his pocket diary out and flicked to 1965. "OK, Sunday January 3rd?"

"Yeah, let's make it then..."

"Can I have your number?" He stalled, frightened that he sounded too forward, like a stalker. "I'll need to check the films on then and call you to make sure you're happy going to see one."

"And agree where to meet." She sounded positive. "I'll have to give you the Warwickshire House number, and my room number.

There's a telephone on the landing so they will put your call through to that. Not very private, I'm afraid."

He smiled. *Not very private, I'm afraid.* He liked, appreciated, the assumption he might want to say something personal, private, to her. Of course he did. But he wouldn't say anything that would compromise what he was already hoping, anticipating, would be a very successful relationship. His first girlfriend in two or so years. A lifetime for a male in his early twenties.

Mark wanted to ask what she was doing for Christmas but bit his tongue. Too intrusive. But Lynda came to the rescue. "What are you doing for Christmas? Away?"

"No! Christmas is always at home, always a family affair. My mother's brother will be over for the whole three days. My dad's sister might also be there for Christmas Day lunch. Very noisy, bit of a drain!"

She laughed. "Yes, just like my mum and dad at Christmas."

* * * *

The first date was a film, *Topkapi*. The second date was a movie. And the third. All at the weekend. It reflected Mark's lack of imagination but in equal measure his desire to 'take things easy', not rush, let any serious relationship between them build naturally, not forced or engineered. Inside him, dying to be articulated in a conversation with her, was his wish, his desire, that their relationship become deep-rooted, lasting.

Lynda broke the weekend-only cycle with the suggestion they eat an evening meal mid-week in the restaurant at Warwickshire House. Male guests could not be taken to residents' rooms but they could be guests for a meal in the very public dining area. The menu was basic, the food very British in presentation, no alcohol, just fruit juice, tea or coffee, and they sat at table shared with others, severely inhibiting

14

their conversation. Afterwards, despite the February cold Lynda suggested a walk in the Bloomsbury evening landscape. She tucked her arm into his and they walked, talked, window-shopped, shared their love of Sinatra, Ray Charles, enjoyed comparing notes on the movies they'd seen before they had met, both learning about each other's tastes, views, likes, dislikes.

At the end of their stroll, back at Warwickshire House, they would tuck into a nearby recess and kiss. At first tentatively, then on subsequent evenings with more passion. On one of their walks they discovered Newman Passage, a poorly-lit L-shaped, dead-end mews, populated by unlit offices. They nestled into a recessed, green-painted door way and progressed to kiss in an intensely passionate fashion. Mark was excited, encouraged, by Lynda's positive response. She was clearly attracted to him, enjoyed his intimacy, his passion.

Walks to Newman Passage and torrid *snogging* sessions became a regular occurrence and, to celebrate her twenty-third birthday in early March, they went to a small Greek restaurant near the British Museum for an early evening meal, followed by their walk to Newman Passage. There, with growing confidence sexual intercourse was attempted for the first time. It was vertical, both of them sunk in the doorway's recess, Lynda hitching her skirt, Mark unzipping his trousers, easing out his erect penis, pulling her knickers away. They laughed self-consciously at its initial messiness, masking it by kissing very passionately. With each occasion they grew in both seriousness and proficiency, enjoying their adeptness at upright sex.

And at the Tolmer cinema they sat on the back row where, on a second visit, a mid-week date soon after her birthday, in the welcome darkness, Lynda slowly, gently, expertly, massaged his penis with her mouth bringing him to a climax, Mark ejaculating into her mouth for the first time, Lynda nonchalantly swallowing all his semen. He was pleased. She had clearly brought other men off in her mouth and had developed a very satisfying technique. When she brought her head up they kissed, her tongue depositing a dollop of spunk in his mouth.

Soon after Lynda told him she was looking for a flat.

Mark's eyes brightened: "For us both?"

"No, just me."

He was crestfallen. He had planned to suggest they look for a flat to share but held off, concerned he might frighten Lynda off the relationship, deciding instead to wait for the 'right' moment' Now she had shot his fox. "Why not the two of us?"

"Let's leave it for a while before we do that. It's only been three months and if we live together it might all go wrong."

Mark couldn't understand her logic. Indeed, there was none but he knew he shouldn't interrogate her, deciding that once she moved, settled in her new surroundings, she'd invite him to live with her.

A few days later she told him she was moving to a flat in Kilburn, one of the girls at the hostel had a friend sharing a flat with two other girls, looking for a fourth. Lynda accepted.

"Kilburn? Not a great area, hope you will be OK."

"It's not that bad. It's a house, on a quiet street. I have my own bedroom, and there's a garden. One of the other girls is involved with a guy called Baz, who owns the house."

Do you know anything else about them?"

"No, just their names, June, Anna, Kay. Our age. They all work in offices, friendly."

"So, what's the street? I can check it on my A to Z, see what tube station is closest."

"Kilburn is the closest, on the Bakerloo. The street is Chatsworth Road."

16

CHAPTER TWO

Lynda's move from hostel in Bloomsbury to room in a house in a residential side street in cosmopolitan Kilburn was an emotionless clinical exercise. But then, she had moved so many times before during her two years in London. She had two large Samsonite suitcases and carefully laid her clothes into their cavernous bowels until both were full, with no need for additional bags. She had learnt to travel light in London.

Kay's boyfriend, Paul, offered to give her lift in his Mini, and he duly arrived on the Saturday afternoon at the designated time, negotiating both suitcases into the back of the car. She placed him as late twenties, excitingly good looking in a late 1950s Dirk Bogarde, Rank charm school way, with dark hair, Brylcreemed straight. And very friendly, monopolising the conversation, his voice an impressive simulation of received pronunciation the McDonald Hobley way.

For the move Lynda had put on her Levi's but sitting alongside this handsome male, she'd wished she'd opted for a skirt to show off her legs. The next time, she told herself. And gave no thought to the fact that she was in a relationship, just as Paul was. She certainly liked Mark. He had, after all, walked into her life at a time when she had become a hermit, tucked up in the foetal position in the dark of her cell in Warwickshire House.

Mark had rescued her, turned on a light, lit a fuse, reminded her that there was life out there. She just required some motivation. And Mark taking an interest in her was just it. But he wasn't the *be all and end all.*

Paul spoke with a confident ease, painting a picture of the Chatsworth Road house as one brimming with fun, parties, loud music, *groovy* neighbours, "...and just a few minutes from Hampstead and the *super-cool* people who hung out at the Flask."

The three girls were at the front door when they arrived, exuding a loud, warm, welcome. Paul lifted the suitcases up the stairs to Lynda's room as she followed him one of the girls shouted they had a party to go to that evening, recommending Lynda dig out her 'glad rags'.

She hadn't told the girls about Mark, unsure whether that might work against her getting the room. They hadn't asked either. It went unsaid that she either had a boyfriend or would collect one at some stage in the near future. Now she felt pressure to say something since she had agreed with Mark that he arrive at the house in Chatsworth Road at seven.

Lynda turned on the stairs and shouted back to the hallway. "I've asked my boyfriend round here. Hope that was OK. We're going for a meal, somewhere on Kilburn High Road."

A disembodied voice shouted back. "That's OK. Have your meal and join us in the Flask. We'll be there til closing time." The voice trailed away, then struck up, "What's your boyfriend's name?"

"Mark."

"OK, look forward to meeting him. If you're going for a meal, try the Sombrero. It's sort of Spanish. Not bad."

"Thanks." Lynda shot up the stairs, into her room where Paul had put both cases on the bed. "What does Mark do?"

"Oh, he's in PR. Works for a PR agency."

"OK. Be interesting to meet him." He hesitated. "June and Anna don't have steady boyfriends and they're constantly trying it on with me."

"Really? In front of Kay?"

"Yes, they have no shame, they're very randy girls. They'll certainly try it on with Mark. I shouldn't complain, take the pressure off me."

"I hope they don't try anything. I've only just arrived, don't want any problems!"

* * * *

As instructed by Lynda, Mark turned right out of Kilburn tube station. He stopped, looked and took in the busy street scene. The large number of West Indians reminded him of Notting Hill Gate. It was just past seven. He was running a few minutes late but knew Lynda wouldn't be too upset. It would soon be St Valentine's Day and he'd bought a large box of Terry's All Gold chocolates, in a special hearts-decorated sleeve. He hoped Lynda would appreciate it.

He pulled a scrap of paper from his A to Z. *89 Chatsworth Road. Off Christchurch Avenue. KILburn 6327.* He found Christchurch, then Chatsworth, walking briskly along the straight road, trees showing the first signs of spring, and got to 89 in a few minutes. The semi-detached house had once boasted a manicured front garden but was now over run, in need of a lawnmower. A few mock Tudor beams adorned the front of the property, its once pure white stucco now a grimy abandoned facade.

His finger pressed hard on the doorbell. *If you don't swing, don't ring.* No, it didn't say that but Hefner's friendly advice outside the Playboy Mansion in Chicago was something that rootlessly roamed his head, seeking a home.

Mark heard a pair of feet clumping towards the door. It swung open. "Hi! You must be Mark! I'm June! Come in!" Her smile was broad, warm, friendly. And in a nanosecond he took in her Cathy McGowan look, dark auburn hair, fulsome at the sides, like fattened panniers, inches short of her graceful neck, shapeless blue shift dress that touched the knees.

He stepped forward, she stood aside, turning her head and shouting, "Lynda, Mark's here!"

No Lynda but the hall filled with two young females and a young male. "Hi Mark, I'm Kay!"

"And I'm Anna!"

"I'm Paul!" He shot out a hand, "Welcome!"

"Come through." Kay broke into a wide toothy smile, "We're all having a coffee!"

"Lynda! Mark's here!" Mark turned. That was June again.

He followed them to the kitchen, taking in their look, their personalities. Kay and Anna were blondes, and he told himself Kay sported a Lesley Gore look, while Anna was more waifish, more Petula Clark.

The kitchen was square, white tiles, red and grey linoleum on the floor, elderly oven and squat refrigerator hardly big enough for one person's food let alone four. "Sit Mark. Coffee OK? Milk?"

He sat, smiled, increasingly uncomfortable as he came to the conclusion he was over-dressed in a suit, white shirt and tie. But it was how he had dressed for every date with Lynda, not thinking that there was any other way, such was his naivety.

"So, what do you do Mark?" Paul said it with a smile but Mark felt it was framed in a *justify yourself, impress us* challenge.

"I work for a PR agency called Welbeck and I've got some technical clients, one of them is Atlas Lighting. I get journalists on newspapers and magazines to write about good lighting." He paused. "And you?"

"I work for Kit Kat, insurance underwriters. Work in the City, not too far from where Lynda works."

"Oh, right..." Mark wasn't too impressed with that nugget of information. He knew Paul had helped Lynda move from Warwickshire House but was unsure of how and why they had got to talk about where Lynda worked. What else of a personal nature had they discussed? Silently Mark cursed his worries, equally unsure of how to control his obvious lack of self-confidence and put it into some perspective.

Mark's regressive introspection hit a wall when Anna pushed a mug of tea across the table towards him, "You look a bit like Steve McQueen with that short hair cut, and your face."

He laughed. "Really? Don't know much about him. Saw him in *The Magnificent Seven* but not much else."

"He's in a new film, *Cincinnati Kid*. You should see it, Lynda will take you I'm sure, and do a comparison. Which one's Mark, which one's Steve McQueen."

"It's about a gambler, a bit of a coincidence," added Paul. "The guy who owns this place runs gambling casinos out in the sticks and holiday places."

"Hi, there!" Mark turned, smiled, got up, as Lynda walked into the kitchen. He moved forward to kiss her but she swerved and left him standing, snubbed, feeling foolish in front of strangers. His eyes followed her as she went to make herself a drink. "You look great!" He was unhappy, bordering on angry but couldn't deny Lynda did look good in a black lace top and black leather skirt, neither of which he'd seen her wear before.

"OK, so what's the plan?" Lynda said it with some force, as if they hadn't discussed the evening or had and he'd been wishy-washy over what to do. He decided to be equally forceful. "We agreed we'd go for a meal. And you mentioned there's a party in Hampstead. Let's go to that afterwards..."

"Yes, come with us to the party!" June broke in. "Meet us in the Flask after your meal. We'll be there 'til closing time then we can all go together. Bring a bottle!"

"You can get a cab to the Flask," added Paul. "Not far from here, not expensive."

Mark felt a little more comfortable, a little less intimidated. Paul was clearly trying to help him relax. "OK. We'll eat then cab it over to the Flask. Do the cabbies know the Flask? It's not a pub I know..."

"Yeah, all the cabbies know it." Paul smiled a smile that said *'you haven't been around much have you?'* He hadn't of course and was glad Paul had kept his comment unsaid. But knew he had to learn fast, get hip, get groovy. Become 'gear'.

He'd read the few snippets about the London scene reluctantly, almost apologetically, published in *The Guardian* and *The Observer* to realise that the groovy and hip went to the newly-arrived-from-Paris discotheques, *Scotch of St James, Blaise's, Phone Box, The Scene, Bag O'Nails*. And each week he bought *What's on in London* to be frustrated to read nothing on hip London, cool London, just the elderly, corpulent London of white middle class theatre, cinema, and restaurants. And, of course, Raymond's Revuebar and the '*We're Never Closed'* Windmill.

Now there was definite pressure to get tuned in. Lynda had shown no interest in 'hip' London in the four months they had been going steady but he sensed that was about to change. She was no longer hiding away in a hostel room. She was now out in the big, bad world, living in a house sharing with other girls. Party girls.

He told himself to get with it, get hip, get tuned in. He had to get abreast of fashion. No more turning out in his business suits for dates. He had to visit Carnaby Street, King's Road, and Soho to check out what shirts, jackets, trousers, shoes were being worn by the trendy, the Mods. And he cursed himself for letting go. In the early sixties he'd been as trendy as any fashion leader with his Levi denim jeans, sitting in the bath full of hot water to shrink-fit them, the white Levi's, button-down Ben Sherman shirts, 'Italian' jackets, Dolcis all leather penny loafers, Annello and Davide Cuban-heeled shoes. Regular visits to Vince Green's boutique in Carnaby Court to acquire some well designed, cut and made trousers. And be intrigued by Vince's obvious homosexuality. Then he lost interest.

And now, five years later, he couldn't escape having to re-invent the wheel, re-invent himself by going back to what he used to wear in the days of the Blue Moon Club on a Sunday night and Cliff Bennett and the Rebel Rousers.

Yes, and the music! He and Lynda hadn't shown much interest in the records played on the radio. He hadn't bothered to tune into any of the pirate radio stations. Sure, there were many top ten records he enjoyed hearing on radio, and he tuned into '*Ready Steady Go!*' every Friday evening. But he hadn't bought a single rock or pop record in almost five years, back in the days when he bought *Billboard* every week, and his last visit to the Ealing Blues Club was pre-historic.

* * * *

"Seem like a bunch of nice people." Mark regretted the observation the second it escaped from his mouth. And he hated using 'nice'. His English teacher in the mid-1950s had told him there was no such word as 'nice'. There was of course but *nice* was a lazy word when with a little imagination a more ambitious synonym could be mined and deployed.

Lynda was a little less warm. "Well, I've only been there a few hours. I'll have a better idea in a month's time. I've shared flats before and it can be a nightmare. We'll see."

"I hope in a few months' time you will agree to us living together."

23

She sighed. "Mark, we've only been going out for a few months. You've got no idea if we'll stay together."

"Why, you planning to break us up?"

"No, silly, I'm not but I've had boyfriends before and they've never lasted. They lose interest, or I lose interest."

"Well, it won't be me losing interest. This relationship is very important to me. I've fallen in love with you."

She looked at him, disbelief on her face. "Have you? I wish you hadn't. Not just yet, anyway."

"Well I have, I'm glad to say."

Lynda ignored the comment. "What are you eating?"

"Spanish omelette and chips. You?"

"The same."

"And a glass of red wine."

"I'll have white, if they have it."

"So, who's this guy who owns the house? Paul said he owned gambling casinos."

"I don't know much more than you. The girls told me he owns four houses, rents them all out, lives in St John's Wood..."

"...and he runs gambling casinos."

"Don't think they're casinos. Sounds like he runs roulette tables in bars and clubs in places like Clacton and Great Yarmouth. And one in Wisbech, near my home town..."

"Nothing more?"

"Don't think so. I haven't had much chance to discuss him. I've only been in the flat a few hours. When I learn more I'll let you know."

"Playboy are opening a club in London next year. Then one in Manchester. You should see if you can be a Bunny."

The sudden change of subject jarred on Lynda. "What made you think of that?!"

"Not sure..."

"They're only interested in girls with massive bosoms and ridiculously small waists."

"Well, that's you!"

"I don't have a large top, nor a small waist. As well you know. I'm very average."

"I think you'd make a great Playboy Bunny!"

She smiled and challenged him: "OK, you find out more about it and I'll see what they say."

"Who knows, you could become a Playmate of the Month!"

Lynda glared: "There's no way I'm being photographed naked!"

Mark joked: "Shame!"

"By the way, I've gone back on the pill."

Now it was Mark's turn to suffer a jarred change of subject moment. "Gone back on? I thought you were already on the pill!"

"No, I wasn't. I came off a few years ago when it gave me bad backache..."

"So when we had sex you could have become pregnant."

"Yes, except we had sex just before my period, and I was wearing my Dutch cap. So my becoming pregnant was unlikely."

"Dutch cap? So, we wouldn't have had sex if it was any other time of the month?"

"Of course not! You didn't offer to wear anything so I had to protect myself..."

"But I did have some Durex gossamer johnnies..."

"...Which you didn't offer to use. Keep them, you may need them!"

"What do you mean?"

"I mean, Mark, I may have to come off the pill if the backache returns."

"Will it?"

"It might. The backache might be a thrombosis so I have to come off straightaway. It's what my doctor said..."

"Your doctor? You didn't go to a birth control clinic..."

"No. No need. Better to go to my doctor than a stranger."

"Won't he tell your parents?"

"Tell them what? That I'm on the pill? My mother's on the pill!"

"Is she? How old is she?"

"Not that old! She's only eighteen years older than me! And she and dad like their sex!"

"What, you discuss their sex life with them?"

"No, of course not! I just know."

"And I'm very glad to be back on the pill!"

Mark said nothing but gave her a look of grave concern. What was she saying? He wanted to ask for some clarification. But this was sex. And this was London. And he had to be *cool*.

"We'll have to buy some wine for the party." Was all he could manage.

"We can get that when we get to the Flask," was Lynda's response. "If we ever do. Have we got to order at the counter in this place, or is there a waiter?"

* * * *

The Flask was packed to overflowing with people standing outside despite the evening chill. Mark took an instant dislike to the place. It played to all his prejudices about trendy places, ersatz cool with its Victorian oak panelling, pictures on the wall of *olde Hampstead* and *olde Flask Inn*, the single bar area heaving with young people breaking sweat as they enjoyed themselves, working hard to have 'fun'.

"Lynda!" It was Paul's voice and as they surveyed the hundred or so heads they eventually saw him, standing against a far wall, his hand waving them onwards. "What are you drinking?"

Mark looked towards the bar – "Let me get them." - as Lynda joined June, Kay, and Anna, standing against a wall, hemmed-in by a group of half a dozen Mods, girls in red and orange stripy dresses, calf-length, white tights, block-heeled shiny shoes, looking like they were off the cover of *Nova* magazine. And accompanied by three guys who were the exact clones of Brian Jones, all aping the look he affected for the cover of the Rolling Stones' *12 x 5* LP.

"I'll help you," Paul motioned towards the bar, hidden by a phalanx of young bodies, all animated in light-hearted conversation, some smoking, blowing blue fog towards the stained brown, once cream-coloured, ceiling. "The girls are all drinking Coke. What about Lynda?"

"We had wine at the restaurant. Guess I better get her another."

"No, Mark, don't. Get her Coke, with ice. It won't take long to drink as wine. We're going to head out of here soon. Too packed tonight. And we've got a party to go to."

"OK. What are you having?"

"Pint of bitter for me. Young's special."

Mark quietly sighed. He hated beer. No taste. Warm gnat's piss, watery, characterless, designed by the brewers to make sure the drinker remains sober enough to buy three or four pints before the bladder finally explodes with shame. He decided to order a whiskey, a single with lots of ice.

Getting to the bar wasn't the problem Mark had imagined. Getting back was. He and Paul hugged to their chests glasses full of volatile liquid that threatened to pour down shirts and jackets, weaving their way through a solid wall of bodies completely unaware of their desire to get the other side of the pub with the minimum of delay and loss of expensive alcohol and Coca Cola.

Lynda looked at her Coke with disdain: "For me? I didn't ask for Coke..."

"No, you didn't." Mark felt superior. "But Paul suggested it, a quicker drink than the wine I was going to get you. He said they weren't staying much longer here, too many people here, not very enjoyable, going on to the party early."

"And what's that? Whiskey?"

"Yes."

"Why not get me one?"

"You don't drink whiskey."

"Gin. Gin and tonic would've been nice, Mark."

Nice. He grimaced, internally, hiding it with a rictus smile, asking himself why she used *nice* when he had explained to her with some force its redundancy. He slid his arm around her waist and she smiled, reciprocating, placing her arm around his waist. He kissed her quickly on the lips, both of them appreciating, enjoying, the modest display of mutual affection.

"So where did you two meet?"

Mark showed no hesitation, "Night school!"

"Different!" Paul laughed. "Where?"

"Princeton College, near Holborn station."

"And you're both studying the same things?"

Lynda joined in: "Yes, both of us. English language and literature..."

"O level," added Mark. "I didn't do GCEs at school so really just catching up. I want to be a member of the Institute of Public Relations and I need O levels for that."

Paul turned to Lynda, "And you?"

"I missed out at school. I was ill for some time and got left behind so failed my O levels. Knew I had to get them at some stage..."

"...no night school near where you work, Liverpool Street?"

Mark became increasingly uncomfortable at Paul hogging the conversation but remained mute. Lynda however was supremely relaxed. "There was something near where I work but I was living at the hostel so needed something close to that. Didn't want to spend too much time getting home late at night." She paused. "What about you? Did you go to night school?"

Paul smiled. "No, I didn't! Did lots of cramming late at night but I managed to get to university and scraped a boring old BA. Don't know how I did it, spent most of the time at university either getting Brahms and List or stoned!"

"Stoned?" Mark was intrigued. "We used to do French Blues..."

"...speed," cut in Paul. "Did those when we had all night parties, or getting through exams..."

"...yeah," added Mark, keen not to be left out of the conversation, "they certainly kept you *compos mentis*."

"Now," he lent forward, whispered on Lynda's ear, "we smoke. Pot. Got some stashed away. When we get back from the party we'll turn you on..."

Lynda smiled. "Sounds interesting. Look forward to that."

Mark was less than impressed at what he saw as Paul's flirting with his girlfriend. In front of his own girlfriend. Didn't she care? He drifted towards the girls.

But his thoughts were too easily diverted by the word 'pot'. He remembered a very long and thorough article in *Playboy* magazine he'd read some years before on pot, 'hash', or cannabis. It traced its use, distribution amongst black Americans, specially jazz musicians, then to the rest of the population, along with its affects on the body and mind, its addictive properties, and its *'coolness'*.

He knew it was illegal but had never got anywhere near able to purchase any 'pot'. But now he was a few feet from someone who not only had actually smoked it, and was promising they'd all get to experience it later. And he recalled taking the French Blues – amphetamines – that he only took because he didn't want to lack physical energy or mental alertness when the prospect of sex with the girl he'd just met offered itself.

It rarely did. Girls didn't do sex until they were in a relationship and knew enough about the boy to make it difficult should he opt to dump them. But there were the odd occasions when sex was offered on a first date and greedily accepted, invariably a messy *shag* in an alleyway, or darkened corner of the cinema car park, her back against the wall, knickers down over stocking tops, the girl better able to roll on his erect penis the johnny he had pulled from his jacket pocket. A dozen pelvic thrusts, tongues deep inside her mouth, moans, and a minute later he had climaxed. He'd remained erect inside her, still kissing passionately before he finally went flaccid and time to remove from her and slide the wet, revolting rubber off his penis.

Mark returned from memory lane in time to hear Paul entertain Lynda further with his knowledge of what journalists were calling *recreational* drugs: "There's a guy in the States I read about and he's got hold of this drug the army's been using. You take it and your mind goes into brightly coloured jungle, lots of leaves, clouds, sun. Then it wears off and you apparently remember everything."

Lynda wasn't impressed. She was censorious: "Sounds like something out of *Alice in Wonderland.* Like children running off into fantasy land. And if you're off into a fantasy land how do you stay safe, protect yourself while your head's in this lovely jungle?"

"Don't know, Lynda. I've only read about it in the *New Scientist*, can't find anything else on it. Just know it's called LSD, can't remember what that stands for..."

"...pounds, shillings, and pence."

They both looked at Mark, nonplussed at the banality of his remark, his pathetic attempt to crack a joke. He felt an idiot but quickly recovered, "It stands for lysergic acid. Think the Americans are giving it to their soldiers in Vietnam, drugging them up before battle, taking their minds off dying..."

"Where did you read that?"

"Probably *The Guardian*. Think the name of the guy in the States is Timothy Leary. He's at a university somewhere, experimenting on students with the drug."

* * * *

The party was five minutes from the pub. Everyone managed to squeeze into Paul's Mini. The three girls sat, squashed, in the back while Lynda sat on Mark's lap on the front passenger seat. Her black leather skirt was knee length but, collapsed on Mark's lap, Lynda could not stop it from riding up, revealing to Mark's delight – doubtless Paul's too – her well-proportioned thighs, wonderfully coated in the expensive sheer, chocolate coloured Wolford stockings Mark had found in the hosiery department at Selfridges, and a gift from him as one of her March birthday presents.

Friends of Paul's friends were the party hosts. The party venue was the two top floors of a four storey Edwardian house on Haverstock Hill, accessed by a daunting external metal staircase. They left their coats in the boot of the Mini, and as they climbed the girls got the slim heels of their stiletto shoes caught in the open, filigree design of the metal steps and landings.

They deposited their bottles of wine in the kitchen on a table already heaving with alcohol in its many forms, using the plastic cups provided to each secure a drink, and wandered into a large room, dimly lit, with about thirty people, some dancing, some standing talking or looking on, blankly. "What's upstairs?" asked June. "Bedrooms," answered Paul. "Must be. But as I've never been before, don't know. Could be a dozen Pakistanis." They laughed, and eased their way around the room, single file, the men in the room engrossed, clearly trying to understand who of the four girls were *attached* to the two men.

31

Mark decided to answer their unsaid question, gently pulling Lynda into the crowded bunch of dancers. This was the first time he'd danced with Lynda in the four months they'd been dating. But, then, it was the first party they'd been to. And he knew he couldn't dance. Lynda could. She moved in time to the music, absorbing its rhythm, slipping easily, gracefully, into a sensuous sway. Unlike him.

Mark cursed. He just couldn't coordinate his arms, hips, legs and feet. And he felt like an idiot. Yet, five years earlier he could *jive* perfectly to rock and roll, like a professional. He had mastered the *Stroll*, the *Continental*, even the maddening, embarrassing *Mashed Potato* and was perfectly capable, enjoyed dancing to the increasingly melodic music that followed rock and roll.

And he enjoyed the party music that he wished he could dance to. He enjoyed the music played on radio. Indeed, his radio was permanently tuned to *Radio London*, the pirate radio station he preferred to *Radio Caroline*. He hadn't bought a *Top 10* record in three or more years yet tuned into both Radio London and BBC's *Top Twenty* hits show every Sunday afternoon.

Mark knew and liked *Glad All Over, Mr Tambourine Man, Midnight Hour,* and every single from the Beatles and the Rolling Stones, aware that 'R&B' was a developing distinct genre, exemplified by records he enjoyed listening to such as *Can I Get a Witness* and *You Really Got a Hold on Me.* Mark agreed with himself: he had to get back into rock music, get switched on, tuned-in. Just as he had to get *cool* on the clothes he wore.

Lynda persevered dancing for almost six records – some fifteen minutes - before she decided she'd had enough of the elbows that pulverised her sides and back in the tight melee of dancers. As *Rescue Me* faded she decided to rescue herself and pushed into Mark, "That's enough for now. I'm getting bashed to death here!" He wasn't too disappointed, "Let's get our drinks. They're over here."

Lynda followed him through the mass of animated bodies, "I'll catch you up. I must go to the loo."

"OK, see you in a sec." And she was gone. He collected his plastic cup off the side board and sipped, looking around. The crowd was definitely Mod, achingly hip, all early twenties, very well turned out, office workers to a man, and woman. But despite being told by June he looked like Steve McQueen he found it difficult to begin to see how he could be as hip as the other partying men around him.

Mark walked the periphery of the room, enjoying the music and the atmosphere, looking for Paul, Kay, June and Anna but if they were in the room they were lost in the heaving mass. And where was Lynda? Still in the loo? In a queue, waiting to get in? Or, mission accomplished, en route back to him? Or, dallying somewhere else? Before he could consider looking for her, his eyes met those of a young male with a broad smile, tousled hair and square jaw. "Hi, it's Mark Dean, isn't it?" Mark struck a guarded pose. "Yes, it is. Have we met?"

"Yep, at Atlas Lighting. I work in the publicity department, on events. I was in a meeting a few months ago, when you were there..."

Mark relaxed, "Sure, I remember...you're Glenn."

"Good memory! Glenn Hardy..."

"Small world! You know the people running this party?"

Glenn laughed, "No, not personally. But my girlfriend does. She knows some of the people. One of them works at her place, and some of them were at party I had a few weeks ago at my place."

"Where's that?"

"Just down the road, Haverstock Hill. And you?"

Mark ducked the question, "Well, I thought I was going to share a flat with my girlfriend but she had other ideas." Then he lied, "So, I'm looking for a place."

"You're living at home then?"

Mark had to drop the pretence. "Yep."

"Well, your girlfriend will probably tell you, if you want a decent place you'll need to share. Look for a big place, like this, your own room but good furniture. Avoid the bedsits, they're rat holes. And don't use an agency. They'll charge you a week's rent for finding a place you could find yourself. They're crooks, real parasites!"

"Well, if you hear of anything, let me know!"

"Sure. And if you fancy meeting up a few of us from the office go to the Coach and Horses in Greek Street for lunch every day. Turn up at one and you'll see us. And the people who run *Private Eye*, Richard Ingrams and Willie Rushton. They drink there every lunch time..."

"Sounds interesting! I'll try to get down there soon. Shouldn't take too long from where my office is, just a few minutes from Oxford Street, then walk down to Greek Street..."

"OK, hope to see you there." Glenn paused. "Is that your girlfriend?" Mark turned round. No, it wasn't. It was June. "Hi! You OK? Who's your friend?" Mark smiled, "Good to see you. Seen Lynda anywhere?"

"Yes," June paused. "She's being chatted-up by some fella. You better go and rescue her."

Lynda wasn't impressed as she saw Mark working his way towards her. She and the male were on their haunches, leaning against a wall, deep in conversation. But as Mark pushed his way through the bodies, Lynda slid her spine up the wall, 'til she was upright, "My boyfriend," as an explanation to him as he looked up, confused, then also sliding his back up the wall.

Mark was bright, "Hi! Wondered where you got to." Lynda didn't reply, instead turning, "Got to go. Nice meeting you!" The guy looked annoyed, disappointed. Mark guessed he'd clearly thought Lynda was at the party on her own, not with a boyfriend. And he wondered whether she'd encouraged him to think that, or not got round to explaining she had a boyfriend.

"Let's dance!" He pulled her towards the mass of bodies. She smiled. He wondered why. Was it a smile of her superiority, having proven her attractiveness while all he could do was display his nervousness, if not jealousy, at her ability to excite the interest of other men?

They danced for five records before *Like a Rolling Stone* came on and proved impossible, other than as a slow dance, and Lynda shook her disapproving head and turned. He followed until she stopped in the kitchen. "Drink?" She handed him a plastic cup and he looked for a bottle of red wine. None but there was a Watney's *Party Four* bitter and a Courage *Jackpot Bitter*. "No wine. You like some beer?"

"Sure. What are you drinking?"

"Got to be beer. There's no wine."

She moved to a corner of the kitchen, a conspiratorial guise on her face. "That guy I was talking to..."

"Yeah, who was he?"

"Called himself Mouse..."

"Strange name."

"He designs clothes, got a shop in Portobello Road. Runs it with two other guys."

"What, you mean a men's shop?"

"No, women's stuff!"

"OK. So, you're going there?"

"Well, yes. They've got a special party there on Thursday. They design their own stuff, one off, not mass produced like Marks and Spencer. Marianne Faithful is one of their customers. And Sandy Shaw. And some new singer called P P Arnold. Do you know her?"

"No, never heard of her. So, you're going to this party?"

"Think so. He said come along. I'll see what the other girls think."

"I could come with you..."

35

"Don't think so, Mark. It'll be a girls' thing. You won't be that interested. You'd be bored."

"I doubt it. I'm very interested in fashion, read *Nova* from front to back."

Lynda gave him an incredulous look but he persisted: "I could stay with you Thursday, go straight to work Friday morning from Chatsworth..."

"Mark," she sounded impatient. "Let me check first to see of anyone else wants to go. I'll let you know."

"OK. What's their shop called?"

"Think he said *Little Red Rooster*."

"Oh, the Rolling Stones song."

Lynda aborted her response when she heard Paul's voice. He was on the other side of the kitchen, hand in the air beckoning them, "We're gonna go..."

"What, right now?" Mark sounded surprised. "We've only been here for a few hours..."

"Yeah, it's an OK party but we want to get back to Chatsworth, have our own. You stay if you wish but we're high-tailing it..."

"We're coming!" Lynda strode forward, stopped, grabbed Mark's hand, "Come on, let's go!

* * * *

What was the living room at 89 Chatsworth Road, at the front of the house on the ground floor, had become what estate agents were calling a 'kitchen dining room' with the removal of the wall that had previously separated both. The one room now had depth and at the kitchen end there was the table at which Mark had earlier sat, while at the lounge end there was a settee and two armchairs framing a large low coffee table, a rug on the carpet. Lynda and Mark watched as the four girls sat on the rug, around the table. "Sit down, join us,"

June implored, patting the space alongside her. Lynda fell to the floor and Mark eased himself alongside Kay with Anna on his right.

Paul entered the room from upstairs, turned off the lighting, "What music shall we have?"

"Same as we always have!" piped up Anna, pouring some *rosé* onto each of four glasses.

"MJQ! Great choice Anna!" Paul opened up the radiogram and within a minute the music, soft, low, filled the room, Mark recognising the melliferous tones of the MJQ's *No Sun in Venice.*

In the limited light from the street lamp that permeated the curtains Mark made out a tin box in Paul's hands. This was it. Mark's memory recalled the *Playboy* article on marijuana. Paul was clearly going to make what was known as a 'joint'.

Paul placed the tin on the table, opened it up, removed a packet of cigarette papers. Mark watched in magnetised fascination as Paul stuck two papers together and filled it with what looked like in the dimness ordinary tobacco. But Mark knew it wasn't. He knew it was cannabis, marijuana, pot, hash, dope. He'd read about it and was now about to experience it.

The cigarette paper was wrapped and sealed around the illicit content. It was long, and thick. Paul placed the end between his lips and lit the end. And inhaled in what Mark thought was a theatrical manner. He passed the cigarette to Kay on his right and as she inhaled Paul asked Mark if he'd smoked any dope before. "No, never!"

"Well you inhale, fill your lungs with the smoke, hold it there, count to ten, then exhale." He paused. "We call these things 'joints'."

"Yeah, seem to remember that from my article." Mark was looking forward to it and watched as Paul began to manufacture a second joint, while Kay passed the joint to Lynda. She inhaled, held the smoke deep inside her lungs and blew it out after ten.

37

"And you will feel very relaxed, very happy, no cares in the world," Paul commented.

"And randy!" added Kay. "Very!"

June passed the joint to Mark and he inhaled long, held the smoke for ten seconds and blew out, passing the joint to Anna. He felt no immediate relaxation, nor happiness or a lifting of cares. But it was a gradual sensation. And as the second joint was sent by Paul in a clockwise direction arriving in his fingers from Anna he inhaled again willingly, deeply, and as he exhaled his body and mind quickly witnessed all the sensations Paul had promised: elation, numbness, light-headedness, a sensation of flying, his cares and worries evaporating, a growing relaxation and sexual desire building inside his mind and body, enjoying in the secretive dark the erection developing somewhere deep beneath his trouser zip.

Mark's thoughts of making torrid love to Lynda quickly built like some rampant culture, in the sun on a laboratory window ledge. Although his grasp on reality was fast fading he watched in the near-darkness as Lynda clearly enjoyed the sensations, head back, eyes closed, opening only when June or Kay passed her a joint.

"This is good stuff." It was a quiet, subdued, disembodied voice from somewhere in the narrow parallel lines of darkness and dim light, female, a comment from someone, obviously high, enjoying the experience. And quickly followed by another female voice, "Must be the best yet, Paul."

"Hey Lindy-lou, d'you mind if I borrow your boyfriend?" It was Anna and Mark smiled as he felt her hand fall gently on the front of his trousers. He wanted to make love to Lynda but she was on the other side of the table, directly opposite, the half-light on her Barbra Streisand looks, the hair mounted high on her head, the black lace top and the matching bra it revealed, the leather skirt, the legs in their sheer nylon stockings.

Paul rolled a third joint, lit it, inhaled and passed it to Kay. "Somebody put the other side on." June rose, slowly, falling forward onto Lynda, both girls giggling at their incapacitated state, June whispering in Lynda's ear. She bumped her way around the settee towards the radiogram, turned the record over and launched into side two of *No Sun in Venice.*

Lynda took the joint from Kay and inhaled, holding it in the air for June to recover. She did and, hitching up her skirt, climbed over the settee, rolled onto the floor, joint still between her fingers. She inhaled again and passed it back to Lynda and as she did June began to slowly unbutton Lynda's blouse. Eyes closed, inhaling Lynda said and did nothing as June's tongue darted out to lick the skin above the black lace bra.

Mark became mesmerised. In the excitingly erotic semi-darkness he watched as another woman licked his girlfriend's breasts, his girlfriend clearly enjoying it. God, he wanted to make love to Lynda there and then, fuck her until she cried, screamed, in unparalleled ecstasy.

But she was on the other side of the table. And Anna had unbuckled his belt, was slowly unzipping his flies, Lynda pulling again deeply on the joint, holding the smoke inside her lungs for the suggested ten seconds, then exhaling, "Of course! He's all yours!" Lynda gave Mark a look that said, '*you're mine and I can loan you out at any time'.* "Tell me how good he performs Anna," she laughed. "Mark him out of ten!"

Mark was almost totally stupefied, but still able, in his soporific state, to understand that sexual license was a very welcome by-product of being *high as a kite.* He watched Lynda as she in turn followed Anna's actions and she blew him a kiss as his erection was eased from his clothing, a powered thrill running along his spine as Anna dropped her head and closed her mouth over the end of his long, hard shaft.

Her mouth was as warm as Lynda's around the head of his penis but, in his spaced-out state, the sensations provided by Anna's tongue and teeth were of a different order and welcomingly complemented the hedonism of his increasingly exhilarating condition.

Despite being high as a kite, Mark was still able to recognise the growing sexual ecstasy of Anna's fellatio and placed a hand on her head, gently forcing more of his erection in her mouth while alongside him Mark became aware that Kay was now fellating Paul. And opposite Lynda had removed her blouse and was unclipping her bra, a hand on June's neck as she kissed one then both of Lynda's nipples.

In the pleasant fog of marihuana and a building sexual ecstasy Mark remained calm, totally at ease, as he watched June raise herself, take Lynda's hand, pull her up, and lead her from the room into the darkness of the stairs. And insulated from anything approaching reality he said nothing as, suddenly without any hint, Anna and Kay deftly swopped places. '*Oh yes!*' he murmured as a fresh, new set of sensations embraced his erection, his hand stroking Kay's neck as she very quickly took all of him in her mouth. She was remarkably more energetic than Anna and he quickly realised he would climax sooner than later. And when he did, some few minutes later, it was an incredible experience, joyous, ecstatic, erotic, and deeply satisfying, Kay moaning her pleasure, sinking down on him as if to ensure none of his sperm went amiss.

He remained inside her mouth until he became irreversibly flaccid. She pulled herself up and he realised that he was no longer high as a kite. The marijuana had worn off. Or perhaps the oral sex was some form of purgative. Kay sipped her rosé, kissed him on the cheek. "For a smallish guy you're quite big. I hope Lynda appreciates it."

Mark ignored the comment. "Where is she? Where did she go?"

Kay smiled, "Don't worry! She's upstairs being fucked by June."

Mark was concerned. "I didn't know June was a lesbian."

Kay laughed. "Don't be stupid, Mark! There aren't any dykes or queers anymore! If you like sex, you like sex. You do it with anyone, everyone!"

"Really?" Mark was unimpressed. And alongside him Paul gave out a soft '*Yes!*' as he climaxed in Anna's mouth. Mark got up but Kay grabbed his arm. "Don't go up there, stupid! Leave them!"

"She's my girlfriend!"

"Yes, OK, but you don't own her! She doesn't own you! You didn't buy her in *Exchange and Mart*!"

He fell back, confused.

"When was the last time you had a girlfriend, Mark?"

"Why?"

"Because it looks like it was a long time ago. Life's changed, girls don't run around like slaves these days, you know!"

"No, I didn't know."

"Well, you do now! Stay here until Lynda comes back down. If she does."

"What do you mean?"

"Well, she and June might just sleep it off. You'll have to wait 'til she gets up in the morning."

"Where do I sleep?"

"Here. Wait 'til we're all gone. You can then crash out on the settee."

"Or you can sleep with me Mark." Anna smiled but the suggestion had no sincerity, no hint of latent desire, no element of seriousness and Mark was able to easily dismiss it, knowing full well that if Lynda woke up and discovered him in bed with Anna it would be curtains for their relationship. And now he had a headache, a pain at the back of his skull, rapidly developing. He silently cursed the booze and the dope.

* * * *

Mark woke up quickly, almost bolt upright, as if someone had run an electrical current through his body. The settee was forgiving and comfortable but sleeping in his clothes wasn't his idea of *fun*. And it was cold. Then he saw Kay. She was making coffee. "Hi!"

She turned. "Hi, sorry if I woke you. Just doing a coffee. Want one? It's not the real thing, just the powdered stuff."

"Thanks, I will. Black." He got up, ran his hand over his hair. "Feel like the bottom of a bird cage!"

"It was a great evening. Really enjoyed it. Good to have you and Lynda there."

He walked towards the kitchen end of the *kitchen-diner*. "So, are you and Paul boyfriend-girlfriend?" He paused. "Can't work out your relationship."

"Don't try." She laughed. "Yes, we are but we're not engaged, we're not going to be together forever, we're just two people enjoying life!"

"So, love doesn't feature..."

"Of course it does! But we're not possessive."

"Strange..."

"No, it isn't Mark. We are not like our parents. Don't know about your mum and dad but mine were born fifty years ago and they have a totally different outlook on life. Got married young, have children, live in debt for the rest of their lives, not much get up and go, not much fun. They live exactly how their own parents lived. But that's not for us. Not now..."

"So now it's 'no' to marriage, getting settled?"

"Well, now life is different. Young people aren't going to live their lives with no opportunities, no money, no fun. We've got to get off our backsides and start taking our own decisions, making our own opportunities, not the ones our parents force on us."

42

"I haven't met many people who think like that. You're in a minority. Only in the pages of *Nova* magazine."

"Maybe Mark but things are changing and there will be more people who think like me and Paul. And Anna and June. I bet Lynda too!"

"Where is she?"

"She's in her own bedroom..."

"With June?"

"No. She's on her own..."

"I'll take her a coffee."

"Don't wake her Mark and start giving her the third degree, it's only eight. Just relax, take it easy. Roll with it..."

"Why are you up so early?"

"Just am. I'll finish, go back to bed and we'll sleep to midday." She hesitated. "Suggest you get into bed with Lynda, have some sex and sleep to mid-day as well."

"Which room is hers?"

"Last one on the left."

He climbed the stairs and gingerly opened the bedroom door. The room was dark but some daylight crept in around the periphery of the curtains. He closed the door slowly, quietly, and tiptoed across the carpeted floor to the bed, placing the cup on the bedside table. He began to undress, stopping only when he saw Lynda's underwear on the floor. He lifted up the expensive Wolford stockings he'd bought her, placing them across the padded stool at the dressing table.

Naked, he pulled the bedcover and sheet slowly away, Lynda stirring, and he eased himself into the bed. She, too, was naked, on her side, back to him. As he took up what little space was on offer Lynda sleepily murmured, "What are you doing?" He hesitated, slid an arm around her waist. "It's your boyfriend. Remember me?" She didn't answer but moved her arm and brought her hand onto his hip, sliding it until it reached his penis. Lynda took it in her hand and it immediately grew. She turned. "Hello boyfriend. How are you?"

He immediately saw the love bite on her neck. "Well, thanks. Much better for seeing you."

She opened her eyes, kissing his lips lightly, then with more passion, his tongue searching inside her mouth before she broke away. "So, boyfriend, how did you enjoy being sucked off by my new flatmate?"

He kissed her again. Her breath was hot, dirty with sex, alcohol, and pot. "It should have been you Lynda, not Anna or Kay." His hand moved serpent-like across her stomach, two fingers sliding effortlessly inside her vagina. Lynda hummed her appreciation.

"Kay?"

"Yes, Kay. Couldn't believe it. She took over from Anna. Like something out of a Godard film!"

"Sucked off by both my new flatmates..."

"And you and June?" He pushed his fingers deep inside her.

"Oh, we had a great time..."

"Didn't know you were a lesbian."

Lynda laughed. "There are lots of things you don't know about me..."

"I hope I get to learn everything..."

"Stop talking, boyfriend. Take your fingers out, get on top and do me!" Lynda parted her legs to the far sides of the bed. Mark pulled the sheets back, lifted his body, dropped into the white sheet space between her legs, surveyed her brown mound of pubic hair, and manouvered deftly to bring the head of his penis to the pink lips of her vagina, effortlessly sinking his fully erect penis inside the open, welcoming channel which, Mark observed, was wonderfully relaxed, warm and lubricated.

Lynda let out a little gasp, placed her arms around his shoulders, kissing him with a building passion as he animated his hips with a

44

piston-like action, slow and considered at first but rapidly gaining speed as his lust consumed him, egged on by Lynda's ever louder moans, until he eventually climaxed, giving out a triumphant '*yes, oh my god yes*!', they both kissing each other with wild passion as he filled her womb with his semen.

Mark crashed back alongside her. He said nothing to Lynda but wanted to tell her it was the first time they had made love in a bed. Not upright against a wall in Newman Passage.

CHAPTER THREE

"Ravi Shankar! It's good isn't it?"

In the daylight, Lynda didn't recognise Mouse. He was taller than she remembered. Frighteningly thin, in a white shirt and worn, green jacket, a round face, a near-constant smile on his face, topped with wild, unkempt sand-coloured hair.

Lynda broke into a smile. "I've never heard that type of music before. I like it. Very soothing!" Lynda accepted his hand as Mouse walked her into the well of the shop. "This is June. We're flatmates. And June was at the party Saturday."

Mouse stepped back. "Wow! Groovy!" He took in June's look. She was in a floral orange coloured mini dress, white stockings, and white leather flat-heeled shoes. "I do like that!" Mouse had a large, white smile. "Where did you get that?"

June greedily consumed the attention. "You're going to hate me but I got it from a catalogue. Freeman's."

"Oh yes, Twiggy and Freeman's!"

"I'm sorry, but this is boring old me!" Lynda interjected with a self-conscious grimace, as she was painfully aware that her dark brown knee-length shift dress was dramatically less than fashionable. Just time-honoured British plain, and lifeless.

"Don't knock it! Thousands of dolly birds wear that look! It's not ours but *Little Red Rooster* is really for girls who want to be different, lead the way, make the trends!"

Lynda laughed, recognising the sell. "So what's here for me?"

Mouse took them both to the back of the shop where two racks presented a sparse collection of dresses. One offered a choice of thigh-length mini dresses in bold, op art-influenced diametric patterns and shocking florid colours, while the other rack was hung with knee and calf-length dresses in busy, tightly-packed, delicate patterns with floral and bucolic influences, square cut necks framed by beads that scintillated in the reflected light.

Lynda hovered over the bucolic dresses. They appealed to her. They were safer than mini dresses or skirts. She was a country girl at heart and these dresses were what she might have seen on people in the Cambridgeshire villages and fields had she been born in 1840.

June appeared with a glass. "Champagne."

Lynda took the glass. "What do you think? Good looking clothes."

"Stupid prices, Lynda! £30 for a dress! Got to be a millionaire!"

"Well, that's why they sell to Marianne Faithful and Sandy Shaw."

"They're not here! Lots of hangers-on but no pop stars."

"Press people are here. Mouse and his mates are trying to get the shop publicity, get it noticed. They want to sell more. can't always rely on pop stars..."

"Lynda, June!" It was Mouse's voice. They both turned and saw him, agitated, thread his way towards them. "Girls, can you do me a big favour?"

"Depends!" responded June.

"The press boys want a photograph of some of stuff on real girls! Can you help? Just take a few dresses and change? They want to do it outside, in front of the shop, and they've got to go soon."

"OK," answered Lynda. "We'll do it. But it'll cost you!"

"Thanks! Promise I'll make it up to you." He smiled, relief written across his face. "Only one changing room, I'm afraid. Behind that." He pointed at a dark blue curtain that hung on a brass railing that projected from the wall and followed a rectangular shape.

"Not very big, Mouse..."

"Sorry about that but if you could both change at the same time it'll save time."

Lynda and June looked at each other and laughed. "We'll try!"

"Wear these!" Mouse hand led them both a mini dress each and they disappeared behind the curtain.

"If you don't mind waiting 'til it's all over there's a little party afterwards. You'd be welcomed. Not at my place, it's at Nick's. He's one of the other guys who runs *Little Red Rooster*. Just round the corner. Powis Square, if you know it."

"Thanks, we'll probably go." June's disembodied voice was cheery, positive. "Can we keep the dresses?"

"Sorry girls, not these." The sorrow in Mouse's voice quickly changed. "But I'd design and make you something. Miniskirts in denim."

"Sounds good!"

"My thanks for doing the pictures."

Outside there were two photographers, each unshaved, rotund middle-aged men, scruffily dressed, cigarettes in their mouths. They leered at the girls and insisted the short dresses were hitched even higher, Lynda stopping at her stocking tops. They mixed plate cameras - with their unwieldy magnesium flash bulbs - with compact single lens reflex cameras, and in five minutes they were finished. "Thanks girls! That was lovely!" One lent forward, his chin stubble tobacco stained: "You girls fancy earning some good money?" He paused. "I do work for *Mayfair, Spick* and *Span* mags, *Reveille, Tit-Bits*. They're all looking for photo models with that *girly next door look*. Good money!" He handed them both a business card. "Give me a call. Eh?"

Then they were gone.

"What papers were they from?" asked Lynda. "Have to keep an eye out for them."

"*Daily Express* and *Daily Sketch*. Not *The Times* or *Telegraph* I'm afraid but beggars can't be choosers!" Mouse hugged them. "Thanks girls. That was a big favour!"

"Creepy guys," shivered June. "Specially that one who asked us to model for him!"

Mouse looked concerned. "Why, what did he say?"

"Wanted us to pose for him. Said it was for *Mayfair...*"

"Ah, the girly mag! Strictly for the dirty old man brigade. You girls need to be in *Town* magazine, far more classy and tasteful!"

Lynda showed some interest. "Is it like *Playboy*? My boyfriend reads *Playboy*. Quite like it but don't think I'd ever model in the nude!"

Mouse stood back. "You girls both have fantastic figures! If you're interested let me know. I have a contact on *Town*."

"I am!" June was strident, bold. Lynda laughed, added her agreement. "If she is, then I am."

Mouse looked pleased. "See what I can do!" And moved off into the throng of guests.

"Do you fancy going along to the Playboy club, see if they'll have us as Playmates?" Lynda gave June a naughty smile, leading the way back to the curtain that passed itself off as a changing room. June responded with a similarly cheeky smile, "Why, are you?"

"Mark suggested it, said he was going to find out more about it." Lynda closed the curtain and both unzipped their dresses "Where's the club?" June ran a finger around Lynda's navel, then down, across the plain white nylon of her suspender belt.

Lynda slipped her dress over her head: "Park Lane." She pushed June's hand away. "Not here! Get dressed!"

"What did Mark say to my love bite on your neck?"

"Nothing."

"He must know we made love..."

"He does. Probably thinks it's a one-off, down to us all being high on that stuff we smoked."

"And is it a one-off Lynda?" She ran her finger over the love bite. "Or are we going to enjoy ourselves again?"

"Yes, June, we are going to enjoy ourselves again. But that's what it is. Just sex, June, so don't get any ideas. I'm not a lesbian, June."

"Didn't think you were. You swing both ways."

"At the hostel I had a couple of girls and we had sex. But that was only because we couldn't find men. I enjoy sex June. Men, women."

"Then when we get back you must come to my room. I've got a dildo. I want to screw you."

Lynda smiled. "Have you? I like dildos."

"And what about a threesome at some time. You, me, Mark?"

"What, you want to screw Mark?"

"Course not! You and him, you and me. He can watch. Or join in!"

"I'll ask him."

Lynda felt some concern. June was beginning to behave in a predatory fashion. The sex with her in the early hours of Sunday was more to do with the influence of the cannabis and a latent desire to state for Mark's benefit she wasn't to be taken for granted. She was her own woman. But June now appeared to assume Lynda was a ready bedmate. Now June wanted to strap on a dildo and penetrate her. Too fast, too soon Lynda concluded.

And treating Mark so dismissively wasn't good. He'd done nothing to warrant her toying with him, like a cat with a mouse. He'd rescued her, and she had to rescue him. Without damaging him, and them, in the process. She knew he wanted to break with his cloying working class background. He had said as much. He was already in

50

a white collar job, a sort of junior managerial position that broke with his father's own family history of the men receiving a threadbare Edwardian education that readied them only as good as labourers and navvies.

Lynda told herself she could help lift him further. Not marriage but support in all but name. She decided to ask him to live with her at Chatsworth Road.

But she had to make it known to Mark this was no rehearsal for marriage, no apprenticeship for wedlock. She had to be free. She was not to be enslaved cerebrally or physically by their de facto *one-on-one relationship*. Nor by anyone. Independence was key. And she knew living as a couple with Mark was almost completely at odds with her desire for personal freedom. It was a contradiction, an oxymoron.

It shouldn't be impossible. Just difficult, Lynda told herself. Mark wasn't a brute. He was intellectually sound. His parents were Socialists, people friendly. Mark himself had been in the Young Socialists, the Campaign for Nuclear Disarmament. Yes, he had left both organizations as he grew in maturity but now, he said, he was a Fabian, a believer in social justice, equality, and a developed regard for an individual's individualism. She hoped so.

* * * *

It wasn't so much a party as a gathering. Mouse introduced Lynda and June to his *Little Red Rooster* partners, Nick and Toby, and the half dozen others in the room. They all sat in the anticipated circle as two joints went in opposite directions. Lynda inhaled deeply on the fat tube of weed, determined to look like she'd been smoking *exotic cheroots* all her life, not the fact there was only her second joint.

She willingly succumbed to the cheroot's lift, its calming, floating, magic carpet ride. And said nothing when Mouse took her hand and, as June had done a few nights earlier, pulled her towards a bedroom. They kissed, gently at first then with a growing passion, Mouse making it known he wanted penetrative sex, she making it known she had no interest in a stranger's erect penis in her vagina. "No, Mouse, can't," she lied. "Time of the month." Instead Lynda energetically masturbated him as they torridly kissed before she finally took him in her mouth for his orgasm.

He seemed pleased, stroked her neck, murmured some words of appreciation. After a suitable interval she got up and left the bedroom. She looked at her watch. It was almost midnight. She tapped June on the shoulder, "I'm going. You coming?"

"No, think I'll stay."

"OK, see you in the morning."

Outside Lynda became aware that Powis Square was worryingly run-down with abandoned furniture, ovens and mattresses littering the pavements. Head down she walked quickly away, not sure of where she was going but clear there was a busy road a few hundred yards ahead. There she saw a road sign, 'Paddington Station ¼' and walked energetically past it, looking back every few seconds for a cab. She breathed a loud sigh of relief when one finally appeared. The cabbie said nothing as she got in but looked with some suspicion at her in his mirror. Must think I'm on the game, a tart thought Lynda. She fell back into the seat, closed her eyes. In less than ten minutes she was outside the house in Chatsworth Road.

There was always a different atmosphere in the office on a Friday. The glorious weekend beckoned and thanks to union pressure no-one in white collar jobs in British Railways had to work a Saturday morning. Not without a massive *time and a half* payment. The only fly in the ointment was Lynda's boss. He made it obvious he fancied her despite being middle-aged, over-weight and married with children.

She had encouraged him. Concerned about her job security she had succumbed a number of times, when she had accompanied him to British Railways' regional conferences, engaging in breathtakingly physical sex which, she had to admit, she enjoyed. Then, one Christmas after a long lunch with wine and whiskey, a few months after getting the job as his secretary, in his office, light-headed and giggly, she had removed her knickers, gingerly placed them around his erect penis and began to masturbate him then, at his behest, she took it in her mouth and brought him off. He kept her knickers and, sober, she went home naked beneath her dress, annoyed at herself at allowing the episode to develop but left with mixed emotions of humiliation, and a undeniable excitement and enjoyment.

Another occasion was again in his office when they were working late on a project document. After dinner in a nearby Indian restaurant, where he gave her a matching silver necklace with a cross, and ankle chain. Back at the office he ceremoniously clipped both on her, one around her neck, the other around her left ankle. Lynda giggled with a disturbing mix of eroticism and embarrassment as she fell to the floor beneath his desk and slowly, lovingly, fellated him to a climax that she had to admit to herself she had enjoyed, the rare event and excitement of a man filling her mouth with warm sperm.

He had been brought up in the same part of Cambridgeshire as she and every Friday littered his conversations with references to where in her home town and surrounding country she'd be enjoying the weekend.

Lynda had not told him of Mark, nor that she'd moved from the hostel to a flat-share. She'd told personnel but they clearly hadn't told him.

Every Friday she indulged him, accepted his invitation for lunch for lunch in the Eastern Hotel but was always careful not to hint that they might slip upstairs to a room for sex. And now she had a boyfriend Lynda was becoming increasingly unhappy at this less than attractive 'personal' relationship with her boss, especially as she'd be seeing Mark later that evening.

Lynda had it planned. He would come straight from work to Chatsworth Road, spend the evening with her, maybe stay the night, then go home. But return late afternoon Saturday. Stay the night, and all day Sunday. Maybe Sunday night. But up early Monday morning for work.

Now that she was living in a flat, not a hostel, she had so much more freedom. Their relationship had much more freedom. And she wanted him to live with her at Chatsworth. If the others were agreeable.

If they were then he'd share their bedroom, contribute to the flat's costs, and have to recognise the girls' need for privacy. If it didn't work out then...well, then, there'd have to be a re-think. Maybe then they'd live together in their own flat. Or maybe it'd be the end of their relationship, the end of Lynda and Mark. Right now, with her leering boss in front of her, across the lunch table, she didn't want the end of Lynda and Mark. She wanted more of it.

CHAPTER FOUR

Between getting home and Mark arriving Lynda had no time to broach with the girls the suggestion that he live with her and, by definition, them. Instead she had a quick shower, ran to her room and dressed in another of her shapeless shift dresses, stockings, high heels, put on eye shadow, mascara and lipstick. And a broad, black-coloured Alice band in her hair.

She slid her arm inside his, said nothing of her plan, as they walked along Kilburn high road in the pleasant warm evening air, stopping at the Golden Egg restaurant to hastily eat omelette and chips before a smart walk to the Kilburn State cinema where the Beatles' second film *Help!* had arrived.

"Very entertaining!" commented Mark as they made their way out of the cinema.

"Looks like they were all high on drugs," added Lynda, squeezing his hand as if to say *'we're in the same drugs club as the Beatles.'*

They walked back along the high road, stopping at the Black Lion pub, with almost half an hour before closing time. It was full, very busy, a fug of grey tobacco smoke in static multiple layers reaching to the ceiling. There was nowhere to sit, forcing them to stand, and as Mark got them both cider, Lynda claimed the side of a column for them to lean against.

Lynda leant into Mark and whispered. "I was going to ask the girls if you could live with me in the flat."

Mark was genuinely surprised, gave her a quizzical look. "Really?! What brought that on?"

"You don't want to?"

He lent forward and kissed her lightly on the lips. "Of course I do, darling." He paused. "Why can't we live in our own place?"

She sighed. "Let's take it slow, Mark, not rush things. Let's see what living together in the flat is like first. If it works out then we can look for our own place..."

"Are we in love with each other? I'm in love with you. As you know."

"That's what I want to see. I really do like you but not sure it's love, Mark..."

"I want to marry you."

"I know you do, Mark. But..." she hesitated. "But, we are really young. Why do you want to get married? It's what our parents did, Mark. Do you really want to be like them?"

"I'm not sure Lynda. One half of me wants marriage, the other half wants to be single..."

"I want to see something of the world before I get landed with a mortgage and kids. Don't you?"

"Sure..." his response was cautious. Mark knew only too well his desire for marriage was motivated by a lack of self-confidence as much as it was by his love for Lynda. And he equally knew that marriage probably wouldn't deliver much else other than a dramatic, further deterioration in his confidence.

"I'm surprised, Mark. With your intelligence I'd have thought you would want to avoid what our parents did and stay free." Lynda slid her hand inside his jacket and squeezed his midriff. "Don't you want to see something of the world? I want to see Australia, Canada,

Cape Town. I don't want to be stuck with a mortgage, scratching around for money, too broke to see a film or go on holiday..."

"I happen to be in love with you, Lynda!"

Lynda sighed. "Are you really? Or is it infatuation, confusion? You haven't had that many girlfriends?"

Mark ignored the remark, despite its essence of truth. "So we live together, sharing your room, at Chatsworth Road?"

"Yes. As long as the others agree. I've only just moved in. They might tell me to get lost."

"Yeah. Can't see them being that happy, having a male about the place."

"Why not? You'll have to pay your share of paying the bills. And that means their share goes down. They won't say 'no' to that!"

"And if we don't get on each other's nerves, kill each other, we move into our own place?"

"Yes, Mark, that's the idea." She prodded him playfully. "But don't you dare tie me down to a date."

He laughed. "Let's say October or November."

"Don't!"

"When will you ask them?"

"This weekend. You've got to be there."

"Sure!" He squeezed her waist. "Drink up! Let's go!" And as they weaved their way from the pub to the street, *sotto voce* he sang: *Help I need somebody, not just anybody...*

* * * *

Apart from Carnaby Street, of which he was deeply suspicious, Mark had little idea where to look for *gear* clothing, *hip* and *cool* jackets, trousers, shirts, shoes. Yes, he adored the Dolcis range of penny loafers and told himself he would never be seduced away. But the rest of wardrobe, what little there was of it, consisted of charcoal grey suits bought from Burtons, John Collier, or the Fifty Shilling Tailors. They were bought for work and were non-threatening to the point of boredom.

Not like the suit he'd bought from John Temple in 1960. An almost silent, mid-green with muted stripes, selecting in stark contrast a post box red lining to the jacket, with ridiculous affectations on the cuffs and turn-ups. Now, five years later, it was an embarrassment that firmly remained in the wardrobe, never to be seen again.

He summoned the courage to ask his more hip work colleagues where to buy *groovy* weekend clothing. They gave him a few leads. Take Five was a favourite but one came highly recommended by the coolest of the office males. It was The Ivy Shop. And it was in Richmond. *Richmond*? That wasn't the centre of cool, Mark told himself. It was a suburban town in Surrey. How could Richmond be *cool, gear* or *groovy*?

The shop was tucked away on a side street with an unassuming double front framing a recessed door. Mark gingerly pushed the door open and was immediately welcomed by the subtle, seductive, pervasive scent of worsted woollen suits and jackets. Its richness enveloped him and when one of the two sales assistant approached him Mark willingly steered himself towards a sales killing.

Mark's head contained a mental list of three items to purchase, jacket, slacks, and shirt. But he knew his meagre finances wouldn't go far at such a *gear* emporium as The Ivy Shop. Unless he paid in part cash and part credit card. And pushed at work for a substantial salary increase.

He fingered through the jackets that hung like fruit on a straining bough, held in a recess in the shop's wall, stopping at one that brought together a palette of intimate, vertical pinstripe rainbow colours, presented on a dark blue canvass. Henley Regatta without the affected, obnoxious stripes, he told himself.

Slacks were simple. Grey flannel. Plus a black leather belt. The shirt was a choice of Ben Sherman, Brooks Brothers, Arrow, or Hathaway. He dismissed the Ben Sherman. He already had two, bought a few years earlier from a hole-in-the-wall shop at the Piccadilly Circus end of Shaftesbury Avenue. The button-down Brooks Brothers Oxford weave in blue appealed, triggering a recall from a fashion spread in *Playboy* magazine.

Gear, cool, groovy, he told himself as left the shop, a bulging *The Ivy Shop* bag held tightly in his hand, and headed towards the station, the cost of his purchases sinking ever deeper inside his head. How will he pay off his credit card?

And what about music? He knew he had to get hip, get himself up-to-date, and wondered if the *New Musical Express* and *Disc* that he'd religiously bought five years earlier was still published, page after page still full of publicity agents' handouts, still with as little genuine interest in popular music. No point in buying *Melody Maker,* as good a weekly musical newspaper as it was. Or *Downbeat* magazine. Neither had any interest in rock and roll music, just modern jazz. He told himself to tune more into the *Caroline* and *London* pirate radio stations, and any other radio stations he could find on his dial. And he would refresh his relationship with Hazel, daughter of the owner of the local record shop. Hazel would know the current hot pop music trends, and any around the corner.

* * * *

Mark checked his look one last time in his bedroom mirror. The new jacket, shirt and slacks looked very impressive. He hoped Lynda would agree. He left home with a cheery 'goodbye' confirming with his parents that he wouldn't be back until late Sunday.

He was buoyed by Lynda's decision to embark on their living together, albeit him sharing her room at the flat. He wanted them to live together in their own place but with Lynda's resistance to the suggestion, for the time being, living with her in the Chatsworth Road set-up was far better than his current situation, one that embarrassed him - early twenties, still living with his parents. It smacked of laziness and cheapness, he told himself, a sure indication of a rooted lack of imagination.

"Hey! You got some new clobber!" Anna beamed a wide smile as she opened the door, a knowing look on her face, one that Mark was sure said *enjoyed sucking you off the other night* but, instead, her mouth let forth an energetic "Groovy jacket!" And she swept into the hall, towards the kitchen, leaving Mark to close the door. "Lynda! Mark's here!"

"OK! I'll be down," came Lynda's voice from within her room.

Mark cursed, asked himself why again Lynda wasn't ready to meet him, why he had to sit in the kitchen with her flatmates, trying not to look uncomfortable. It didn't enter his head that he was not only an unsociable type but someone who lacked the skills to communicate at ease on a social setting. He was fine at work where there was no margin for *niceties*, just an undiluted concentration on the job in hand.

"Mr Cool! Great jacket! Where did you get it?" June gushed, quickly followed by Kay, "And the shirt. Looking very good, Mark. Great taste!"

He smiled, limply, "You like it?"

"Sure we do! The jacket looks like a college or university. Is it?" Kay lent across to inspect the vertical stripes.

"It's Ivy League. No particular university, just a style."

"I like it! I must get Paul to get some new threads. Where did you go?"

"The Ivy Shop in Richmond. Coolest place in town."

"So, where you and Lyndy-loo going tonight?" asked June, an accusative look on her eyes.

60

"Maybe go see Donovan. He does a regular show at a pub near Goodge Street..."

"Donovan? The folk singer?" June looked surprised, as if watching Donovan perform revealed a lack of enterprise and imagination. "What happened to him? He had a few hits then disappeared."

"Well, he's still around." Mark responded, careful not to sound too much like someone selling tickets to a show no-one wants to see. "I've never seen him but got his new LP the other day and it's not bad..."

"Poor man's Bob Dylan isn't he?"

"Well, once I've seen him I'll be able to let you know."

"Ooo, you look smart!"

He spun round. It was Lynda. He got up and gave her a quick kiss on the lips. "Great looking jacket. And shirt. You look very handsome!"

"Thanks. Makes a change from wearing a business suit all the time..."

"Where we going tonight?"

Mark hesitated for a second or two. "Thought we'd see Donovan. He's on tonight at the Duke of York pub near Goodge Street..."

"OK." Lynda sounded positive. "Think I've been there. Some of us from Warwickshire House went there ages ago to see Ewan McColl..."

"And we could eat first somewhere nearby." Mark injected an upbeat tone to his voice. "So, if you're ready we'll shoot off."

Lynda raised a hand to stay him, and turned to the other girls. "Mark and I have got a big favour to ask you..." her voice trailed off as she glanced at Mark. He affected a serious look and nodded. Lynda took his hand. "Would you hate it if Mark was to live here, sharing my room?"

There was a silence, eventually broken by June. "No problems for me!"

"Well, Lynda, not very sure," Kay looked uncomfortable. "This is a girl's flat. Not sure what it would do if Mark was living here. What about you, Anna?"

"Not sure either. Living in sin!" Anna also looked uncomfortable. "What about privacy? How would that work? And why don't you just go and share a flat, get your own place?"

Lynda squeezed Mark's hand. "We might well do that, at some time in the future. This way we can see if we're going to get on..."

"So you plan to leave us?"

"Well, not tomorrow. Not soon. But it might happen. It might happen anyway. You know what life is like, living in flats..."

"So, you'd be leaving in, what, three months, or less?"

"No plans to leave at all, Kay. I've only just arrived and want to stay. And if Mark lives here he'd be with me in my room. He'd use the bathroom but he wouldn't stop you using it. He'd pay his contribution to the rent. That means the rent's paid five ways, not four. And that goes for all the other costs like electricity, coffee, tea. We'd cook our own meals, clean up afterwards. And Mark would do all the repairs around the house..."

"Sounds OK to me, girls!" June continued to be positive. "Just as long as he doesn't pinch my knickers off the clothes horse!"

"What about Baz, June?" Kay continued her concern. "He's not going to like it if he finds out."

"Why would he? I won't tell him."

"He has a habit of turning up without warning. If he sees Mark here..."

"Then it's Mark visiting his girlfriend!"

"OK, Lynda," Anna sounded less worried. "But on the basis that if it doesn't work out Mark goes, no ifs or buts!"

Lynda smiled, "OK, thanks for that. What about you, Kay?"

"Agree with Anna. Give it a try and if it doesn't work for any reason, Mark has to leave. No debate. OK?"

Lynda smiled, broadly, "OK!"

* * * *

It was Friday and Mark decided to squeeze two hours from his lunch break, not that he ever took a recognisable break. He had clients who enjoyed calling him across the lunch period and had learnt from past errors and omissions to remain at his desk, gobbling unhealthily an expensive shop bought sandwich, along with a packet of crisps, and sinking a bottle of Coke or R White's Lemonade.

Office automation was a subject that mesmerised him and the regular articles in the *New Scientist* that predicted the arrival of time-saving word processors and the fantastical sounding transmission of facsimile documents over telephone lines across the globe excited him and he wanted to be part of the *'white heat of the technology revolution'* promised by Prime Minister Harold Wilson, if only to free up his lunch time for a few moments for himself.

Mark slipped from the office at noon, telling the receptionist he'd be back 'around two'. Outside he experienced a bizarre mixture of guilt and freedom as he quickly marched south down Baker Street, determinedly turning left onto Oxford Street.

In his suit pocket he had three addresses – One Stop Records in South Moulton Street, The Magic Phonograph on Soho Square, and Harlequin Records in Brewer Street. The mission was simple – get abreast of what was *cool* in music, what was *hip, gear, groovy.* Gather the necessary information to more than hold his own in any conversation with anyone who regarded themselves as 'super cool'.

Entering One Stop Records was a revelation. For Mark it was the equivalent of going from grey conformity and entering a rich hinterland of colour, warmth and promise. The music that greeted him, belching from the large wall-mounted speakers, wasn't anything he'd heard on *Top of the Pops* or *Ready, Steady Go!*

It was a loud, compelling, creative cocktail of pressurized rock and blues music. "Stones," was the answer to Mark's question from the guy behind the counter. "Great R&B, eh?"

"Not heard anything like that on the BBC!"

"Nope, you won't. It's not released in the UK. It's an import. It's what we do here. Sell American imports. So don't ask for Cliff Richard or Gerry and the Pacemakers or any of that crap! You'll be shown the door!"

Mark laughed. "Promise! What else have you got?"

He gave Mark a quizzical look. "What are you looking for?" He paused. "You don't look like our average customer. They don't wear suits. You from the council?"

"No, I'm not from the council! I work for a PR agency!" Mark was aggrieved he could be mistaken for a faceless supernumerary. "So, what do your customers wear then?"

"They're musicians from rock bands or students from the LSE, and suits aren't their style."

Mark nodded his head, "Understand..."

"We get new albums in each week, it's always changing here. Right now we've got the US version of *Help!*, *Highway 61 Revisited* by Dylan, second one from the Pretty Things, and American outfit, Paul Butterfield Blues Band."

"I got some Dylan a few years ago, his first two. What's the Stones LP you're playing?"

"This one's called *Out of Our Heads*, not released in the UK, it's got *Satisfaction* on it."

"What about American groups?"

"Bands. Got Big Brother and the Holding Company, Great Society, Warlocks, Moby Grape, Iron Butterfly. They've all been privately recorded, live, so they've got plain covers..."

"Like those dodgy girly magazines?" The remark was ignored and Mark moved swiftly on, "They've all got great names. What do you recommend?"

"Try Great Society. They're more folk-rock. It's just in, great sound!"

"What about British groups?"

"Bands." He admonished Mark. "They're called bands..."

"OK, bands."

"Pretty Things, Kinks, Yardbirds. Not a lot yet but they'll catch up. You can see them live. Lot of them are making records right now but not yet released."

"Who?"

"Fairport Convention. They're folk-rock. Pink Floyd. They're really experimental, do amazing things with their guitars, great sound, great light show too..."

"Where do they play? Where can I and the girlfriend see them?"

"You need to look for gigs at universities and colleges, like Regent Street Poly, LSE, local pubs. These bands can't get gigs anywhere else. You could try the Marquee, Countdown Club, Electric Garden, the Ricky Tick clubs, Eel Pie Island or the blues music places like Ealing, or Country Club and Klooks Kleek..."

"Where's that?"

"Klooks Kleek? That's at the Railway Hotel, West Hampstead station. The Country Club is near there, at Belsize Park. Great music at both places!"

"Not too far from where I live..."

"We do a good music gig guide." He handed Mark a lurid yellow-coloured foolscap sheet, covered both sides with a closely-typed list in chronological order. "There's an all night party on at the Roundhouse next weekend." He proffered Mark a wildly designed and coloured leaflet. He eagerly received it, reading out the title, *"The Dream Sroom Bash."*

Mark hesitated as he attempted to understand the giant mushroom image. "Mushroom? And Sroom?"

"Yeah, you know. Magic mushrooms..."

"Ah!" Mark's penny dropped. "Mescaline!" Mark smiled. "Looks like the guy who designed this was on something!"

"Some good bands! Should be a great gig!"

Mark surveyed the list of acts. He recognised the Pretty Things but the other half dozen or so other band names meant nothing to him. However, he conceded names like *Steam Packet, Soft Machine, Bluesbreakers* and *Social Deviants* offered promise.

"If you want more good music gigs you should read *The Village Idiot*."

"What's that?"

"It's a paper for hip people, comes out every fortnight." He handed a copy to Mark. "For people looking for good music to inspire the soul, people looking for something better than the rat race. Looking for an alternative way to live..."

"Sounds revolutionary..."

"Counter-culture. One shilling if you want to buy that."

Yes, please. What about that album you mentioned? Great..."

"Society. Great record. Fifty-nine and six. No purchase tax, it's an import."

Mark dug his wallet out, looked at the cover, plain except for the rubber-stamped title, *Great Society Live at The Matrix SF.* "Expensive."

Mark left the shop, greatly heartened by the information on *hip, cool* bands he'd been given, and the list of gigs where he and Lynda could see them. He decided to return to the office, vowing to visit The Magic Phonograph and Harlequin on another day.

* * * *

Under the resentful gaze of his mother, Mark moved from the family home a week after the Lynda-led short discussion with the Chatsworth Road girls had produced the guarded, conditional approval to his moving in.

No Paul to provide a lift in his car but then Mark had little to move. A few business suits, shirts, shoes, his new *groovy gear*, the collection of some twenty LP records, and a few paperbacks. It all fitted in his two, cheap-looking suitcases, and he booked a local hire car service for the journey from Hayes to Kilburn.

Behind, he left some fifty or so 45 rpm records, his collection of James Bond Pan paperbacks, *Private Eye* and *Playboy* magazines, the ephemeral flotsam of his boyhood: Eagle annuals, Ian Allen loco and bus spotting books, and his album of photographs taken on the series of Kodak Brownie 125 cameras he had received at Christmases through the late 1950s. All were carefully boxed up, assiduously secured with doubled-up sisal, labelled, and put into the garden shed.

To his surprise and delight Lynda opened the door. She beamed brightly. "Hi! Good to see you!"

Mark didn't reply directly. Instead he took a punt on some humour. "Hi, honey, I'm home!" It clearly meant nothing to Lynda who gave him a look that said *strange person.*

"Upstairs!" she commanded. And he dragged the two suitcases up the carpeted stairs, careful not to disturb any of the carpet rungs.

Inside what was once her room but now theirs, she closed the door and threw her arms around his shoulders and kissed him with a building passion, almost animal. He responded positively, much heartened by Lynda's obvious lust and he deftly steered her onto the bed, her arms still locked around his neck. He quickly unzipped his flies, unceremoniously grabbed his erection out into the open, pulled Lynda's knickers down and hurriedly penetrated her.

She hung onto his neck, her eyes closed, an almost imbecilic, simpleton smile on her lips as his hips thrust energetically. For his part he was thankful that regular sex with Lynda had slowly built his resistance so that he no longer climaxed with a minute or two. He could now take lovemaking beyond ten minutes and by the time he ejaculated he was more at ease, his head less fogged with worry and doubt, sure Lynda had also enjoyed some of it, if not all.

He collapsed alongside her and they kissed. When they broke she pointed at the wardrobe. "Your clothes on the left, mine on the right. If it can't fit in then you'll have to leave it in your case."

"Have I got one of the drawers for my underpants and socks?"

"Yes, the top drawer. You'll have to share with my bras."

"OK. I've only got three suits, half a dozen shirts..."

"Did you bring your records?"

"Yes. But you haven't got a record player."

"No, you'll have to put them in the living room, next to the record player..."

"Really? They'll be ruined in no time. Or nicked!"

"No they won't, Mark. You've got to share, you're now sharing a flat. And, anyway, you've got to make sure they're not ruined or pinched. Your responsibility!"

"Paul's got some records here I think."

"Has he?"

"Yes, think that MJQ record is his." Mark paused. "Any idea why Paul's not sharing with Kay?"

"No idea." Lynda got up. "Maybe they don't want to live in each other's pockets."

He ignored the remark. "OK. I'll unpack."

* * * *

68

Mark walked slowly down the stairs with his LPs carefully tucked in his arms. Half-way down he was greeted by June, then Anna and Kay, eyes bright as he laid the LPs on the table. "What's this?" Anna pulled a couple off the pile, answering her own question: "Ray Charles. What else?"

Mark was guarded, "Mainly my rock and roll LPs. Jerry Lee Lewis, Elvis, Everlys, Roy Orbison, plus some Beatles and Stones..."

"No Sinatra?" Lynda sounded pained.

"Didn't think anyone here would want to listen to Sinatra..."

"I would!" Anna sounded genuinely enthusiastic. "My dad had *Come Fly With Me!* and played it all the time. I used to love it!"

"I'll bring it in. Maybe with some others..."

"*Songs for Swinging Lovers.* That'll be good!" Lynda squeezed his arm, "And *Ring-a-Ding-Ding!*"

"And I got this one yesterday." Mark pushed the plain cover across the table.

"What's this?" Anna picked it up, turning the anonymous cover in search of some information. "Very suspicious Mark. What is it? Christine Keeler sings *Love for Sale*?"

Mark laughed with the others, "No, it's an American band, Great Society. Recorded live in San Francisco."

"Let's put it on then!" Anna walked to the radio-gram.

"And there's this." Mark handed Kay the leaflet. "There's a music gig on at the Roundhouse next weekend. Looks good. We should all go!"

Kay handed the leaflet to June, "Yeah, looks interesting. Sure Paul would like to go..."

"What sort of music?" Lynda took the leaflet.

"R&B, rock and roll. Really looks very good. We should go. All of us!" Mark was bullish.

"OK, let's go!" Lynda sounded enthusiastic. "June?"

"Yeah, I'll go if everyone else is going!"

CHAPTER FIVE

Behind the excitingly fresh design of the front cover of *Nova* magazine lay the equally excitingly and equally fresh women's fashions that Mark observed were beginning to deliver an identity to what some style arbiters were calling '*the swinging sixties*'.

Nova harnessed a new, young eye in its fashion spreads, all of which deployed revolutionary layout, photography, and typography techniques. Mark had walked passed St Martin's School of Art building in Charing Cross Road many times and was now assured it had found a role in shaping *cool, hip* London if not the rest of the country.

Mark appreciated the publishers sending him the monthly *Nova* media pack, especially since he had no clients likely to buy space or get involved in any other form of promotional activity. And with the bonus of sharing each edition with Lynda, the magazine had become a flourishing object of delight.

Lynda was careful not to leave the magazine lying around the flat. She wanted to read it while travelling the tube from Kilburn to Liverpool Street, and back again, alleviate the boredom, and the endless delays with trains held between stations in cramped, claustrophobically entombed conditions. Only when she was finished with it would *Nova* be left on the kitchen table for the others to consume.

Mark knew he was on far from firm ground when it came to fashion. Yes, he'd started to get *cool, hip* but he had a long way to go. One expensive Ivy League jacket, shirt and pair of slacks was just one swallow, not a summer. But he wanted Lynda to change her look, swap her dull, 'safe' wardrobe for the new exciting clothes that packed the covers of *Nova*.

Given his own predilection for conservative wear, Mark knew he couldn't directly criticise Lynda's look, her taste in fashion. It was 'safe', anonymous, as was his charcoal grey suits, white shirts, plain ties. Like so many young females Lynda clearly wanted to merge into the background, disappear into an almost inky phalanx of nothingness.

Her dresses fell into two styles, shapeless, and fitted, both knee-length, while skirts adhered to and reflected the same modesty. Would she, he wondered, ever consider wearing mini-skirts? They spilled out in dramatic *photo-spreads* from almost every page of *Nova* but he had no hint on Lynda's views on *swinging London* fashions. The buzz in his office amongst the young women was not good. They all dismissed the style as one invented purely for Twiggy-type models to wear.

Mark suspected Lynda held the same views, *'good to look at but not for me'*. And he had to tread carefully in urging her, no matter how subtly, to get *hip* with some *cool, groovy* fashions. He did not want to provoke any resentment with a withering *'don't make me over!'* accusative evocation of the Dionne Warwick hit record.

He decided to broach the subject with a joke: "Why don't I get you a late birthday present. Or an early Christmas present?" But he didn't wait for Lynda to respond, rushing ahead, "Get you a couple of mini-skirts or dresses."

Lynda was downbeat: "I don't have the legs for mini dresses."

"Don't be silly, course you! You have great legs!"

"Really? You haven't said anything before." She rose from the kitchen chair, pulling up the hem of the skirt.

"Yes, I have Lynda. You weren't listening!"

"So, where are we going? Somewhere trendy?"

"Thought we'd go to Oxford Street, walk along there, see what's on offer, then go to Carnaby Street..."

"What about Portobello Road? Or King's Road?" She paused. "I could show you Mouse's shop in Portobello Road."

Mark feigned ignorance. "Mouse?" He halted for a few seconds, to emphasise his simulated disinterest. "Oh, you mean the guy you met at that Hampstead party." Another pause. "OK, we'll do Portobello first, then King's Road. Can always go on to Oxford Street, or do it another day."

Portobello Road was a revelation. As it snaked ahead of them they both stood, open-mouthed at what they agreed was a bizarre confluence of fresh fruit and vegetable stalls, antiques traders and a handful of clothes shops, with an even odder thronging mass of people, down at heel locals, *Hooray Henrys*, and hip young. Plus some - he and Lynda – presenting themselves as un-cool, drop-jawed *out-of-towners,* lumpen proletariat, tourists.

They quickly decided to hide themselves in the mass of bodies funnelled between the stalls, displaying a mix of genuine interest and sated boredom at brass kettles, bedpans, '*Edwardian*' wall mirrors on one side of the road, with West Indian mangoes, guava, pawpaw, and yams – and other exotic Caribbean produce - far removed from the roast beef, runner beans, potatoes, and Yorkshire puddings Mark and Lynda had been brought up on.

"Where's this shop? Mouse's place?"

Lynda peered into the busy river of people. "Don't know exactly. It's called *Little Red Rooster.* We'll find it."

And a few minutes later, weaving their way through the massed ranks of their fellow tourists, Mark spied what could only be a shop selling *groovy* clobber. The outside was painted an intriguing mixture of gypsy caravan on amphetamine and art school licence with large explosions of vivid, torrid competing colours in a variety of shapes from obvious flowers and plants, including mushroom, to fantastical forms simulating waves, sun-rays, moonbeams. Above the main window it told him the shop was called *The Hedgehog and the Toadstool* and six small vertical tubes of silver metal hung, gathered in congress, from an extended hook, chiming softly in the breeze.

Inside, the muscular aroma of joss sticks caught the back of Mark's throat, while Lynda pulled a face at its pungency. A reel-to-reel tape machine released a stream of pleasant Bert Jansch folk while clothes hung at every imaginable level, and the further he ventured into the shop's womb the darker it got, greater the claustrophobia and Aladdin's Cave effect.

Lynda dug along a rack of dresses as he surveyed displays of rings, chains, beads, and scarves sporting the CND symbol, American and British flags. Then the music changed and the pastoral riverbank music of Jansch was replaced by the loud, starkly revolutionary tones of the Kinks, accompanied by a young girl appearing from with the deeper recesses of the Aladdin's Cave. She smiled at Mark, "Hi! Let me know if I can help..." Her voice was ethereal and as it trailed Mark could see she was high. He smiled back at her. "Thanks. Just looking."

"That's what they call the shop few doors down." She laughed. "Cool."

"Thanks!" It was Lynda, moving towards the exit.

"Bye!" Mark walked quickly away.

Outside he caught up with Lynda. "Not interested? Nothing there?"

"Let's go to Mouse's shop."

The shopfront of *Little Red Rooster* and the two floors above of exposed brickwork was, predictably, covered in deep red with a massive reproduction of the ubiquitous image of head, shoulders and beret of Che Guevara overlaid on the scarlet, from the shop window to the roof gutter. Mark was impressed. "Che Guevara."

Lynda wasn't. "I know who it is Mark!"

He ignored the protest, seduced by the music that floated from within. He'd heard something like it on the Beatles *Help!* film, told himself it was Indian or Oriental.

She walked inside leaving him still adoring the giant sized image. "Hello, is Mouse here?"

He was young, good looking, slim and incongruously dressed in a red, Victorian-era British army jacket, replete with bright, golden-coloured sergeant's stripes on both sleeves, all straight from *Zulu,* Lynda told herself.

"No, Mouse is away this weekend. Anything I can do to help?"

"You Michael Caine?"

He laughed though she could tell he wasn't overly amused or impressed. She quickly moved on, "I was here a few weeks ago at the party. I was with a friend, June, and we put on some of your dresses for the press photographers. Remember?"

It slowly dawned on him. "Of course! You must be Lynda!"

"Yes, that's me..."

"Good to meet you! I'm Nick, one of the three who run this place. The other one is Toby, and that's him over there." He raised an arm and waved behind him. "But Mouse is away this weekend. He's gone home, be here Tuesday."

Mark joined them. "This is my boyfriend Mark..."

"Hi, I'm Nick. Good to meet you."

"And don't say anything or joke about *Zulu* or Michael Caine!"

Mark was very impressed with Nick's uniform. "I wasn't going to joke, darling, but I'd like to know where Nick got it from!"

"Trade secret I'm afraid!" He laughed, moved away, turned, "What can we do for you beautiful people? *Little Red Rooster* is at your service!"

"Mark is going to buy me a mini dress." She hesitated. "But I'm afraid not at your prices! Much too expensive for us ordinary mortals."

Nick smiled. "Don't worry about that! We know we can't sell our clothes to people in the real world so we're selling them for a lot less than we'd charge pop stars!"

"Really?" Lynda sounded encouraged.

"You try something on. If you want it, let's talk, make us an offer! I wouldn't want you to go to *Biba* or Thea Porter, buy any of that tourist crap!"

Lynda laughed, Mark swallowed. *Biba* was on his list, a place to visit after King's Road. And Thea Porter was hardly crap. Just pretentious Indian-mystic, *mega-bucks* expensive, and nothing he wanted to see Lynda wearing. However, he made a mental note to get hip, brush-up, get aware of the difference between *cool* and *super-cool*. He knew in the early sixties Levi '501' blue denim jeans were *cool* but white Levi's weren't. He knew it was *cool* to buy and laud black American rhythm and blues records but not the versions, *covers*, made by white American singers.

He knew it was *cool* to read Orwell but not Fleming. But he had bought every James Bond book in Pan paperback form he could find. He rationalised that by telling himself the juvenile Buchan-est *Boy's Own* plots were rescued from total embarrassing parody by Fleming's commendable literary style, his eye for detail and his employment of sinewy, information-rich sentences.

So, *Biba* was off his list as he watched Lynda pull one, then a second, then a third mini dress off the rails, immediately bolstering his positive feelings, noting that each of Lynda's selections were virtually identical to those he'd seen on the pages of *Nova*.

Lynda appeared three times from behind the blue curtain that masqueraded as a changing room in the *Che Guevara-ed* world of *Little Red Rooster*. Mark liked all three. They were essentially white canvases on which Mouse – or someone – had planted large geometric boxes in vivid orange, blue, and red, all slashed with vertical lines that ran on a bias from shoulder to hem.

"I'm getting this one." Lynda held it up and Mark nodded his agreement, following as she went to look for Nick.

"Good choice!" Nick appeared pleased. "It's a really hip look. Super cool!"

"Yeah, I like it. Really do!" Lynda handed him the dress. "How much?"

"That will be ten pounds, Lynda."

She turned to Mark and he dug his wallet out.

"You could always have two for fifteen pounds."

"No, thanks. Just one!" Lynda was decisive. "May not take to it. Can't really see myself in it..."

"You'd wear it at a party, or happening." Nick cut in, his voice concerned. He didn't want any second thoughts.

"Happening?" Lynda surrendered her face to a quizzical expression.

"Yes, darling. Like the one we're going to at the Roundhouse next week."

"Oh, right. That's a happening is it?"

"Sure is!" Nick folded the dress and shot it into a paper bag with *Little Red Rooster* stencilled across both sides, and handed it to Lynda. Mark handed him a ten pound note.

"You won't be able to wear stockings with this dress. It's far too short."

Lynda looked blankly at Nick.

"You'll need some tights." He pointed to the other side of the shop. "Ten shillings, just white. Made in Austria."

"You mean tights, as in the things they wear on stage?"

"Yes," Nick walked to display and took a pack. "They're all one size. You can wear these with any length of mini dress and keep your modesty."

"Ten bob is expensive."

"They're made in Austria." He looked at the pack. "By Wolford."

"OK, we'll have a pair." Mark dug out his wallet again. "What's the music? Really like it."

"Yes, it's great isn't it. Some Indian guy. Hang on and I'll tell you." He walked to the back of the shop, lifted an LP cover, and read out the text on the cover. "Pandit Ravi Shankar. *The Three Ragas*."

They walked from the shop. "That was a lot of money, Mark. I hope it's not wasted." She squeezed his hand. "Let's get something to eat. I'll pay."

* * * *

Mark didn't want to sound like a *know-all* but knew the Roundhouse had been saved from demolition by Arnold Wesker who transformed it from a derelict husk to a new venue for experimental visual and dramatic arts, calling it Centre 42. But Mark just had to pass on his scrap of knowledge so confided in Lynda as she sat at the dressing table, in a black bra, applying make-up. He shouldn't have been surprised but was when she quoted the titles of a few of Wesker's plays. And glad he had such an erudite girlfriend.

"I saw *Chicken Soup With Barley* and *Chips with Everything* a few years ago with a boyfriend. Went to the Canonbury Theatre. Have you been there?"

Mark smiled at her jousting. "No, I haven't. Where is it? Never heard of it."

"Islington. Not too far from King's Cross. We got there on the Northern Line. Just a few stops."

77

"I'll have to find out more about the place. And see if any Wesker plays are on anywhere."

"They normally are. There's always one being performed somewhere." Lynda paused. "But don't get any tickets without speaking to me first. OK?"

"Sure. I wouldn't anyway. And are you still interested in seeing *Passion Flower Hotel*? Tickets have just gone on sale."

"Of course! Make it a Saturday night. We'll go for a meal before, somewhere near the theatre..."

"Prince of Wales theatre, near Leicester Square. Should be plenty of places to eat round there."

"Are we going with the rest to the Flask? Or eat first?"

"Let's eat first, then go to the pub..."

"Or straight to the Roundhouse."

"They're my flatmates, Mark. I can't be anti-social..."

"OK."

"Right, I'm putting on my mini dress!"

Lynda slid the dress over her head and shoulders, pulled it down and stood on front of the mirror. "Arrgh! This is so not me!"

Mark was supportive but also defensive. "It looks great Lynda! You look amazing! Very *groovy*!"

"I look like that LP cover for *Anatomy of a Murder*!"

"You don't look anything like that, Lynda. You look just great, really trendy!"

"I look like something out of a magazine Mark! Real girls don't wear things like this..."

"It's leading fashion, Lynda, and you're leading the rest. All the girls will be wearing dresses like this soon, once they catch up with you! You're a trendsetter!"

"I'm a bloody circus act, Mark! That's what I am! They're going to look at me like I'm some freak!"

"Show the girls downstairs, they'll be knocked-out! Believe me!"

"Where are the tights?"

Mark lifted the pack off the bed and gingerly opened it, handing the contents to Lynda.

"I don't think I wear knickers with tights," she questioned but didn't wait for Mark's answer as she removed hers, falling into the bed, peeling the white opaque tights up her legs.

She dug a pair of black, low-heeled wedge-shaped shoes from the wardrobe and stood in front of the mirror. "I'm not taking a bag, Mark. You'll have to look after my keys and money."

"No need for keys. We'll have mine."

"Let's go downstairs then, see what the girls think about this dress."

Downstairs, in the kitchen, the four girls jointly let out a series of 'oohs' and 'arghs' as Lynda entered. "Wow! You look great!" was said alongside "You look very trendy! Right out of *Nova*!" And as the voluminous welcome faded both Lynda and Mark saw the guy standing against the sink. "This is Baz, our landlord!" June waved a hand towards him. "Baz, meet our new flatmate, Lynda. And her boyfriend Mark."

"Hi!" Lynda smiled, guessed Baz's age was thirty or so, but was unsure about his nationality. He was swarthy with a developing beer belly, a day old dark beard, looked Italian. Mark remained quiet but Lynda decided to be friendly. "You've got a great tan Baz. Don't think you got that here!"

Baz smiled, wriggling his body like an infant receiving attention from a cloying aunt. "No, I'm not British. I'm from Malta." He paused and attempted to admire Lynda's dress but, to her, it looked like a leer. "You look smashing!" And he smiled broadly, a set of very white teeth on display, "Just like a model from a magazine!"

He then dropped his smile and adopted a serious tone. "Let me tell you Lynda what I tell the other girls." He paused. Lynda went cold, expecting a rise in rent. Instead it was a request. "I run gambling in cabaret clubs where British people go for holidays. Great Yarmouth. Clacton. Hunstanton. Blackpool. I looking for croupiers. Young girls. Pretty girls. British like to gamble. I make money. I pay well. I reduce rent for any girl who wants job as croup..."

"Just for summer?" Lynda's interest was kindled but took care not reveal any keenness in her voice.

"Maybe more, all depends. Give me a call if interested." He handed Lynda a card. "I go now. You enjoy Saturday night." And he walked from the kitchen to the front door, June following.

"Any of you interested?" Lynda scanned their faces.

"I'm not personally. I'm happy with my job. Don't fancy a summer job, getting the push in October."

"Pay's not too bad, around two pound an hour. And you only work in the evenings, nine to midnight or one. It's all cash up front, no tax or national insurance, you have to sort that out yourself."

"He gives you training in roulette and blackjack. Has a room at his house in Brent set up like a casino."

Lynda surveyed the card *Baldassar Debono.* "Might give him a call."

Mark was concerned. "Hope you're joking."

She looked at him with a *not amused* face. "Just to find out more." She hesitated. "You never know."

The concern on his face doubled and he wanted to argue her out of any such move but, instead, bit his lip, making a mental note to discuss it later, addressing Anna, Kay and June, "You still going to the Roundhouse?"

"Think we all are. I am!" Anna was clearly enthused. And June. And Kay, "Paul's taking us, but first we're going to the Flask."

"We're going straight to the Roundhouse!" Lynda was adamant, Mark confused. "Thought we were going for a meal first."

"No, Mark I'm not going to a restaurant in this. Get us some fish and chips, we'll eat here."

* * * *

Lynda had her arm inside Mark's. "Did we just get in for nothing?" She had a wide-eyed disbelief in her voice. Mark ensured they moved forward, away from the two people collecting money, before answering. "Think we did. They must have thought we were pop stars." Then he stopped and looked around, then up. There were no tables or seating. The vastness of the circular space was not immediately apparent, the milling throng of people masked the immenseness of the space, telescoping its lateral radius to something more intimate.

Above them the domed roof rose in a creeping darkness. To their right was clearly a stage, lit brightly, and a band producing a lot of music, or was it, Mark asked himself, just noise? Then the smoke. It sat some five feet above them, a horizontal blanket of blue-grey, the aroma rising around them. Lynda squeezed his arm, "Dope." They laughed and quickly kissed each other on the lips. "So, this is a 'happening'." He surveyed the scene. "Guess so!"

They strolled around the perimeter of the crowd, in the manner of a Victorian couple promenading around the Royal Albert Hall during a concert. It slowly dawned on both that many of the females were dressed as Lynda was, achingly trendy, superlatively *cool.* And Mark observed many of the males appeared to be students, younger than he and Lynda, cheap-looking shirts, tops, and well-worn jeans. "They look like they've just left school."

Yet, there were liberal sprinklings of both sexes of Mark and Lynda's mid-twenties age group, males dressed smartly in suits, jackets. If not *uber-cool* in Portobello Road-acquired drapes, they were almost certainly *Ivy League* from the pages of *Playboy*, while the females clearly were *Nova* readers, hip to Mary Quant's entreaties.

They passed a bar. "Drink?" Lynda looked, considered but declined.

When somebody stepped from the throng and photographed them in a massive explosion of light from a flashbulb they both laughed. "Who was that?!" Lynda asked, pushing her body into Mark's. "Has to be *The Times* society page!" joked Mark. "They must think we're somebody!" Mark kissed her on the cheek, "Of course! You're Barbra Streisand!" She squeezed his arm, "You saying I have a large nose?"

"No, darling, of course not! But you have the Streisand look! It's unique!"

Lynda wanted to answer but didn't. The music from the stage was louder, and in front of them the crowd thinned to reveal the stage, the band, and a small group of about thirty people, male and female, *St Vitus* dancing, un-coordinated, bodies bouncing, arms flailing, little connection between the movement of body and the insistent, repetitive beat of the music.

Mark and Lynda stopped, almost open-mouthed and gawped at the group. "Looks like they're possessed," observed Mark. Lynda was more prosaic, "More like drunk."

"Or..." Mark hesitated, "...high on dope."

"You think so?"

"Bet on it...." Mark's voice trailed and the space in his head drifted to memories of the days when he did dance to rock and roll. The jive, the stroll, the continental, and the ludicrous mashed potato. But he didn't throw his body around as though it was suffering surges of electrical power directly off the national grid.

"It's not the music," Mark qualified. "It's rather good rock music, similar to the Stones." He turned to Lynda. "Wonder what band this is..."

"Don't know. Does it matter?" She gave Mark a look that he received as *you're too old for this sort of music.*

"I like good music Lynda, rock, jazz, folk."

She ignored the riposte. "Come on, let's find the others."

He looked at his watch. "They're still in the Flask."

"No, they won't be. They don't like staying there to the bitter end, too many pseuds."

"Pseuds? I like that word, as in Pseuds Corner in *Private Eye...*"

"Thought you might like the word." She pulled him forward and they slipped between *St Vitus* dancers and the elevated stage. Mark looked up. The singer eyed Lynda, grabbed his crotch and shoved it forward. Mark laughed, Lynda pretended not to see. Mark followed an urgent Lynda but managed to see *Social Deviants* on a drum box. He made a mental note. Must see if they have a record out.

"What's that?" Lynda pointed to a stall, set back in the red-brick darkness of the un-lit perimeter. It was decked out in multi-coloured, hand-drawn shapes in a variety of forms, either side of a sign that read, in lower case letters, *welcome from the happening.* They both walked over, and were welcomed from within the gloom by a loud, energetic male voice, "Hi, friends. Welcome from the happening!"

In front of them Lynda and Mark were presented with two trays. On one, labelled *alice's wonderland* were twenty or so large, flat biscuits, each mid-brown with a rough-looking texture into which were sunk what appeared to be small chunks of chocolate. On the other tray, labelled *mad hatter's oven* sat a similar number of small brown cakes. Both biscuits and cakes were one shilling each.

Mark decided to look cool. "What's in them?"

The accent was American, the voice *sotto voce*, and, in what little ambient light on offer, his round, soft face was delivered out of the gloom with a thin beard, concentrated around his chin. "Good honest ingredients friend. Good honest ingredients!"

"What do think? One each, or share?"

Lynda smiled, "Share. We can always come back for another."

"OK. Biscuit or cake?"

"Biscuit."

They walked as they ate, beginning another encirclement of the crowd, now denser than when they first arrived. "What's in this?" asked Lynda.

He lowered his voice. "My guess is cannabis."

"How do they get away with selling it?"

"Don't know. But who's here to stop them?"

It took about five minutes then both began to experience their mutual high, the light-headed floating, the warmth, the soporific sensuousness, the collateral desire to engage in sexual activity. They pushed through the bodies and joined the *St Vitus* dancers, dancing separately at first, with Lynda soon hooking her arms around Mark's shoulders. "I feel very sexy Mark. What about you?"

He answered in the affirmative with a passionate kiss, then broke away. "Me too."

"Let's go somewhere."

"Where? Can't go outside. Never get back in."

She didn't hesitate. "Somewhere dark. Against a wall. Like the old times."

"Newman Passage." He liked that. "Let's find a place."

He took her hand and they strode out of the harsh pool of light that flooded from the stage, off the dance floor, and hundred yards into the dark of the perimeter, between some large anonymous storage cases. The music and noise of the crowd was of another world, somewhere over there, both enjoying a real sense of freedom and sexual licence, heightened arousal, not a perception, but the *actualites*, delivered by the cannabis.

"Have you got a handkerchief?" Lynda whispered with some urgency, bringing Mark down to earth.

"What?"

84

"A handkerchief, Mark. Handkerchief!" She paused, calmed herself. "I'm not wearing any knickers. I don't want your stuff, your spunk, running down my leg, thank you!"

Mark's penny dropped and he dug his handkerchief from his slacks pocket, taking care not to spill on the floor coins or keys.

They resumed kissing, passionately, as Lynda unzipped Mark, eased out his erection while he slid her expensive, white Wolford, made in Austria, tights down off her buttocks. She lifted her body and brought her vagina down on the hard, thick shaft. "God, you feel big." was Lynda's only comment, whispered conspiratorially as he moved his hips up and down.

It took only a few minutes before he climaxed. He wasn't sad, and sensed Lynda wasn't too frustrated. It was just too public, despite being walled in by large storage cases. Newman Passage worked because no-one ever went there late at night. The Roundhouse late at night during a *happening* was a *different kettle of fish.*

They walked back into the light, arm in arm. "I'm perfectly sober," Mark affected a sad voice. "Shall we get another biscuit?"

"Yeah, let's do that!"

"Good to see you folks back! Like another cookie, or one of Martha Washington's finest cakes?"

"We'll have a cookie."

"Lynda!" They both spun round. It was Mouse. Plus a very young, thin girl in a mini dress, matchstick legs. "Hi, Mouse! How's tricks?"

"Fine!" He looked at Mark. "This your boyfriend?"

"Yep, meet Mark!" Lynda paused, wondering who the girl was. "And this is your girlfriend?"

"Yeah, Suzie!" He stepped back to admire Lynda's dress. "That looks really good on you! Glad you came back to the shop."

"Thank Mark. He insisted I get hip with the fashion. I might get another..."

"We're having made up some denim mini-skirts, my design. Should be in around two weeks' time. I'll call you."

"OK. Look forward to that."

"So, what do you think of this gig?"

"OK. Not done much so far. Just walked round..."

"And got high on a biscuit. Getting high again."

"You mean the guy running the stall? Yeah, that's Gene. He's a student at the Regent Poly. Does some tasty *gear*."

"Just pot?"

"No, if you want some acid or coke he can generally get it..."

"Is this it then?" Lynda interjected. "'*The 'happening'*. Or is there more to come?"

"This is it. Music, *gear* and booze. Get in the groove and get stoned."

"I like the Social Deviants," commented Mark. "Great music."

Mouse ignored the comment, "Why don't you two come with us tomorrow, we're going to Primrose Hill."

"Primrose Hill?" Mark was interested, enjoying the influence of the biscuit's dope. "Never been there..."

"It's the highest place in London, stunning views. You can see as far as Brighton."

Mark laughed. "Hey, we can get high again tomorrow!"

The remark fell on deaf ears.

"What time you going?" Lynda sounded interested.

"Come round my flat at twelve and we can go for lunch. There's an Italian in Praed Street. We can eat there first."

"OK, where's your place?"

"Above the shop! Portobello Road!"

Mark felt like an idiot. "OK, didn't know you also lived there. We'll be at yours at twelve."

They then parted and as he and Lynda resumed their circular perambulation Mark felt obliged to comment about Mouse's girlfriend. "She said a lot, didn't she?"

"Probably nervous, shy..."

"Think she was really high. Too many of Gene's cookies."

"Skinny legs. Shouldn't be wearing short skirts."

"Bitch!"

They laughed, Lynda squeezed his hand. "Where are the others?"

* * * *

The door to the flat was at the bottom of Che Guevara's left shoulder, as deep red as the rest of the building's painted front. Mouse opened the door – "hi, great to see you!" - and Mark and Lynda followed him up the bare, uncarpeted stairs, Mark registering the music, rhythm and blues of the type he'd heard from three or so years before.

Reaching the first landing Mouse turned, revealing a long room, bare, dark-stained floorboards that ran from front to back of the house. At the front, overlooking Portobello Road, two sash windows illuminated an area occupied by a work bench, supporting an industrial-sized sewing machine, surrounded by tailoring accoutrement with, alongside, floor-standing tailoring dummies, replete with measuring tapes garlanded around shoulders.

To the plain wall were taped dress patterns, photographs, and a line of hooks held a miscellany of pattern books, giant scissors, small pyramids of chalk on sisal, tape measures.

And away to the back of the room it was a jumble of sofas, armchairs, low table, a kitchenette, and large wooden dining table.

"What's the music?" Mark walked towards the record player.

"Yardbirds."

"Name rings a bell." Mark picked up the LP cover, surveyed the cover, then flipped it over.

Mouse was enthusiastic, "Great band! They're always on at the Marquee and Klooks Kleek. You should get to see them. Great live!"

"Think we should see them, Lynda."

"Take a seat!" Mouse waved towards the sofa, and as Mark and Lynda made their way across the bare floor Suzie hoved into view, stretched out on the sofa, reading the *Sunday Times* colour supplement. "Hello!" Suzie sounded bright, slid her feet off the sofa to make space.

"Wine?" Mouse held up a bottle of red.

"OK for me. Lynda?"

"Yeah, sure."

Mark noticed the large pot boiling on the hob. "We still eating at the Italian restaurant?"

"Slight change of plan." Mouse paused. "Thought we'd eat here. I'm doing spaghetti Bolognese. I'm a dab hand at it!"

"No Primrose Hill?"

"Sure, we'll go there after we've eaten."

"Hope so! We're looking forward to it!"

Mark enjoyed being the disc jockey selecting Dylan, Ray Charles, Booker T & the MGs, plus the Stones, and Beatles.

The meal, however, was a perfunctory affair. Spaghetti, slopped over with minced beef cooked in a tomato-based sauce, showered with Parmesan cheese, accompanied by baguettes of bread. The conversation was a two-way inquisitive process, Mouse clearly probing to elicit any help – financial or otherwise - with *Little Red Rooster,* while Mark and Lynda alternately undertook a gentle interrogation, attempting to discover more about him and his background. Stowe public school but instead of university, a drop out, member of a long-disbanded music group, designing clothes for stick-thin females, learning the rag trade basics, partnership with Nick and Toby "for a laugh, see what happens".

When the wine ran out a bottle of R White's lemonade was brought from the fridge, enough for four glasses. "Party time!"

"What?" Mark was anxious.

"Party time!" repeated Mouse. "How about we all turn on, tune in, drop out?"

"More dope!" Lynda sounded sated.

"Not quite," qualified Mouse. "This is magic mushroom spirit. Time to see your inner me!"

"*Inner me*?" Lynda did not hide her incredulousness.

"Expand your mind. Find out who you are! Get rid of your demons!"

Mark affected seriousness while inside him he really wanted to experience magic mushrooms. "You're talking about mescaline?"

"No, that's something else. This is magic mushrooms. Just a drop in your drink..."

"No, Mouse, not here!" Mark was assertive, had an idea. "Let's go to Primrose Hill! Get out in the open, out in the sun!"

Mouse shrugged his shoulders. "OK, I'm easy. Let's go!"

They ambled along the Regent's canal, the towpath at times both narrow and crumbling, black, oil-slicked water lapping their shoes, passing the occasional fellow Sunday afternoon walker. It took an hour before they finally arrived at Regent's park, climbing the embankment onto the road, crossing over onto Primrose Hill, the open, inviting peak above them, a seductive straight paved footpath running skywards.

"Here, take this." Mouse offered Mark, then Lynda, a sugar cube. He then dropped a small pearl of clear liquid onto the sugar. "Go on, put it in your mouth, suck."

Mark looked at Lynda. "You game?"

"If you are."

Mark popped the cube into his mouth. Lynda followed. Then Mouse and Suzie. Within a few minutes Mark began to walk up the hill, quickly, leaving the others behind, while Lynda, Mouse and Suzie ran off the path, onto the grass, whirling wildly in circles, a crazed imitation of Julie Andrews running over the Austrian alps, alive with the sound of music.

At the top of the hill Mark fixed his view south, to the distant Thorn House skyscraper, plus the familiar silhouettes of Nelson's Column, and Houses of Parliament, along with a nest of tower cranes. He raised his hands and let out a loud, and long, 'yes!' The handful of people sharing the peak of the hill, gave him, variously, looks of shock, worry and disgust, and quickly moved away.

Inside Mark's head he was standing on the brow of hill, overlooking a green, verdant valley, sweeping away before him, his vision framed by waving large rain forest leaves, beads of water running off them. In the centre, his vision presented in the bed of the valley a snaking river, sparkling silver as it reflected the large, burning orange ball set in a cobalt blue sky, against which swept prehistoric animals, silently, slowly.

The music in his head was the infectious rhythms of Ravi Shankar, the notes he'd heard in the boutique in Portobello Road.

Mark was oblivious to others who zig-zagged across the paved path below him, unaware that they appeared to be sharing together their own psilocybin mushroom-induced hallucinations. For him his mirage gradually faded, then accelerated, as reality very quickly repossessed his mind. He was alone, on his back, on the grass, the sky above him a less vibrant blue and the sun markedly anaemic. There was no sign of the others.

He groaned as he pushed himself up on his feet, checked his watch. It was five and he realised he'd been engrossed in his hallucination for almost three hours. He walked down the hill and back to the towpath, worrying about Lynda and where she had got to. He assumed she was back at Mouse's flat but wondered why she and the others hadn't taken him with them.

It was another hour before he got to *Little Red Rooster*, remembering accurately the way back. The door was eventually answered by Suzie, naked under a bedcover. He followed her bare buttocks up the stairs, intrigued as she said nothing to his few gentle questions. She continued up to the top floor and there, in one of the rooms, in the dark, was a large bed, containing a naked Mouse and Lynda.

The vision left him cold, annoyed at Lynda, betrayed by her. But, inside his head, he quickly corrected himself. He had to be *cool, hip, with it.* Men do not possess women. This is the sixties and women are no longer chattels. He repeated it silently to himself, desperate to be *hip and cool*, desperate to be a fully paid-up member of the *youthquake* Nova magazine revolution.

Mark smiled. Lynda smiled. Mouse smiled. "Come and join us!" Suzie took his hand, pulled him towards the bed "Yes darling!" added Lynda. "Take those things off, come and join us!" He quickly disrobed, Lynda opened the sheet, her breasts large and inviting. "Mouse is so virile! He's had both of us, now it's your turn!"

She took the joint from Mouse and inhaled as he fondled her breasts, exhaling before they kissed. She broke off, "Come on darling! You're missing all the fun!" He finally pulled off his underwear and climbed into the bed, his penis growing hard with anticipation. Aroused, he kissed Lynda passionately. She was obviously high Mark noted, probably the joint, maybe a hangover from the magic mushroom.

He blanked Mouse from his vision, despite his close proximity, and deftly penetrated Lynda, she linking her arms around his shoulders, bringing her mouth to his. And as he moved his hips in a gentle thrusting action Suzie ran her fingers up and down his spine.

It irritated Mark and when he finally climaxed he collapsed into Lynda's arms telling himself he had no interest in sex with Suzie.

He was in love with Lynda and told himself he had to find a way back to the beginning of their relationship and the time when she clearly entertained no interest in other men. When the relationship was so simple, embryonic and unattended by the need to be *hip, cool, gear*. The days of night school at Princeton College. The days of Warwickshire House, seeing the latest West End movies, simple sex in Newman Passage and the Tolmer.

CHAPTER SIX

On Thursday July 1st Mark had no idea that his relationship with Lynda had six weeks of life left before it rapidly crumbled around him, sucking his life into a vortex of fear, confusion and, in time, a form of loathing. But, on July 1st he remained an innocent and busied himself with arranging a weekend away in Dieppe for the middle of the month. It was essentially a reprise of a week spent with friends some four years earlier. Then, he and his friends had spent a mid-summer week driving along the Normandy coast, from Dieppe to La Havre, Caen, Fécamp, Deauville, and back, staying in cheap hotels or sleeping on beaches, always being moved on by the police.

A mid-priced hotel in Dieppe was traced via the local *syndicate d'initiative* and in a letter Mark booked three nights, Friday to Sunday. It would be a base for them to travel, by train, along the coast, especially Deauville where they'd gamble in the resort's famously opulent casino. Lynda booked the train and ferry, raiding her stock of privilege tickets amassed as an employee of British Railways. She also arranged acquisition of two SNCF season tickets for collection at Dieppe.

Booking the weekend was no substitute for a two-week holiday in Spain or Italy but, Mark reasoned, it was a start and, importantly, a move to consolidating his relationship with Lynda. He couldn't kill off the desire in his head to engineer an exclusive relationship, the one he wanted at the beginning of the year, the one he believed Lynda also wanted, in those far-off Warwickshire House days.

And, he also believed, she still did, despite her actions. They were, he told himself, political, a statement that she wasn't anyone's property. They were also lessons he had to learn about relationships. She knew their backgrounds were identical: working class, parents brought up by Edwardians, latter-day Victorians, with fiercely defined, if ersatz, morals but, like him, she wanted to participate in the, albeit slow-moving, social revolution that was developing in the post-Profumo, *That Was The Week That Was* young people's world.

Mark told himself the weekend in Normandy would provide some time to discuss with Lynda exactly where they were and, gingerly, attempt to steer her towards the exclusive, loving relationship for which he ached.

* * * *

Lynda waited until her boss was away at a meeting and she had half an hour to herself. She dug out the card from Baz and called him. The voice that answered was female, young, didn't ask who Lynda was, or why she was calling.

Baz came to the phone, his voice bored, tired, southern Mediterranean accent. "Yes?"

"Hello, it's Lynda Fowler. We met at the Chatsworth Road house a few weeks ago..."

"Sure. You're the new girl there." He laughed, throaty, dirty, phlegm rising in his gullet. "You wanna be a croup?"

Lynda held the phone away from her mouth, in disdain, as if she was about to catch an infection. Bringing it back she was firm, "I was thinking about it. That was all. I wanted to know more about it."

"You need to see me and the operation I have here."

"Operation?"

94

"Yes, I got tables set up to train you. You work during day?"

"Yes..."

"Then come tonight. I tell you everything."

"Where are you?"

"Brent tube station. Heathfield Gardens. Nineteen. You come out of tube, turn left, then next left. See you at six." He hung up.

Lynda left on time, five p.m., and, to avoid her boss landing her with a last minute 'urgent' letter, covered her typewriter at speed, shuffled papers into a pile, grabbed her handbag, and ran from the office, forgoing the loo and a make-up fix. At Liverpool Street station she jumped a Central Line train, travelled one stop to Bank, changed to the Northern Line, the painfully slow-moving train, tightly packed with home going commuters, eventually exiting the deep tunnel at Golders Green, with an equally slow trundle into Brent station, the bright summer evening light flooding into the cramped, elderly carriage.

She was wearing her brown shift dress, over a patterned caramel chiffon blouse. At Mark's behest she had shortened the dress by a few inches and at her boss's behest she wore the seamed stockings he had given her, a subtle light chocolate hue. Her handbag covered the welts of the nylons the shortened skirt revealed, as well as reducing any risk of a glimpse of the vermillion-coloured knickers she had opted to wear that day. Mark had showered her with underwear, bought from a shop in Soho's Berwick Street, and while she much appreciated his interest she voiced some reservations about his desire for her to adorn her body with *tart wear*.

Her boss had also given her an expensive Gossard underwear set of bra, knickers and suspender belt, his plan that she would wear it for their lovemaking when they were away on business somewhere. It was a plan that had eventually matured twice when on two separate occasions his desire to consummate their *relationship* was realised, following Lynda's two office-located sex acts of fellatio.

At Brent station, consumed with an inexplicable emotion, she decided to wear the ankle chain her boss had given her one Christmas. She pulled it from her purse, bent low and clipped it to her left ankle. She then strode towards nineteen Heathfield Gardens. There, Baz opened the door with a large, white-toothed smile, "Hello Lynda!" He was in an open-necked white shirt, revealing olive skin, and a gold chain resting on his androgens-stimulated chest hair.

She smiled and entered.

"Upstairs," he beckoned in his growling southern Mediterranean accent, and followed her, Lynda aware that, behind her, his eyes were consuming her.

At the top of the stairs, she halted, three rooms facing her. "In here?"

"Yes." He waved her in. The room was full of green baize tables, some rectangular, containing roulette wheels, others kidney-shaped with their baize covered in a series of small yellow-lined boxes. And a girl, Lynda's age, sitting at a roulette wheel. She smiled at Lynda. And Lynda smiled back.

Baz wagged a finger. "They are roulette tables, and they are blackjack tables. I will learn you both." He paused. "You wanna drink? I have some Algerian wine. Very good. My brother makes it. You like?"

Lynda shrugged her shoulders. "OK."

Baz turned to the girl. "Nicola, you do the drinks, please." The girl got up, wearily, and left the room.

"What sort of operation have you got?" Lynda walked into the well of the room, flicking a roulette wheel.

"I run the gambling in all these clubs, all over country..." His voice was softer.

"Where?"

"Great Yarmouth, Blackpool, Fakenham, Hunstanton, Caister, Boston, Skegness, lots of places. Gambling big business in UK."

"What are these clubs? You mean British Legion?"

"What this British Legion? I mean cabaret clubs. They have entertainers, singers, magicians. We have two, three tables at the back of club. They either sit looking at stage or come back to tables to gamble. Big business."

"What, you share the takings with the club?"

"I take eighty per cent, they take twenty. I take more in some clubs, ninety per cent, where lots of people want to gamble, big income, big profit, everyone happy."

"And what do the croupiers get out of it?"

"I pay good. Each girl gets five pound an evening. That thirty-five a week if you work every evening. You pay own tax and insurance. In some places I have caravan where you can stay, no cost to you. Other places you stay in bed breakfast, very cheap for you."

"And this is where you train the croupiers?"

"Yes. Two weeks you learn roulette, blackjack. Learn how to check wheel every evening, make sure it not cheating people. And you learn how to stop people stealing..."

"Stealing?"

"People steal chips, run off very bad..."

"You on duty at these clubs?"

"No, just a few. I drive to clubs in evening to check things all OK. Can't do them all. I drive you to Great Yarmouth and Blackpool when you first go there but you to drive yourself to other clubs, on your own."

"I don't have a cat..."

"You have money to buy car when you become a croup for me!" He paused, smiled. "You also get tips. People who win lots like to tip. Big tips!"

"OK." Lynda hesitated for a second or two. "I'll need to give it some thought. You need me to start straight away after the training?"

"Yes. If you good I need you in club straight away, making us all lots of money!"

"It's just for the summer, nothing after September?"

"No! It go on all year, not just summer. I have gambling in country clubs, all year round! Big money! You go on working all year. If you good, club like you, punter like you, I raise you pay to six pounds every hour at Christmas!"

Nicola handed them the glasses of Algerian red wine. Lynda sipped. "You want to try roulette?"

Lynda looked across the room. "OK," and put down her handbag, walked to a table.

"Nicola show you how. I watch."

Lynda sat at the table, Nicola spoke. "You turn wheel one way, very gently. Shoot ball the opposite way, very gently. The ball falls on red or black number, or zero. The customer put their chips on a number, black or red, or split bet, and you have three sets of odds, five to one, ten to one, and fifteen to one. Five to one is for five shilling chips, ten to one is for ten shilling chips, and fifteen to one is for one pound chips."

"Zero?"

"The table keeps the stakes, no-one wins..."

"Except Baz."

Nicola laughed. "Don't complain! If you're good Baz will give you a little extra!" They both smiled at Baz.

"Chips?"

"Punters buy them from you. When they win they hand back the chip, you pay them cash, work out the odds in your head. Pull in the dead chips with the rake, leave the winning chip on the number, tell the punter what he's won and once he agrees you rake in the chip and pay him cash."

"Where's the cash?"

"In a drawer." She pulled it open, out on Lynda's lap, to reveal a tray similar to a cash machine's in which sat coins and notes." Nicola paused. "Remember to always keep the drawer shut unless paying out."

"You mean there's no security in these places?"

"None. The clubs don't want to know, expect you to make sure there's no trouble. You may get a few people run off with chips. They think it's money. Tossers!"

"Two weeks training?"

"Yes, you'll also learn how to croup blackjack."

"You the teacher?"

"Yes, that's me. And Baz. But I *do* get to go out to the clubs. When Baz lets me out!" She gave him a big smile. "And, by the way, on duty in the clubs you always dress like me." Nicola pulled back. "You always wear a dress or skirt, stockings, high heels, very smart, low cut dress or top, lots of make-up, attract the punters. They're always men."

Lynda gave out a wry laugh. "Short skirt, low cut dress, but not too *tarty*?"

Nicola nodded. "You got it!" She laughed. "And the men, some of them, will try to pick you up, ask if you want a drink. Play it by ear but you mustn't get yourself compromised, where they could try to get you to cheat for them."

Lynda struck a quizzical look. "They'd try that?"

"You bet! So, watch it!"

"I will!" Lynda was positive. "How many tables in the clubs?"

"Four in the big ones, two wheels, two blackjack. Just one, a wheel, in the small clubs."

Baz interjected. "I give you blackjack rules. You read, understand. When you come back you ready to learn."

"Why don't you stay? We've got three girls coming this evening to learn, never done it before. You could join them, just on the wheel.

We finish at nine, then we go for a drink." Nicola paused. "Come on! You'll enjoy it!"

"I give you a lift back to house!" added Baz.

"OK," Lynda sounded a little resigned, cornered. "Can I phone my boyfriend? Tell him I won't be home till later?"

She rang the house, spoke to Anna, left a message, aware that Mark would not be pleased. She decided not to leave Baz's number, Mark could get that from June. Not that Baz would allow Lynda to talk until the evening's training was complete.

At nine Baz called it a day, thanked everyone and suggested they go for a drink. At the pub the three girls and Lynda got on very well, joining together protectively, like members of the same group or club. Lynda learnt that Nicola was Baz's business partner in the gaming enterprise, sometimes, like June, sharing his bed when his wife flew back to Malta to reunite with family. And Nicola suggested Lynda meet with one of Baz's business associates, a guy called Apollo, owner of a large house in Hampstead. "I sense you're a girl who likes a challenge, not frightened of the future. You'll get on well with Apollo, lots of *business* opportunities!" Lynda picked up on the emphasised *business*. "You mean drugs, prostitutes?" Nicola nodded, "Yeah, amongst other things."

And almost two hours later they spilled from the pub, laughing, giggling, like naughty schoolgirls, Baz providing Lynda with a lift back to Chatsworth Road in his Mercedes Pagoda. He pulled into a gap a few yards from the house, turned off the engine, killed the headlights. She did nothing when he placed a hand on her knee and, clearly pleased she wasn't violently protesting, began to gently squeeze the nyloned knee, then stroke it, the hand moving slowly along the thigh. The conversation consisted of Lynda's questions - and his answers - about the caravans where the girls lived, the owners of the clubs, how many girls he had crouping for him.

When his fingers reached the front of her knickers she unzipped his flies, eased out his small but very hard penis and vigorously masturbated him for a few minutes before he ejaculated. His sperm spilled out onto her fingers and she lifted two to her mouth and licked them. Only then did she remove his hand from inside her skirt. "OK, Baz. I will call you in a few days, let you know." She then leant forward, whispered, "And if it's 'yes' then you can do me! On one of your roulette tables..." She kissed him, "Bye!"

* * * *

Mark bit his tongue. He wanted to protest volubly at Lynda's unwelcome news that she was seriously considering abandoning mouthwatering job security for what he regarded as a very insecure life as a croupier. Not at a glamorous Mayfair casino but instead running around the country, working in cheap *'kiss me quick'* holiday resorts or rural, backwater *cabaret* clubs.

Instead he held his fire and decided to use the time during their weekend in Normandy to broach the subject, not just to campaign against the idea, but also to understand where they, as a couple, were heading.

When Lynda finally walked through the door, well past eleven, from her meeting with Baz, Mark really tried hard not to behave like a Donald McGill cartoon wife, waiting with rolling pin behind the front door for the errant husband to stumble home drunk.

Yet he sat in the lounge, watching *Good Old Days* on television, holding off sleep, waiting for Lynda to walk through the door. When she did Lynda strode straight up the stairs, aware the television was on and someone was watching it, but disinterested in knowing who or why. Not so *laissez-faire* for Mark.

He quickly turned off the television and rushed after her, careful not to shout out since everyone else had gone to bed. "Lynda!" he whispered as she reached the landing. "Where the hell have you been?"

She turned, a fierce expression on her face, disappearing into the bedroom.

"Unzip me!"

He obeyed, standing behind her, unzipping her dress. "They're not the stockings I bought, are they?"

"Probably not."

"And I didn't know you had an ankle chain..."

"What's your point Mark?"

"Nothing." He sensed she was annoyed, or possibly tired. "How did it go tonight? With Baz?"

She turned, wearily: "Can we talk about it tomorrow, Mark. Not in the mood now. Get undressed, let's get to bed, you can ravish me. I'm in need of a good seeing-to..."

"Keep your stockings on, and your chain..."

"I was going to..."

"I can do you like a whore..."

"Yes, please!"

They made love with a visceral passion, she shoving her hips fiercely, physically, down on his erection, legs wrapped around the small of his back, teeth biting his neck, tongue deep inside his mouth, finger nails sinking deep into his shoulder blades. When Mark climaxed he bit deep into her neck and she growled a low appreciation, the ecstasy kidnapping her senses, running away with them to a wondrous place of colliding blacks and yellows somewhere deep inside her head.

When he finally exited from her body, she shoved a tissue into her vagina to soak up his sperm, and turned to embrace sleep. Mark placed an arm around her waist and lightly kissed the nape of her neck. "Did you fuck him?" he whispered.

102

"No, Mark, I didn't." Her voice, quiet, clear, was the model of weariness.

"But you wanted to."

"Yes, I did, even though he was a short, fat, hairy dago, I wanted to do him!"

"Did you..." he trailed off, a sadness in his voice. "Are you going to work for him?"

"Let's talk tomorrow, Mark. I'm very tired."

"OK, tomorrow." He ran his hands down to her stockings. "There's a party tomorrow night. American independence party, Earl's Court..."

"OK, let's go to King's Road tomorrow, see what's what. We can then go the party from there."

* * * *

Mark awoke first, slipped slowly, smoothly from under the sheets, careful not to wake Lynda, wrapped his naked body in his dressing gown, checked the mute alarm clock – nearly 9 - and went to the bathroom. He showered and shaved, deoderized his arm pits with Mum, then splashed a few drops on his cheeks of the expensive Trumper's after shave Lynda had given him for his birthday.

Back in the bedroom he dressed, quietly but not too successfully as he heard Lynda rouse, turn under the sheets, head hidden, murmuring 'coffee'. He smiled, "Hi, good morning little school girl. Or, should that be my little whore?"

"Oh god, I've still got my stockings on. What a slut!"

"I'll get that coffee."

When he got back she was sitting up in the bed, sheet wrapped around her body, radio on, tuned into London's *Kenny and Cash* show.

"You've got to get a car, Mark."

"Have I?"

"Yes! Everyone I know has a car. Only you don't."

"Can't even drive."

Lynda's throat released a derisory *hmm.* "Then learn to drive! I did! Take some lessons. Must be hundreds of driving schools round here..."

"Then I have to buy a car, pay out on insurance, road fund, petrol, expensive hobby..."

"Don't bellyache, Mark! Just do it!"

He was resigned and the tone of his voice emphasised it. "OK."

"I'll help you buy the car. Get a second-hand Mini. Not too old, not a crock. Sixty-three. Nothing older. Twenty thousand on the clock, and no more!"

"There's a second hand dealer on Kilburn High Road. We can take a look there." He hesitated. "So, how did it go last night?"

"It was OK. Baz has got this place near Brent tube where he trains all the croupiers. And this girl, Nicola. She does the training..."

"And he runs gambling in clubs out in the sticks?"

"Yeah, places like Great Yarmouth and Hunstanton..."

"Hunstanton? Where's that?"

"Not too far from where I come from, know it well. It's about ten miles north of King's Lynn. Big holiday place, we'd all go there in the summer, for a day out..."

"So, what are going to do? You going to train as a croupier?"

"The money's very good. He said I'd get thirty-five pounds a week if I work every evening..."

"And what do you do when the summer season is over?"

"Go on working. He says gambling goes on all year round. He doesn't just run gambling in seaside towns. He's got clubs in the countryside. Says it's a big business."

"So, you're going to be a croupier?"

"Don't know Mark." Lynda stared at the ceiling. "I've got a very secure job at British Railways. Not likely to get the push there. If I jack that in and become a croupier it might not work out. He might sack me. I might mess up the takings. And if I fall ill there's no pay, maybe no job..."

"And us? If you take this job you won't be living in London. That'll be the end of us..."

"...doesn't have to be. You could come up at weekends, we could see each other. Get a car and it would be a doddle..."

Mark was annoyed, anger welling up inside him but he remained calm. "Shame. Thought we had a great relationship. Can't believe you want to kick it into bits..."

"Don't be so dramatic, Mark. I haven't made my mind up. I'm still thinking about it."

Mark knew when to stop the interrogation. He told himself he would return to some gentle quizzing of Lynda on their weekend in France.

* * * *

Mark had never been to King's Road nor, he admitted to himself, any part of Chelsea. He had, in the early sixties on a hundred or more occasions, hand-dropped press releases and invitations to press launches to newspapers in Fleet Street, magazines based in Covent Garden, and south of the river in Waterloo's Stamford Street, but had never ventured to Chelsea.

For Lynda it was not virgin territory. With other girls living in Warwickshire House she had been to parties in Chelsea, had drunk in at least two King's Road pubs, *The Chelsea Potter* and *Markham Arms*. But she had never shopped in King's Road.

They caught a Circle Line train from Paddington, after a ride from Kilburn on the Bakerloo to Baker Street, exiting at Sloane

Square. The sun was bright in a near clear blue sky and they both slipped on their dark glasses or, as Mark joked, *'our don't-want-to-be-recognised-at-the-airport-glasses'*.

To his right he immediately saw the Royal Court, the theatre he'd read so much about in *The Observer*, almost every Sunday, presented on its arts pages as the cockpit of the London theatrical revolution. He recognised the title of their offering - *Happy End* - from *The Observer*'s notice as a Kurt Weill and Bertolt Brecht musical comedy that had influenced *Guys and Dolls*, a musical he knew very well having bought the film's soundtrack LP.

It slowly dawned on both that the street which beckoned before them offered a different experience. There appeared to be few people older than thirty. Indeed, the street was occupied by a tribe of very *groovy, hip* people, young, lively, confident. King's Road was their parade ground, their tribal capital, their *Big Top*.

This tribe had a uniform. It distilled to short skirts, garishly coloured tights, and large floppy hats for females, and velvet jackets in deep green for males. Some girls wore faux feather boas, some men wore brightly patterned scarves that cascaded down their equally floral voile shirts, knotted tightly at the Adam's apple. Others occasionally presented a visual shock, wearing bright red Victorian British army jackets, doubtless, Mark commented, sold off by the wardrobe people after completion of the *Zulu* film.

"We don't look anything like them," Mark whispered. "We look like the *VoPo*."

"VoPo?"

"East German police. The people who eradicate any independent thought or action. Like in George Orwell's *1984*."

"Then we have to get with it, Mark. Don't want to look like the secret police!"

With a frenetic energy they raided every shop along the loud, lively, bubbling artery, drinking in the seductive atmosphere, redolent of last-day-of-term *sans rules* freedoms, the swirling rock, blues, and raga music in every shop meeting to collude in delivering an anthem to self-expression, courage to look authority in the eye and not blink first. With the music came the aroma of the *youthquake*, pot openly smoked in the *hip, groovy* shops, a clear provocation, a transparent invitation to those in power to display their *uncoolness*, exert their mentally-frozen rigidity, by reacting with censure and arrest.

It took three hours but when they reached World's End both realised that they'd come to the end of King's Road's strip of *cool, hip* boutiques and the expensive mock-Mediterranean restaurants with their excruciatingly well-heeled *in-crowd* patrons. Mark was pleased to see, at long last, the place where comedic estate agent Roy Brooks was based, from where he composed his weekly advertisement in *The Observer* with its belly-laugh descriptions of his client's properties *'reeking of damp with plaster coming off the walls'.*

"OK, that's it," Mark turned to look back along King's Road. "We go back. But, this time, we do some shopping. I'll buy you that denim mini skirt in the Westerner shop. OK?"

Lynda squeezed his hand, "Sure. And I'll get that woollen dress I saw somewhere..."

"Top Gear or Kleptomania, maybe Bazaar."

"I'll need to buy some more tights..."

"Pantyhose, darling. You don't need to wear knickers with them."

"You're an expert, then?" Lynda gave Mark a sly smile.

"Of course. One of us has to be if I'm going to get you to wear miniskirts."

Mark paid for the denim mini, Lynda bought the woollen dress, a purply background on which sat a series of horizontal soft, muted coloured bands. And to Dolcis where she bought a pair of cream coloured shoes, and Mark added to his small but growing shoe collection with a pair of desert boots. Mid-afternoon they decided to eat a late lunch, and found a small workmens' cafe at the back of King's Road, next to the large black double wooden-door entrance to Thomas Crapper's builder's merchants yard. They ate egg and chips, accompanied by two rounds of buttered bread and cups of tea. "Days of wine and roses," joked Mark. "Living high off the hog."

"We can't go to the party with these bags. We'll have to go back to the flat."

Mark pulled a face that said 'agreed' but voiced a wish. "Let's get a drink at The Pheasantry. I'd like to see inside. Get a proper look."

"What's The Pheasantry?"

"It's on King's Road, near the Markham pub, looks like something you'd see in Venice."

"Surrounded by water?" Lynda attempted some humour but Mark was in serious mode.

"It looks like some Italian palace. I went there a few years ago, delivered some lighting fittings there, to a photographer. He had a studio on the second floor but the place looked like it had a restaurant, bar, God knows what else..."

"What, we're going to just walk in?"

"Yep. I can always flannel my way in, ask where the photographer's studio is, say I'm going to be delivering some stuff for photography later in the week..."

"OK, let's go." Lynda was courageous. "They can only throw us out."

They walked through the arched portico, across the tiled courtyard, up the steps, pushing on the wooden double doors. Inside, they stalled, intimidated by the inky blackness. It was clearly a hallway, mock Grecian, an unassuming stone staircase sloping upwards to a higher floor. And steps down to a basement from where came the barely audible sounds of Sonny & Cher's *I Got You Babe*.

The darkness on the stairs remained inky but nearing the bottom some light seeped forward and as they entered a back-lit bar, harlequin-coloured by a row of upturned spirit bottles, distributed some illumination. In the reluctant light provided by the bar they both discerned a quad formation of Chesterfields, surrounding a low coffee table.

A girl wafted past them. Waif-like, dressed in what looked like a plain thigh-length slip but, Mark decided as she floated past, was a dress, and semi-diaphanous. He gave Lynda a knowing smile, and whispered. "Think she's high." Lynda nodded.

She turned, walked back towards them. "You folks tourists?" The voice was soft, American.

"No, we're locals." Mark was keen to immediately ensure she didn't get the wrong idea about their provenance and dismiss them as *outoftowners*.

"OK." She smiled, engaging Mark's gaze. "Just saw all those bags, looks like you're visitors."

Mark ignored the remark. "What goes on here?"

"The Pheasantry Club!" Her voice went from soft to an exaggerated incredulous tone. "You never heard of The Pheasantry?"

"Yes, I have." Mark countered with a superior tone. "I was here a few years ago for a photo shoot, upstairs..."

"Is that what's upstairs?" The girl looked chastised. "I've never been up there."

"So, what's the Pheasantry Club? A discotheque?"

"Yeah, coolest place on earth. Epicentre of cool!"

"Tonight?"

"Yeah! Tonight!"

"What time?"

"Don't get here before eleven."

"Do you have to be a member?"

"Yes, but don't worry about that, we'll make you an associate member at the door. Just for the night. Just ask for me, Janie. I'll sign you in."

Mark turned to Lynda. "OK, we'll be back." He paused, "Can you do us a drink now?"

"Sorry, guys, no. We're not open for anything right now. And you two better skedaddle!" She smiled. "My boss will be in soon and I gotta get this place cleaned up!"

Back in the daylight they agreed to return to Chatsworth Road, but also agreed to return to The Pheasantry on another day.

Lynda affected her *must make a date in the diary* voice, "I'd like to go to that place. Looks interesting."

"Yes, it does. Very hip. The *epicentre of cool*!"

"What other places like that are there, Mark?"

"Good question." He put his arm around her waist. "Don't know the answer, have to investigate, see if there's anything in *What's On*, maybe go back to the record shop and ask the guy there. He seemed pretty switched on."

She was insistent. "We've got to get switched on, Mark, start meeting the people who make things happen!"

"The *movers and shakers*, the *music makers*, you mean?"

"Yes, the *ring-a-ding-dingers*. The people who make things *hip* and *cool*, Mark. There's no reason why we shouldn't be them!"

"We're not rock singers Lynda, not film stars!"

"Maybe not." She paused. "But we've got to get with it!"

"OK, Miss Fowler, let's get with it! Tonight we've got this party. We give that an hour and if it's no good we leave, go The Pheasantry! How's that sound?"

Lynda smiled, "Yeah, let's do that!"

110

The flat was empty when they got back and, after Lynda had hung up her new clothes, they made coffee, switched on the television and watched the end of *Grandstand* and the beginning of *Dr Who*, with the curmudgeonly William Hartnell in the title role. "You got the address of this party?"

Mark reassured her. "Certainly do!" He dug out his wallet and pulled a slip of paper from it. "It's a July Fourth party! Thirty-six Earl's Walk, off High Street, Ken. And there's a pub on the corner, the Scarsdale. We'll have a drink there first."

"Dig out the A to Z, make sure you know where it is."

"Will do boss..."

"And we'll eat at the Spanish place in Kilburn, then go to the pub."

"Sounds good." Mark paused. "You watching this?"

"*Dr Who*? Not really. It's for kids, isn't it?"

"OK, let's go upstairs for some discussions of a *Ugandan nature*."

"Ugandan nature? What *are* you talking about?"

"*Private Eye* in-joke. Another way of saying *let's have sex*."

* * * *

They walked from High Street Kensington station to the Scarsdale pub, Mark carrying a bottle of *Mateus Rosé* for the party. Dressed in her brand new denim mini skirt, white Wolford tights, skimpy rainbow-striped top, neck hidden beneath a vermilion boa, Lynda was unimpressed with the walk. "How much further is it?"

"It's off Edwards Square. Find that and we'll find the pub."

And Edwards Square eventually greeted them, the pub secured a few minutes later with, alongside, Earl's Walk, a cobble-stoned mews, lit at either end by two feeble street lamps hanging off what,

Mark told himself, were two unbroken, facing rows of Georgian houses.

Mark went to the bar, leaving Lynda in charge of the Mateus, searching the heads of the people who crowded the pub. "Where are the others?"

"It's only ten. They'll be here." Mark surveyed the pub's patrons. They appeared to be a mix of elderly local residents and an uncomfortably large contingent of young *Hooray Henry* types, dressed in blazers, cravats, flannels, a uniform that branded them for Mark as louche, lazy unearned inheritors of daddy and mummy's wealth. *Upper class twits,* Mark told himself.

But that was no barrier to their being predictably predatory males. Within minutes all the men in the bar had clocked Lynda, her long legs and short skirt, and three of them decided to engage her in conversation. Mark became edgy as they jokingly introduced themselves, not to him, only Lynda, pointedly ignoring Mark, marginalising him as he watched Lynda clearly welcoming their interest as they ingratiated themselves, leaving him to concentrate on ensuring they didn't *laager* her, leaving him an outcast, looking at their backs as they vied amongst themselves to be the first to talk her into bed.

Inside his head he grew increasingly annoyed with Lynda, expecting her to display some loyalty but tried hard to accept she was an attractive female who, quite naturally, enjoyed the attention. He despaired as they coached from her she was at the Scarsdale as a preliminary to a party 'round the corner', worked at British Railways as a secretary, lived in Kilburn. Just a passing mention of him as the boyfriend.

Then, to his shock and amazement, one of them invited Lynda to pose for *Penthouse*. Mark piped up. "Don't think that's a good idea!" He got a look of fierce condemnation from Lynda. The *Hooray*

Henry was encouraged. "Come to our office. We're in Bramber Road, Fulham, near North End Road market, not too far from here!"

Mark felt like walking out on her, going to the party by himself, leaving Lynda to the *Hooray Henries*. But he was rescued by Paul's voice, somewhere behind him. Mark turned, waved, "Hello! You made it!" His face succumbed to a very broad smile as he watched Paul and the three girls weave their way through the bodies.

"How's tricks?" Paul was a breath of fresh air, and he offered Mark a way out of the intimidating Hooray Henries propositioning his girlfriend.

"Who are your friends?"

Mark pulled a sad face. "Not mine, Paul. They saw Lynda and made a bee-line for her..."

"Looks like they're throwbacks from a 1950's boat race day..."

"Chinless fucking wonders. And Lynda's falling for it, hook, line and sinker!"

Paul pushed forward, "Hello, Lynda! Come and join us!"

Her eyes lit up and she welcomed Paul with a smile. "By lads! See you!" The three cravated males parted and Lynda moved through them. Mark couldn't help a sardonic remark. "Oh, good to see you! I'm Mark..."

"Shut up, Mark!" Lynda wasn't amused. "They were three nice guys! Good to meet them..."

"Posing nude in *Penthouse*?"

"Yes, that sounds interesting..."

"Really?" Mark decided not to let the subject go. "Seem to remember you saying you wouldn't do it for *Playboy*!"

Lynda ignored both the riposte and Mark, engaging with her flatmates who all expected Paul to fight his way back to the bar for a round of drinks. "I'll help out," offered Mark, and they both weaved their way through the massed ranks of *Hoorays*.

113

When they got back, drinks on a tin tray, the four girls were surrounded by a small group of cravats and blazers. And so confident were they, the excited *Hoorays* stood their ground when Paul and Mark arrived. Both shared the same feeling of being somewhat ostracised. "Are they trying to tell us something?" inquired Mark. "Before you arrived I had three of them sniffing around Lynda, and she was lapping it up! Disgusting!"

"They're telling us *you don't own us!* That's women for you. All that women's lib guff from America! Just grin and bear it. They still need men to stroke their egos!"

Mark laughed while, inside his head, he couldn't agree with Paul. His socialist parents and his own reading of modern history told him women were exploited, continued to be exploited but, as he read in *The Observer* and *New Statesman*, many in the arts were beginning to rebel.

"So, who's party is this?"

"It's a friend of a guy I work with." Mark was confident with the statement but continued in a less assured tone. "Don't know anything about him. But if the party stinks Lynda and I are going onto The Pheasantry."

"What's that?"

"It's a place in King's Road. Interesting building, got a discotheque type club in the basement. We sussed it out today, looks interesting."

"OK. If you decide to go let me know and me and Kay will join you. Be good to find another place to go to. The Marquee and 100 Club get a little boring!"

"There's also the Country Club in Belsize, Blaise's in South Ken, the Countdown Club..."

"Never heard of these places. Where did you hear about them?"

"One Stop Records. The guy who runs the place seemed pretty au fait with what's *cool* and *hip*. He told me about the do at the Roundhouse. He got that one right!"

"Let's go to the Country Club. Belsize Park isn't too far from Kilburn..."

"We're away next weekend, in France, so we'll make it the weekend after."

"How you getting there?"

"Train and boat. Haven't got a car."

"You should get one. You won't get far without one."

"Got to pass my test first, take lessons."

"Try Thanet. They're in Kilburn High Road. They use Austin Eleven Hundreds. I learnt on one a few years ago."

"Where did you get your Mini?"

"Second hand jalopy. But it gets me around. Bought it off a bloke in Harrow." Paul hesitated. "If you want a car, I can help. This bloke does up cars that are write-offs, makes them good for the road again. Very clever geezer!"

"Minis?"

"Yeah, if that's what you want. Get your provisional licence and you can then get a car, drive with Lynda, L-plate on the back, Bob's your uncle!"

The *Hooray Henries* bought a bottle of wine as their passport to the party, appended themselves to the girls as they all exited the pub at fifteen minutes past eleven, the landlord demanding all its patrons immediately leave, having consumed more than the allowed *'ten minutes drinking-up time'*. Lynda tucked her arm around Mark's as the group lazily made their way over the cobble stones of Earl's Walk, heat from the day caught, retained, between the mews' Georgian houses.

"That's it there." Mark pointed to the open door and the welcomingly loud music pouring into the mews. He joined the singer on the record being played *there she was just walkin' down the street singing do wah diddy, diddy, diddy, dum diddy doo.*

Like a rash the party had spread all over the house. People crammed into every corner and hideaway of the claustrophobically-dimensioned house, spilling from every room, littering the stairs, populating the small grassed garden. The ground floor was split into two rooms, one at the front, dark, crammed with bodies dancing to friendly hit records that beckoned Mark. On the other side of a wall, the kitchen shone bright, its linoleum-covered floor swimming with beer and wine, spilt by uncaring partygoers, none of whom would be around in the cold light of dawn to clean up.

Scented waif-like girls, hair towered high on the head, black panda eye shadow, glided by or shoved their way through gyrating bodies, all dressed in shapeless miniskirts that Mark much appreciated as they revealed well-proportioned legs, while one or two other females had gams he considered offensive weapons, log-girthed limbs that should have remained hidden from the eyes of cultivated society.

The males were a strange mix of early twenties LSE students, and people like Mark, also early twenties, but gainfully employed *super-cool, hip*, executives. And four *Hooray Henries* gathered from the Scarsdale pub.

He followed Lynda and the others to the kitchen where he deposited the *Mateus Rosé* eyeing an opened bottle of Bull's Blood. It was a rough, meaty wine but it was a lot more fulfilling than rosé, white, or the anaemic, urine-coloured Watney's Red Barrel. He poured the red wine into two paper cups, handing one to Lynda. "Cheers!" and she was gone. He stood, feet planted on the wet lino, as she walked into the forest of bodies. Did she expect him to follow, like some unquestioning dog displaying unconditional loyalty? Or, was she saying it's *a party Mark and for an hour or so I'm going to*

116

enjoy it, something I can't do if you follow me around like some lost dog.

Well, two can play at that game Lynda Fowler. *I'll pick up some girl, take her to the garden and fuck her, or at the very least, have her suck me off.* Except that he didn't want any of that. He wanted Lynda, alongside him, boyfriend, girlfriend, a perfect relationship, made in heaven, just what their parents would have wanted for both of them.

He freed his feet from the kitchen floor and swerved his way to the front room where, to his dismay, he couldn't avoid but see that Lynda was already dancing, with one of the *Hooray Henries*. Salt in the wound. He put his cup down and walked to June and Anna, dancing together, joining them with a broad smile, he mouthing the words of the song they were clearly enjoying *my temperature's rising and my feet are on the floor twenty people knocking 'cos they're wanting some more let me in baby, I don't know what you've got but you'd better take it easy, this place is hot...*

Mark began to enjoy himself. He was dancing to records that had his feet tapping, and dancing with two girls who had no intention of walking away from him as soon as they could, after the first record faded. June and Anna were clearly enjoying themselves, moving arms and bodies sinuously, energetically, like wind-driven waves insistently lapping on a beach. All three of them fed off each other, each injecting fun, pleasure and a frisson of sexual excitement, their gyrations becoming increasingly flirtatious semaphores signalling a desire for coitus.

But, Mark told himself, with Lynda somewhere in the party, he wasn't looking for sex. He was, above all, concentrating on avoiding her discovering him having casual, gratuitous sex with a girl he'd only just met, whose name he probably hadn't bothered to elicit. Instead he told himself he could *pull* any *bird* at the party, given his prowess as a *cool, hip* dancer to any Top 40 record.

When June and Anna finally indicated they wanted a break they'd all been dancing for an hour and only then did Mark become aware his shirt was ringing with sweat, his deodorant giving off a sickly-sweet odour, the heat in the room finally registering with him. "I'm going to see if there's anything left to drink." And in the kitchen there was nothing but the water in the tap. He poured a cupful and slipped into the garden, pleasantly surprised at the warmth of early hours summer London. "Where are the fireworks?" he asked, crouching down by a girl sitting on the paved patio. "Thought it was meant to be a July fourth, independence day party."

"Didn't know that." The voice was quiet, tone disinterested, delivery slurred. Mark deduced she was high, presumably from smoking dope, and the assumed knowledge sexually aroused him, something he didn't fully understand but enjoyed the emotion as, beneath his dark grey slacks, his penis grew. The arousal arrived wrapped in an envelope of sensuous warmth, visiting on him a confidence.

"Have you got any dope?" he whispered, conspiratorially, leaning forward, kissing lightly the side of her forehead. She turned, smiled a schoolgirl giggle, took his hand and stood up, Mark pulling himself to his feet. They walked slowly through the mass of bodies, in single file, she holding onto his hand, stupefied but clearly aware, and as they climbed the stairs he became aware of her figure. She was very skinny, her upper body in an olive-coloured t-shirt, chiselled to a narrow waist, merging to small, pert buttocks held in black velvet hot pants.

She turned into a darkened bedroom, dropped Mark's hand, climbed over the legs of two males leaning against a wall. He watched as she dug under a pillow on the bed, retrieved what he discerned as a tobacco tin. They shared a smile and returned to the stairs, then to the garden. This time she wasn't intoxicated. She was very much awake, determined. In the garden's shadows she handed

118

him the tin. "Roll two." The order was delivered in a quiet but, Mark noted, menacing tone.

He had never rolled a cigarette before but had seen Paul and Anna do it so gingerly opened the battered, yellow-coloured tin with the words *Old Holborn* on the lid, desperate not to spill its contents, poured tobacco into the folded paper, rolled it in his fingers, licked the gum, giving it a final roll. Mark handed the completed work of art to the girl. "Light?" He looked blankly at her and she turned to a group standing a few feet away. One of them recognised her. "Hi, Cheryl!" and handed her a box of Swan Vesta matches.

In an unsaid display of solidarity they lit their joints, inhaled, held the smoke in their lungs for ten seconds then exhaled. Mark expressed his appreciation. "Good!"

"Yeah, it's good stuff." She paused. "Your first time?"

He assumed she meant smoking cannabis. "No!" His voice carried a degree of incredulous pain. "No, we've smoked quite a lot!"

"You don't look like a dopehead."

"Don't suppose I am. I don't smoke morning, noon, and night."

"You should turn on as much as you can. Clear your head, think straight ahead."

"Don't think anyone I know will show any sympathy if I go to jail..."

"Paranoia! Eating away inside you!"

"So, what sort of job do you do so you can smoke all day long?"

"A fun one..." she looked at him. "You here with anyone?" A sly smile broke across her face.

"My girlfriend, Lynda. Haven't seen her though since we arrived, and that was..." he broke off, looked at his watch, "...three hours ago."

"Looks like she's pulled, whatever your name is."

119

"Mark..." He gave her a look that plainly said *should I go and look for my girlfriend or stay here with you?* He dropped his head, embarrassed. "Better go and find her."

"OK. Best of luck!"

He walked briskly across the short patch of grass into the kitchen, the few deep puffs of cannabis having no obvious effect on him, telling himself he'd fallen at the first hurdle. It was a test and he failed miserably. She was offering sex, he was sure, but he'd decided to run away, frightened, so middle-class, so *un-hip and un-cool*

Back inside he soon found Lynda. She was dancing with a worryingly good looking older man, her arms linked around his neck. He stood in the darkness, out of the light that seeped in along the hall from the kitchen, spying on her. *You've lost that loving feeling* moaned the song on the record player. Then he noticed she'd looped her tights around her neck. God! She's had sex with him! And were her knickers in his pocket? A trophy? Then they kissed and he fled the room.

Cheryl laughed as he approached. "You found her! Don't tell me, she's upstairs in bed being poked by some fella!"

"Not quite. She's dancing with some older bloke. I left when they kissed. She had her tights around her neck, so it's looks like they have done it!"

She put her arms around his neck, "Ahh, you poor thing! Your girlfriend's been stuffed by another bloke..."

"It's not funny!" He cut across her mocking.

"What's not funny, you twit, is you thinking you own your girlfriend!"

"I don't think I own her!" Mark protested.

"Yes, you do! You think she's a possession! That's why you're angry!"

"What ever happened to loyalty, whatever happened to boyfriend-girlfriend relationships?"

"Still around, just the rules have changed. You men can't go treating women like meat. You've got to start respecting women. Life's changing, old man! Get in the groove or you'll be left behind, yesterday's man!"

"Thanks for the advice Jill Tweedie!" Mark was unimpressed, began to pull away.

"Hey, where you going?" She linked her hands together to halt his exit, kissing him lightly on the lips.

"Good question..." his voice trailed off. "Think I can safely say this party has turned into a disaster."

"Let's go to your car."

"Don't have one."

"That's a drag. I was going to cheer you up..."

"You mean..."

"Hey, the penny dropped! Yes, I mean...like I mean, I'd like a poke..." she broke off. "Unless that's your girlfriend coming this way..."

Mark turned. It was, and he told himself Lynda was slightly tipsy, maybe she'd also been sharing a joint or two.

"What are you up to?" She addressed Mark while giving Cheryl an interrogative look.

Mark felt like the boy caught with his hand in the cookie jar. "Just enjoying the party and the warm night air. You?"

"Talking, dancing, drinking, meeting people, whatever you do at parties..."

"How's your boyfriend, the one you were snogging?"

Lynda paused, recovered. "Oh him! He became a bore. Wanted to take me back to his quarters. Just didn't fancy him that much!"

"Quarters?"

"Yes, he was Household Cavalry!"

"And your expensive Wolford tights?"

Lynda looked down at her legs. "What about them?"

"Saw them around your neck..."

"...yeah, took them off. It was too hot for them. It was like a furnace, dancing in there!"

Cheryl laughed. "He thought you and your guards officer had been doing it!"

"Did he? Sorry about that! He's got it on the brain..."

"...that's OK." Cheryl smiled. "Think you'll find he's in love with you."

Mark was uncomfortable. "Let's go." He put his arm around Lynda's waist but she pushed it away. "Yeah, let's go. I'm tired and need some sleep."

Mark sloped behind her, wondering where Paul and the other girls were, unhappy that it didn't look like any of them would be going on to The Pheasantry.

CHAPTER SEVEN

Most of the week following the Earl's Walk party developed into a small, private hell for Mark. Lynda revealed her displeasure with him, perhaps, life in general, by limiting their conversation to monosyllabic exchanges, finally informing him her period had started. He looked at the calendar and admitted to himself that their weekend in Normandy would probably be *sans sexual intercourse.* But, at risk of darkening the weekend's atmosphere, he would find an opportunity to ask Lynda why she hadn't worked out the date of her period when discussing their French trip. He suspected a conspiracy.

His plan had been to make the weekend a memorably enjoyable escape from the confines of their room at Chatsworth Road, the peripheral nature of the subjects of conversation around the kitchen table, and the *ska* face of Kilburn High Road. The only likely fly in the ointment would be his intention to discuss with Lynda their relationship and to discover finally whether it had a future, or was a lost cause.

Thursday evening, they packed their clothes into a single suitcase, one of Lynda's fashionably expensive Samsonites, made cheese and ham sandwiches for the journey, packets of Smith's crisps, put their passports and tickets into a buff British Railways foolscap folder, and booked a 'mini-cab' for Friday morning. It would be driven by a middle-aged Asian, someone who, Mark told himself, had the destination not been Victoria station, would have got very badly lost. In the event, the very white Cockney driver bulleted his Ford Zephyr in a straight line down the Edgware Road, Park Lane, Grosvenor Gardens and into the station forecourt.

The train journey to Newhaven was speedy but the crossing over what the French insisted was *La Manche* was lengthy. On board the goodship *Villandry*, the sparsely numbered French crew spoke English reluctantly and poorly. Both Mark and Lynda found their couchette, he bought two cups of coffee, they dug out their sandwiches and crisps, and ate as the sun-drenched waves outside rose and fell.

Douane at Dieppe was a nightmare as the French uniforms examined in meticulous detail every page of every British passport, their loathing of the perfidious British or, at least, English writ large on every face. "Bloody-minded frogs," Mark whispered as the shaven-headed demi-warriors insisted each suitcase was opened, each uniform taking great delight in rifling contents, leaving disorganised heaps for mute, hapless tourists to make good.

Fortunately, the walk from the ferry terminal to the hotel was a friendly few minutes along *Avenue de la Republique*. Inside Lynda's room they unpacked, Mark making little attempt to check his own room since he would not be using it for sleeping. They walked down to the beach. "Brighton," observed Mark as they noted the long sweep of pebbles that ran away before them to a narrow strip of eggshell-coloured sand, lapped by the channel waters.

Using the Kodak Brownie 125 camera he'd owned since his school days, Mark snapped Lynda and she snapped him, stopping a couple to request a shot of them together, arms locked around waists, big, happy smiles.

They walked along the sea front to the casino and agreed to eat in its horrendously expensive restaurant prior to experiencing the gaming tables. From there they drifted towards the town centre, both agreeing that it was a little jaded, if not downright shabby. Yes, it had its restaurants, bars, intimate-looking hotels, *boulangerie, boucherie*, and candle-stick makers but no fashionable shops, nothing *hip*, *groovy* or *gear*. In a small, stone-framed *epicerie*, with a window jammed full of produce representing every imaginable food stuff, they bought a bottle of red wine and four hand-made pastries.

When they found the train station they hunted down a window and Lynda asked for the pre-booked *billets* for their day-trip further along the coast to Fécamp and Deauville. Her fractured French and the SNCF supernumary's refusal to speak a word of English metamorphosed the simple, basic request to a parody, akin to a sketch from *Not So Much a Programme, More a Way of Life*.

"What a nightmare that was!" Mark was laughing at the comedy of the situation but annoyed that the strident protectionism of their language made the French such sad, marooned figures of fun. She reproved him. "We should learn French if we're coming to visit their country." They sat at a table outside a bar and ordered, in perfect French, *cafe au lait deux, s'il vous plait.*

Back in their hotel room Mark flicked on the radio, oddly sunk into the bedhead, twiddling the dial, searching for music. He hoped he would be lucky and find water-borne pirate radio stations, Caroline or London, but drew a blank, having to settle for the only station the radio would recognise, one that offered a male speaker who spent ten minutes hectoring his audience in manic French before reluctantly playing two minutes of music, of a genre he'd last heard on *Housewife's Choice* sometime around his tenth birthday. He cursed and switched it off.

Lynda removed her dress, hung it up in the wardrobe, wrapped herself in her housecoat, lifting herself onto the bed. Mark laid out Kleenex sheets on the bedside table, placed two of the pastries on the virgin white fresh tissue, then dug out of the case the two plastic cups and corkscrew they'd packed, opened the wine, lying alongside Lynda on the bed. They ate in silence, sipping the cotes du Rhone, and when Mark slipped a hand inside the housecoat Lynda said nothing, made no move to stop him.

When he slid a hand inside her bra, gently massaging her breast, then fingers squeezing a nipple, she turned and they kissed. Her hand moved to his crotch where she located his zip and pulled it open. The hand moved inside and eased out his penis, stroking it slowly but firmly, pulling determinedly down on the foreskin, until it was fully erect. Then she broke away from kissing him, dropped her head, sinking his erection deep into her mouth.

He placed a hand on her head as it rose then fell, slowly at first then with an increasing pace. "Oh, my God Lynda, that's so good!" And a few minutes later he climaxed, four spurts of sperm filling her mouth. She brought her head up and kissed him, her tongue depositing a dollop of the warm creamy issue in his mouth. They then fell asleep.

* * * *

For the first time in their seven month intimate relationship they showered together, Mark laughing at Lynda's shower cap, she studiously ignoring his erection in the water's heat, he intrigued by the inch or so of tampon string that exited from her vagina. When they did eventually kiss Lynda fought off the temptation to engage in anything sexual. Instead she stepped from the bath, wrapping the miniscule towel around her frame, sitting at the dressing table, launching into her make-up ritual.

Mark shaved his face, sprayed his chest and cheeks with Trumper's eau de cologne, his armpits with Mum rollette. He dressed in a simple mid-blue Ben Sherman button down shirt, grey slacks and loafers. Lynda had brought three dresses, all with muted

126

floral patterns, conventional knee length. "Can't see the mini skirt having got to Dieppe." Mark concurred. "If you wore a mini skirt to the casino they'd ban you from entering."

In the casino's restaurant the extravagantly presented menu distilled to a half a dozen *le plat principal*, bookended by *appetizers* and *desserts*. Despite their fractured French neither could fail to recognise *sole meunière* and, assuming it to be locally fished, they ordered it, with *hors d'oeuvre* of *champignons* in a sauce for Lynda, and *pâté en terrine* for Mark, plus a carafe of red wine, the waiter displaying faux shock at the ordering of the wrong colour wine to accompany fish.

While he maintained a conversation with Lynda over dinner comprising mainly peripheral subjects, deep inside his brain he wanted to talk about 'us', attempt to discover exactly what was deep inside Lynda's brain. Yes, she'd told him she had no interest in marriage, no interest in behaving like her Victorian parents, marrying young without seeing anything of the world that existed outside their village. He found it difficult to accept but she clearly had no desire to commit, telling himself that was only Lynda's short term view. Mark was quietly desperate to achieve some understanding of what the long-term future offered, believing Lynda, deep-down, wanted stability, firm foundations, not quicksand.

But while their conversation ranged over numerous subjects including his job and exactly what he did day in, day out, plus his need to take driving lessons, discovering dope, music, films, and the tickets he'd promised to buy to see Barbra Streisand in *Funny Girl*, they studiously avoided discussing the future of their relationship and the threat of Lynda going off to the countryside as a croupier.

After the meal they climbed the ornate marbled staircase and entered the casino. The room was long and wide, thick, plush carpet under their feet, opulently decorated, gold leaf on walls and ceilings, rich red drapes at tall windows, all impressively presented in homage to a long dead French king.

In front of them two lines of tables, alternating roulette and blackjack, ran to the horizon, each table busy with gamblers, the room's air busy with the low hum of polite society at play.

Lynda linked her arm in Mark's and they walked imperiously between the two lines, observing the play and the people. A few of the older men were dressed in dinner jackets and black bow ties, their ladies in sparkly gowns. Mark hummed the James Bond theme music, Lynda laughed, "Are they shaken or stirred?"

At the end of the room, Lynda released Mark's arm and joined the group around a roulette table. She watched intently at the mesmeric spinning wheel, and Mark observed her. The croupier was young, slim male, dressed in a red patterned waistcoat. Lynda appeared hypnotised as the croupier languidly spun the wheel, releasing the little white ball in the opposite direction, with noticeably more energy, his cultured voice informing all *rien ne va plus.*

Mark told himself it wasn't his imagination, Lynda clearly was seduced by the thought she might one day be a croupier. Perhaps not in a French casino surrounded by James Bond lookalikes, perhaps only in *cabaret clubs* in Great Yarmouth or Fakenham race course, perhaps only with shirt-sleeved farmer's lads and their *birds* as punters. But, he told himself, she could so easily move from *hicksville* to the Cromwellian Club, assuming she wanted to trade on her rural gaming experience, and her good looks. He felt depressed, leant forward. "You're not going to play are you?"

"No, I'm not." She turned to face him. "We don't have enough money." The tone was accusative.

"We might have some left on Sunday. You could always come back here, they're open all day, blow some francs, five to the pound."

"Let's take a look at the blackjack table." She moved across the floor, he followed shaking his head. Again, she appeared hypnotised, this time by the svelte speed at which the cards were brought from the antique-looking wooden shoe and placed down in front of each punter, multi-coloured chips pushed across the green baize with impressive ease. She stood watching for ten minutes, rooted to the spot, before finally breaking the spell. "Let's go!"

"Fancy a film?" He gave her a broad smile.

"You mean the one they're showing here?"

"Yes. *High Wind in Jamaica*. They've got it on at eleven."

"Looks like a kid's film."

"It might look like that but I bet it's a lot more adult."

"What are we going to do if they've dubbed it into French?"

"Good question." He paused. "We should be able to follow it. It's made for American audiences so should be a doddle to follow."

They walked from the casino, down the stairs to the cinema but as they did Mark's concentration was lost to his concerns about Lynda's fascination with the glamour of being a croupier. He knew, just a she did deep-down, the *cabaret clubs* in the English rural countryside of East Anglia were as far removed from the glitzy opulence of Normandy's casinos as the *Queen Mary* was to a rust-bucket merchant ship.

As they both surmised, *High Wind in Jamaica* was, as the Americans would say, a *turkey.* It was, Mark observed, a film that wanted to reprise the *Jolly Roger* element of Walt Disney's take on *Treasure Island*, a film he recalled fondly from his childhood, a film that set him on a course of devouring English literature classics, courtesy of F W Woolworth's *Heirloom Library* books, from his eighth birthday to his fourteenth. He took a visceral dislike to any film that attempted to usurp any of his priceless childhood memories.

Back in the hotel, in their room, they undressed, climbed into bed, kissing passionately, Lynda masturbating Mark in a muscular

129

fashion, a pair of her knickers wrapped around his erection. When he climaxed his body shook, Lynda released her grip, turned and instantly fell asleep.

He got up, cleaned himself, slipped back into the bed and lay awake, the room's near darkness heightening his hearing's acuity, sounds that would be lost during the day – the clanking of a steam locomotive and wagons in the harbour – as clear as a bell, entering through the open window, as if to woo him, seduce him, encourage him to slip out through the window's gap, fly to *Neverland*, a growing sense of isolation enveloping him before he, too, fell asleep.

The hotel had one hour set by for *le petit déjeuner* beginning at seven. At eight Mark woke Lynda. They showered, dressed and walked to the nearest cafe, ordered *pain, fromage, jambon,* and coffee. An hour later they presented themselves at Dieppe station seeking the train to Fécamp. The journey took a very brief twenty minutes, with very few others for company. They sat opposite each other, said little, Lynda buffing her nails, Mark absorbing the countryside, occasionally gazing at her until she looked up. "Yes, what do you want?"

He shrugged his shoulders. "Nothing. Just thinking how beautiful you are."

"Of course! Tell me something I don't know!"

"Tell *me*, darling, something I don't know!"

"What's that?"

"Tell me why it's me who loves you but you're not in love with me? And why you don't see any future for us." There, thought Mark, I've said it!

Lynda was not amused, and her voice heavy with boredom. "Oh, God, Mark! Do we have to talk about this now?"

"Why not?" He paused, not sure if he had the courage to continue, discovering he did when he heard himself being brave. "I know I'm being very juvenile, wearing my heart on my sleeve, but you're the first girl I've fallen in love with and it just knocks me for six when I don't get any encouragement back, any feeling that you care."

She let out a sigh. "Of course I care, Mark. I wouldn't be here today if I didn't. You've got a great personality, great sense of humour, we get on really well, same wavelength. But..." she halted. "As I've said Mark, I'm not interested in getting married. Not just yet, we're far too young..."

"I know that, Lynda. I know we're not going to get married any day soon. We both know we're too young for that, don't want to repeat our parents' mistakes...I just want to know you're not going to lose interest, run off somewhere."

"How do I know what I'm going to do, Mark! I'm young! You're young! Why do you want to map out your future? You can do that when you're thirty! This is swinging London Mark, not some village in India with my father picking out my husband when I'm ten years old!"

He pulled a face of resigned acknowledgement, nodding his head, turning to the window then back again, wanting to cry but biting his lip. "Guess I'd better enjoy you while I can!" She got up and sat alongside him, tucking her arm in his. "Aw come on, don't be sad, darling. Let's have some fun together!" He smiled, kissed her forehead and looked back out at the passing countryside, depressed at Lynda's words, but not surprised, telling himself he had a choice. Be the one to end the relationship, or continue and wait for the inevitable moment Lynda brought the shutters down. There was no choice. He couldn't bear to be apart from her.

* * * *

They arrived back at Chatsworth Road mid-afternoon expecting an empty flat, everyone out in the sun, but instead found a full house, flopped out on settee or armchair, either reading newspapers or paperbacks, or watching *I Love Lucy* on television. And the fading aroma of enjoyed joints. "Hi, you two!" Paul greeted them with a broad smile, dropping his *Sunday Times* colour supplement. "How was France?"

"We had a great time!" Lynda was bullish, pleasing Mark.

"Buy any chic French frocks?" June looked up from her book.

"Not in Dieppe..." Lynda's tone was mocking, prompting Mark to cut in.

"We could have in Deauville. Really trendy place. Or go to the races!"

"So, where did you go?"

"We based ourselves in Dieppe but went by train along the coast. Fécamp, Le Havre, can recommend it!"

"Is there any food?" Lynda sounded pained. "We haven't eaten since breakfast. We're famished!"

"We had roast beef for lunch." Paul pointed towards the kitchen. "Should be enough left for a couple of sandwiches."

"Thanks!" Lynda was relieved. "We'll unpack first, get our dirty clothes in a bag for the launderette."

Paul got up. "You unpack. I'll make you both a sandwich. Mustard on the beef?"

"Thanks, Paul! That's very kind."

"My pleasure!" He gave Lynda a broad smile. "And a date for the diary! We're having a party here next Saturday!"

"OK..." Lynda's voice trailed off. "Any reason?"

"No, not really. We just thought we should have one, can't keep going to other peoples' parties so thought we'd have our own. And it's summer. We can use the garden to get high!"

Mark smiled. "Sounds good! Let's get together on the music. Must make sure we have good music!"

* * * *

132

Lynda spent all week looking at Baz's card. Every morning she took it out of her purse, leant it against her card index box. It looked enticingly back at her. And every evening she put it back into her purse. But finally on Friday, after lunch with her boss, she returned to her desk and, perhaps emboldened by the lunchtime wine, she rang Baz's number. Nicola answered and they agreed she would start her training on Monday evening, continuing every consecutive evening for two hours until she and Baz were assured of Lynda's proficiency as a croupier, or bring it to an inglorious end should she not make the grade.

She didn't want to tell Mark but knew she had to. He would be angry and annoyed. She told herself he would absorb it as a comment on him as partner and a person, implying a lacklustre nature of their relationship, leaving him wondering what magic component in boy-girl love affairs he clearly didn't possess. He might even cry she thought, an act of self-pity she would find difficult to counter.

In the event Mark took the news with a resignation prompted by the inevitability telegraphed in their conversation on the train to Fécamp. He slumped on the bed, depressed, his head searching for ways to analyse the news, devine his next steps, try to work out some plan to save the relationship, understand why he couldn't cope with not being loved by a person he was so besotted with.

"So, you're going every evening to train being a croupier. Then what happens?"

"If they think I'm up to it, I'll hand in my notice and start working soon as I can."

"That's a week's notice?"

"No, a month's unless I can get out of it. I might be able to get it down to a fortnight. Depends on my boss."

"OK." Mark's depression slid a few floors deeper. "So, you could start as a croupier end of July?"

"Could be. Or mid-August if I have to work a month..."

"And your new mate Baz is willing to wait a month."

"He might not. I'll spell it out for him on Monday."

"What about the flat? You giving this room up? If you are then I'll leave, find somewhere else to live..."

"No. I'm only living in caravans and bedsits when I'm working, moving from one place to another, I'll leave my winter clothes here, and I'll be back here every weekend I get off..."

"Unless you go to your parents."

"Should be able to see them during the day, especially if I get a car. I can drive to them in an hour if I'm working in places like Fakenham."

"A car?"

"Yes, Nicola said I'd probably get one, just to make sure I get from one club to another. Can't rely on British Railways. I should know, I work for them!"

Mark stood up. "Are we going out for a meal?"

"Yes, don't want to stay in."

"OK. It's just that Paul had asked me to help him get the booze for the party."

"Booze? People will bring their own."

"We need some to start with."

"Where you going for it?"

"A cash and carry he knows in Cricklewood. Should be back by nine."

"That's too late to go out, Mark. Get us some fish and chips on your way back."

* * * *

Paul was in charge. He gave everyone a handful of duties. They shared pushing furniture back against walls, covering the TV with a table cloth. Mark muscled an elderly Qualcast mower across the overgrown back garden lawn until every inch has been cut to cricket pitch perfection, collapsing at the end, his arms heavy with ache and tiredness. The toaster was taken from the kitchen – "somebody will nick it if we leave it there" – and put in a cardboard box along with valuables the girls were advised not to leave on their dressing tables. Paul opened the loft hatch, jumped from a chair into the darkness with the box, and tucked it away from sticky fingers, closing the hatch with a sly smile.

A friend of Paul's would be bringing his collection of hit 45s for the party and Mark was asked to ready the radiogram for a night of heavy duty use. He did so, scooping up those LPs in his collection he treasured, hiding them beneath the bed, leaving behind a few for which he had no special love.

The girls went to Kilburn High Road to acquire fresh French bread and celery to accompany the cheese and crisps Paul and Mark had bought at the cash and carry. In Woolworth's they bought red lamp bulbs to ensure the lighting for the party was appropriately subdued.

At lunchtime they broke from preparation duties and walked to *The Old Bell* pub where all six bought pints of beer and rounds of dog-eared ham sandwiches. Mark and Lynda sat under the metaphorical spotlight as the others quizzed them about the trip to France and Lynda's decision to take Baz's shilling and learn to be a croupier. She presented it as a temporary summer job, one that would end with the arrival of autumn. There would be no change to existing arrangements, the rent would still be paid, her clothes would still be in the wardrobe, and Mark would wait for her return. "Well, that's the plan," he commented, his voice clearly implying there could easily be a change.

At closing time, Anna and June jumped a 16 bus to Church Street market, while the others walked back to Chatsworth Road where Paul and Kay slipped to her bedroom, and Mark and Lynda to theirs.

The carnal knowledge denied Mark in France while Lynda was enduring a period was a fast-fading memory. There was now no such impediment to full sexual enterprise and Lynda was once again voracious, almost animal, in her desire for sexual pleasure, satisfaction, and fulfillment.

After an hour they fell asleep, waking only when Paul banged on their door. It was six in the evening. Lynda showered first as Paul's friend with the music arrived and they played a selection, Mark listening in, enjoying the irresistible dance records that included *Black is Black, 123, Mr Tambourine Man, Hard Day's Night, It's All Over Now.*

Lynda wore a loose white top, bought in Deauville, sporting the *Oui* magazine logotype, her blue denim mini skirt, and flowery tights Mark had bought her during their King's Road excursion. He opted for his Levi 501s and a plaid Ben Sherman button-down shirt, both of which had labels hidden away from sight that boasted *Made in America by Americans.*

Mark had invited half a dozen people from work and a few clients while Lynda similarly invited girls from British Railways' Liverpool Street typing pool, a few from Warwickshire House, as well as Mouse and his girlfriend Suzie, plus Mouse's business partners, Nick and Toby.

A small group of guests gathered from ten and for an hour the party looked doomed, everyone standing around, nervously looking at each other and the large gaps between themselves. Then the pubs closed and a swarm of people descended on 89 Chatsworth Road and within half an hour there were clearly a hundred or so people covering every inch of carpet and lino, dancing to *hip, groovy* records.

Lynda remained with Mark for a lot longer than he imagined she would, both dancing together for appreciable periods, occasionally breaking off to introduce him to her workmates, friends from

Warwickshire House, he returning the courtesy with introductions to his work colleagues. Then they parted, agreeing to play at being hosts, circulate, ensuring people were enjoying themselves. Mark didn't want to part from Lynda but he had to tell himself to be *grown up*, thank God for small mercies. At least she hadn't dumped him. Yet. She clearly had some feelings for him. He wasn't husband material but he wasn't a complete *Charlie*.

The people Mark knew and invited to the party had atomised. At the beginning of the party they had coalesced into groups but, now, were individuals either dancing or deep in conversation. He slipped past them unnoticed, facing the inevitable drift into the garden, just as he had two weeks earlier in Earl's Court. And there, equally inevitably, he found Mouse and Suzie, sitting on the newly mown lawn, in a small group, smoking dope, passing around joints.

He invited himself into the group, and welcomed the joint, dragging on its fulsome body, holding the smoke in his lungs for ten seconds, exhaling, coughing an endorsement, "Good stuff!" And it was. He immediately felt its lift, his mind easing, his body relaxing, listening to the inconsequential conversation, only coming out of his soporific repose when he heard Suzie ask after Lynda. "She's fine. Indoors somewhere." He paused. "We'll have to come to the shop someday soon, see what's new."

"Lots! Come tomorrow! Some of the shops are opening on a Sunday. Against the law, but what the fuck!"

"You don't want them closing you down."

"If they do, they do! But this is 1965 and if we want to open seven days a week we should be able to. People want to shop at weekends..."

"Sure, of course!" Mark wasn't interested in the travails of their business but feigned concern. "So the shop is doing fine then?"

"Sure is! We'll be in *Nova* next month and we had American TV news people film there last week." She inhaled on the joint, handing it to Mark.

"So, you and Lynda living here together?" Mouse had a Cheshire Cat smile on his face. *You're as high as kite* thought Mark. "Sure are! It's a great flat. Share it with three other girls!"

"Sounds interesting! Bring them to the shop one day!"

"Think you met one of the girls. June? She came with Lynda to your party."

"Sure! They modelled some of our gear for the *Express*."

"Yeah. What happened to that? Was it printed?"

"No, the buggers never used it in the end!"

"Shame!" Mark got up. "I'll get and find Lynda, bring her out." He smiled, turned, and stumbled forward, righted himself. *Powerful stuff!* he thought, and indoors he made for the kitchen, pouring cold water into a paper cup. Taking a few gulps he searched for Lynda but she couldn't be found.

He walked up the staircase. Their bedroom door remained locked but Kay's bedroom door was ajar, an inviting narrow shaft of dim light beckoning him. As he got closer to the door he heard the low vibrations of some slow, mesmeric blues-influenced jazz music he told himself he knew as the work of the group put together by Don Rendell and Ian Carr. He gently pushed the door. The room was lit by two candles, and sitting on the floor he saw the shapes of three people, his nose enjoying the aroma of cannabis.

As his eyes acclimatised, the shapes become recognisable. They were Paul, Kay, and someone he hadn't seen before. And, bizarrely, June standing face to the wall her arms tracing a large arc above head, arms moving in time with the lazy, seductive music, her hips swaying. He watched her, transfixed, like a rabbit on a country lane, a prisoner of car headlights.

Paul looked up at him, grinning but not initially speaking. When he did his voice was slurred, sounding, Mark told himself, more the worse from alcohol, not drugs. "Mark! Good to see you old chap! Where's your lady?"

Mark crouched. "Don't know. Thought she might be here..."

"Far too independent, old chap! Got to keep your woman under control!"

Mark went a shade of red in the dark. He didn't need or appreciate any relationship advice from anyone, specially a drunk anyone. "June appears to be enjoying herself!"

"Mesco time! She's mellow yellow old chap!"

"Hope she finds that happy valley!" Mark got up. "I'll find Lynda and we'll come back, join June..."

"You do that, old chap!"

Downstairs, the party had thinned. The music was still frenetic, still the spirit of *Ready, Steady Go!* And the thirty or so dancers clearly enjoying it, including Lynda, her dance partner a tall swarthy male, slim, good-looking, probably Spanish, Mark told himself. He stood on the sidelines, fixed his gaze on Lynda. When she finally noticed him she waved, stopped dancing, clearly apologised to the swarthy male, and made her way to Mark.

As she got close she raised her arms and brought them down on his shoulders, kissing him very dramatically, superficially at first, then with some passion before breaking off. Mark was very impressed. "You pleased to see me?"

"Of course I am darling!" she paused, looked around. "You enjoying yourself?"

"Yes, I am. It's been a good party, not over yet." He stopped, looked across to the dancers. "Who was that you were dancing with?"

"Thought you'd ask me that." She took his hand and walked towards the kitchen. "That's Baz's business partner. His name is Apollo."

Mark was shocked. "What's he doing here?"

"He's with Baz..."

"What, he's here?"

"Yes."

"How did he know about the party? You didn't tell him did you?"

"No! Of course not! I don't want the landlord at our party. Must've been somebody else."

Mark dropped his voice. "Well, I was going to invite you upstairs to Kay's room. There's a little party going on there. June's high on mescaline, climbing the wall, Paul's high on pot..."

"Then we don't join them until Baz and his partner leave."

"They may not."

"They will. They're going soon. Got something else to do."

"OK, let's go to the garden. Mouse is out there. Wait there 'til they go."

And they waited in the garden. Mouse and his group sat on the grass in a large informal group, a few of the faces illuminated by the lighting spilling from the kitchen, one of them was Anna, arms wrapped around a good looking young man, her happy expression and bright, laughing eyes indicating the fruits of inhaling what *Private Eye* would call *exotic substances.*

Mark left Lynda to do the talking, engaging Mouse and Suzie with her croupier news, and plans to flee London for the flesh spots of East Anglia. They were shocked she should ever consider leaving the centre of the known universe for hicksville, confidently informing her that it was a seismic error of judgment that would have her running back to reality. Mark was asked for his views and he willingly gave them his feelings of deep regret, only to be admonished for allowing Lynda's plans to leave London to develop.

140

He resented the uninformed blame but, inside his head, realised he was culpable, his lack of authority, lack of firmness providing the vacuum Lynda was able to all too readily exploit.

"They've gone. OK, let's go!" Mark got up, extended his hand and pulled Lynda onto her feet. She turned, explaining their imminent departure with a conspiratorial smile. "Little party upstairs. Come with us!" They tagged on behind and all four snaked their way through the dancers, the records still loud and insistent *she said that living with me is bringing her down, she would never be free when I was around.*

Mark gently pushed the door and they all filed into the candle-lit mystery, dropping to the floor to join the others. The music on Kay's record player was now the MJQ, perfect thought Mark for the room's near-darkness. June was no longer hugging the wall but sitting, cross-legged, hips and torso still moving to the music, hands clasped, waving slowly above her head.

Stupor cloaked the room. Nobody appeared to notice that four people had entered the room and were now sitting with them. "They're all high as a kite," whispered Mark. It was a statement of the blindingly obvious, eliciting a firm *sotto voce* "Right on!" from Mouse. He pulled from a pocket his tobacco tin and began to produce a joint, slowly with care in the shadowy light from the candles. He lit it, inhaling, passing it to Mark to inhale, then to Lynda who did likewise, passing it to Suzie. As it circulated Mouse rolled a second one, and as he lit it Paul surfaced from his stupefaction. "Hey, Marky! Good to see you!" And was offered the joint by Mouse. It was inhaled and passed to Kay. "Where's Lyndy-loo?" "I'm here!" chirped Lynda. "Groovy!" Mark watched as he jerkily got up, stumbled across to the dressing table, opened a drawer and removed what looked like a small box, and returned, falling back alongside Kay.

141

He shoved the box towards Lynda. "Marshall McLuhan time! Timothy Leary time!" Lynda pushed his hand back. "Not for me Paul. Once is enough. I'll stick to this." She held up the joint she'd been handed. Paul wasn't upset. "OK! Your loss! Just think of all those groovy pictures in your head you'll be missing!" Lynda said nothing, passed the joint to Mark and got up, whispered: "I'm going to our room. You coming?" Mark got up. "Sure. But who's going to lock up when the party is over?"

"You are. You're the only one who isn't totally doolally on Paul's mind benders..."

"I'll go downstairs, get rid of people."

"Don't be long."

Mark walked downstairs with some trepidation. He'd never stopped a party before and expected to be lynched. He would have to lie and the only one he could think of deploying was the threat that the police would be on their way if the noise continued. He turned off the record player to loud moans but was unnerved and pointed to his wrist watch. It was past three in the morning and apologised for the sudden bringing down of the shutters. Fortunately they put up no resistance and filed good-humouredly from the house into the warm Chatsworth Road night.

In the garden he found half a dozen, all under the influence of *exotic substances* he told himself, all incapable of understanding his entreaty. He locked them in the garden and went upstairs.

He entered the room to Paul repeating his declaration with a schoolboy glee: "Marshall McLuhan time! Timothy Leary time!" Lynda surveyed the box in his hand.

"Take it!" Paul dropped in her palm. "Take off, enjoy! Don't come back 'til you're ready!"

Lynda turned to Mark. "You going to join me?"

He nodded his head, some trepidation on his face. "OK."

She opened the box. Four sugar lumps. Mark peered. "One each. No more."

They both each took one of the small cubes and handed the box back to Paul. And a few minutes later the fantasy images began to build in Mark's head until he was entirely consumed, a return to the valley and puffs of cloud moving across a blue sky he had witnessed on Primrose Hill.

When he awoke there was daylight, he was fully clothed, in his and Lynda's bedroom, laid out on the bed, which hadn't been slept in. He pulled himself up, feeling perfectly well, no hangover, no aches or pains. He pulled back his shirt sleeve to check his wristwatch. Ten. Where was Lynda? Downstairs Anna and Kay were cleaning the kitchen. "Hi, can I help?"

They looked up. "Clean the walls, lots of mess on them." He dug a cloth from under the sink. "Where's Lynda?"

"No idea. She not with you?"

"No. Just me in the bedroom."

He took the wet cloth to the patterned wallpaper where wine and beer had been clearly splashed. But it was the last thing he wanted to do. He wanted to know where Lynda had got to. And he wanted to shower, get out of his clothes into something fresh. Mark cursed, asked himself where June was, to where Paul had disappeared. He persevered for some twenty minutes before summoning the courage to tell Anna and Kay he had to shower, clean himself up. "Where's Paul?"

"He went home."

"June?"

"Must be still asleep."

Mark showered, noticed the bathroom has been cleaned. He dressed and, downstairs, was asked to clean up the garden, gather up the party detritus. He filled two plastic shopping bags, placed them in the dustbin and walked to Kilburn High Road to look for Lynda.

He strode down one side to well beyond the State, then back again on the other side, didn't find her, bought *The Observer*. Every shop that wasn't selling newspapers was closed. The pubs weren't open. He got back frustrated, annoyed. Why hadn't Lynda left him a message?

In the kitchen he found June, sitting at the kitchen table, in a shabby towelling robe, hugging a coffee. "Any idea where Lynda is?"

"Yeah. She's gone off to do some croupier training."

Mark spluttered. "I don't believe it!" He crashed onto a chair, opposite her. "It's Sunday! Why the hell can't she keep Sunday free, like everyone else does!"

"Think you'll find, Mark, you were spark out. She had no idea when you'd come round. You were on a mesco trip..."

"So was she!"

"No, she wasn't. There was nothing on her sugar lump, just yours. You went off, telling everyone how beautiful it was, climbing the walls. She took you off to your bedroom..."

"Did she? Where did she go?"

"Don't know. You better ask her."

"I will!"

"What are you doing today?"

"Well, I was planning to spend it with Lynda! Not much chance of that now!"

"Do you fancy going with me to some friends of mine? They live in Blackheath, having lunch."

"Lovely idea June but I think I should be here for Lynda."

"Don't waste your time, Mark. She's not going to be back 'til much later. You'll be sitting around here all day doing nothing!"

Mark moaned his annoyance, looked blankly at the kitchen table, the neatly folded *Observer*. Then brought his head up, faced her.

"OK, June, I'll come with you." He paused, sighed. "Can't sit around here all day, moping, reading the paper."

She got up, her robe falling open. "That's the spirit, Mark! You'll enjoy it!" Then she noticed Mark wasn't listening. Instead he was transfixed by her naked, bra-less breasts, and the little black knickers she wore. She laughed and pulled the robe off her shoulders. "You like?" Mark didn't answer but quickly averted his eyes, noting that June's breasts were smaller than Lynda's but firmer, with nipples that dominated, mesmerised him. She walked around and stood behind him, lent forward and whispered. "Come upstairs, Mark, and do me." She paused. "Please."

She kissed the top of his head. "There's no-one here, Mark, they're all out, not back for hours." She dropped her hand and squeezed his crotch. "You've got a hard on, Mark. Great shame to waste it! Come upstairs, Mark. Let's have a great little fuck! I'm on the pill, no need for a johnny!" He got up, dropped his head and kissed, then bit her right nipple, a finger pushing inside her knickers, then into her vagina. She hugged him. "That's better, you sexy man! I've wanted you to do that ever since you arrived!"

They climbed to June's bedroom where she fell on the bed, removing her knickers while Mark undressed. He joined her and they kissed passionately, she guiding his erection into her vagina. His hips crashed wildly into hers as they mutually enjoyed the unbridled lust for ten minutes, June letting out a series of loud moans, before he finally climaxed, depositing four spurts of spermatozoa inside her. He collapsed alongside her but June raised herself. "No, Mark! Get dressed! I've got to get a shower. You wait for me downstairs!" She smiled. "Mini skirt?"

"What?" He looked blankly at her.

"Would you like me to wear a mini?"

He shrugged his shoulders, not particularly interested in what she planned to wear for their day out in Blackheath. "OK. Wear a mini."

"Tights with knickers, or tights with no knickers?"

He laughed. "Tights with no knickers! Of course!"

Downstairs he read the paper but his head became increasingly populated by a strange mixture of guilt, having been dramatically unfaithful to Lynda while also viewing the sex with June as a way of spiting his girlfriend, getting back at her, a form of balancing the relationship books. He also wondered how long June would keep it a secret. He told himself she was sure to use their tryst against him at some stage. And he also enjoyed a modicum of self-satisfaction, having given June 'one' to the appreciation of all concerned, and without resorting to rolling on a johnny.

He looked up as she walked slowly down the stairs. It was a complete transformation. June had piled her hair high on head, put on her Dusty Springfield panda eyes, a khaki top, and a mini in a dogtooth check, tan tights. Halfway down the stairs she stopped, lifted her skirt. "No knickers!" He laughed and they left the house, her arm in his, a bottle of Macon red she'd bought at Thresher's.

It took an hour to get to June's friends. The threadbare tube service was more than matched by the emasculated Sunday train schedule from London Bridge. Her friends were Debs and Sally, met at university, now trying to survive in London living on a typist's pay. Their flat was the ground floor of a 1920s semi-detached house.

June and Mark were welcomed by the very Sunday aroma of roast beef, and after an hour of gentle, polite conversation they gathered around the dining table where Mark was asked to carve the joint. Despite watching his father carve roasts and the Christmas turkey, it wasn't something he'd done before, and his failure to slice the hot beef evenly was a source of amusement. He blamed the blunt carving knife but joined the others in enjoyably devouring the pink meat, home-made Yorkshire pudding, and vegetables that hadn't been boiled to a bland tasteless state.

There followed home-made baked Alaska, coffee and, to stave off falling asleep, they resolved to walk across the heath to Greenwich. At the observatory they voiced their admiration for Wren's naval college, gazing down to the Thames as it snaked one way to the west, and the other towards the North Sea. And after touring the observatory buildings Mark peered at his wristwatch and declared they should be getting back. "Not me, Mark." June whispered. "I'm staying with the girls tonight. Be back tomorrow, after work." The penny instantly dropped. Debs and Sally were lesbians or, at least, swung both ways.

He smiled at her, knowingly. "OK. Have fun!" June turned to Debs and Sally. "Mark's off now!" They jointly said their goodbyes. "You can get a train to London Bridge from Greenwich station, just down the hill and on the high street!" June kissed him lightly on the cheek and swept away with the other two, back towards Blackheath and the flat, sans knickers.

Mark stood, rooted, transfixed as the three slowly disappeared into the distance, a direct co-relation between their diminishing size and his growing feeling of being very alone and abandoned. Thirty seconds and sun's heat on the west side of his face brought him back and he quickly began his walk down the hill, his head now free to worry about Lynda and what she'd been up to all day.

At Chatsworth Road there was no Lynda. Kay and Anna sat with Paul in front of the television watching *Pinky and Perky*. "Hi, Mark!" Anna was cheery, Kay and Paul surveying him as he sat with them. "Any sign of Lynda?"

"She rang, left a message." His heart lifted, then crashed. "She won't be home 'til much later. She's gone to some club to look at the gambling. She's gone with Baz and his mate..."

"This guy Apollo?" His despondency deepened.

"Yep, think that's his name. You know him?"

"No, I don't but he was here last night with Baz."

"Baz was here last night?!" They all looked at him with fear and worry written across their faces. "Shit! What the fuck was he doing here?"

Mark was less concerned with the landlord spiriting himself at the party than Lynda with two men he didn't like or trust. "Where have they gone to, what club?"

"She said Great Yarmouth. But they might go to other clubs. Said she'd be back late."

"Thanks! Not very impressed with her, shooting off on a Sunday, the one day of the week we should be doing things together!"

"Come with us. We're going to the State to see *Emily*. Looks good, Julie Andrews and James Garner."

"I might just do that. What time you going?"

"Half six. We'll get a swift half in at the pub before."

Mark was impressed with the 1940s London captured in *The Americanization of Emily* even despite its complete failure to dress its cast in authentic period clothes and hairstyles. But cursed silently that he hadn't seen the movie with Lynda, that she had taken off from their Sunday together. He told himself as he had a girlfriend going to the pictures was a couple's activity, not something you did with flatmates.

They got back at ten thirty and around the kitchen table sat Lynda and June. Mark gulped, shocked to see June who had clearly decided not to stay the night with her Blackheath girlfriends. He was suddenly afraid June had boasted about seducing him. Would she? Or decide to keep quiet? And if she did would Lynda say anything? Or keep it to herself but use it to influence her attitude to him? And he wanted to show his annoyance at her deserting him on a Sunday, their one day together to relax, walk in the sun, visit parks, tube it to the West End, drink in a pub on the river, window shop, eat omelette and chips at a Golden Egg, or bangers and mash at a Sizzling Sausage, end a beautiful day at the Academy cinema, the one that

148

anonymously tucked itself away next door to M&S in Oxford Street, where he saw *Fellini 81½, The Trial, The Servant*, and many other films he regarded as being highly creative, the very antithesis of the low quality mush Hollywood was spewing.

She got up, "Hi there boyfriend! How's you?"

"Very sad and upset! Missed you and all the things we could have done today!"

She put her arms around his shoulders. "Ahh, poor thing!" And kissed him. He wanted to break away, to show his displeasure but couldn't. He loved her too much, his planned frigidity melted, and as she searched his mouth with her tongue, so he did hers with his. When she broke off she took his hand and they walked upstairs.

In their room they undressed and climbed into bed, Lynda declaring immediately she was offering an insatiable appetite for physical, aggressively active sex. Mark responded, releasing the day's tension that flowed from her disappearance with an equally visceral performance. Once he had climaxed he wanted to quiz her about her day but surmised her desire for torrid sex was an attempt to frustrate his interrogation. He was right. She immediately fell asleep while he remained awake for another twenty minutes, mesmerised by the curtains that gently lapped in the warm summer evening breeze that flowed, in tandem with the moonlight, into the room. But he, too, eventually succumbed, slipping into unconsciousness.

* * * *

All day he'd been dreading going home. There'd be no Lynda arriving at six or seven. It was Monday and her first evening of training to be a croupier. She'd go straight from work at Liverpool Street to Baz's place in Brent, and spend two hours learning to run roulette and blackjack tables. Instead of Lynda cooking them a simple meal he was on his own.

He was the first one home and after changing came down to the kitchen and looked blankly at the table, then the hob. He had never cooked anything in his life before. It had always been either his mother, a chef in a restaurant, or Lynda.

On their shelf in the fridge sat eggs and bacon, some cheese, cooking fat, remnants of a small loaf and a tub of margarine. He stood gazing at the food, paralysed with fear and indecision, his trance broken as the front door opened. He didn't turn to see who it was but instead pulled the egg box from the fridge, in an attempt to look decisive and active.

"Hi, Mark! What you up to?"

He recognised June's voice and turned. "Hello!" He paused, gave her smile but felt inside something more than just the perfunctory, automated welcome between people who know each other. And he sensed June also saw in his smile something more than a bland welcome. "I'm about to cook myself something. There's no Lynda so I have to do it myself. How do you make an omelette?"

She arrived alongside him, a hand squeezing his thigh and, looking down at the egg box and giggling whispered, "Am I wearing knickers, Mark?"

He laughed, looked down at her bare thighs. "You're not wearing tights so I'm assuming you're wearing nicks." And he pulled the hem up her thigh until the white lace nylon was revealed. "They're white. virginal white, as befits a virgin who's never been poked."

She smiled. "I'll cook you, us, an omelette. Then, afterwards, we'll go to my room, and you can do me."

He looked back at the egg box, his head finding it very difficult to simultaneously hold two thoughts, a desire for someone else to make him a meal, and the need for him to prove to himself he was able to stand on his own two feet. And the third, worrying, thought that grew rapidly, banishing the other two to the sidelines. How could he willingly have sex with June when his girlfriend lived under the same roof?

"Don't think that's a good idea, June."

"Why Mark? You worried about Lynda?"

"She happens to be my girlfriend, June." He paused. "I'm in love with her, not interested in playing around, not interested in anyone else..."

"So, what was that we did yesterday, in my bed, Mark? Don't think we were crocheting!"

"That was me not thinking June. You caught me at a very low moment. I got very high at the party on that mescaline, woke up, no Lynda, she'd shot off with Baz..."

"Not Baz, Mark. She went off with this guy Apollo. And, do you know what Mark? He did her, twice!" She paused. "He's got a big cock Mark, and Lynda likes big cocks!"

He groaned. "What, she told you that?"

"Yep!"

"She was boasting, showing off."

"Don't think so Mark. No need to. She's not in love with you. She doesn't want marriage, mortgage or kids. None of us do!" She stopped, pushed him aside. "Go and sit down. I'll make us an omelette."

He dug out knives and forks and placed them alongside worn raffia mats, complementing them with napkins, pepper and salt sellers, and the long-serving bottle of HP brown sauce that sat in a cupboard with an equally tired looking bottle of Heinz tomato sauce. And he sat, first looking blankly at the table, then turning to June, watching her back as she moved along the hob, cracking the eggs, whisking them, grating cheese, melting margarine in the pan, pouring in the egg, then adding the cheese. "I'll do some bread and marg."

"OK. But don't get in my way."

She cut the omelette in half, placed the halves on plates and sat at the table. He smiled. "Thanks, looks very eatable."

"Edible you mean."

"Yes, that too."

"Well, you'll have to learn how to make an omelette. It's basic!"

He ignored the advice. "So, I've got to accept Lynda doesn't love me and we've got no future?"

"Love, no, but whatever comes just below love..."

"Deep affection."

"Yep, that sounds right. You should take it as it comes, not try to force it. We're all free to run our own lives and those days are all gone when we all left school, worked as typists waiting for Mister Right to come along, got married, then screaming kids. All gone!"

"If she starts working as a croupier, that's the end of the relationship. She'll never come back to London."

"Wouldn't be so sure. She'll give it to the end of summer then come back, get a secretary's job somewhere and the two of you will be back to normal."

Mark was not reassured, feared the worse. "Hope you're right but can't see it happening. She's going to be away for six weeks or more. She won't even be back at weekends. It's going to be so lonely without her, like living on after someone close has died."

June wasn't impressed. "That's a bit dramatic, Mark. You'll hardly be on your own. You'll have us girls. This is your opportunity to get to know us, don't be so stand-offish!"

CHAPTER EIGHT

Mark bought a copy of the Highway Code, booked himself fourteen one-hour driving lessons at the Thanet School of Motoring, and began to acquire some understanding of how a car worked, the roles of the three pedals at his feet, and how to manoeuvre his vehicle, to him as big as a tank, on narrow streets busy with what looked like equally giant-sized mobile warriors.

Every evening at seven he climbed into an Austin 1100 and nervously drove Kilburn's residential streets, crawling along at studiedly slow speeds, his caution frustrating the seasoned motoring graduates. And while he drove his mind constantly returned to Lynda, wondering how she was progressing, learning to be a croupier, wondering if she was thinking about him as he manfully progressed towards mastering the art of driving a car, and onwards to a full driver's licence.

Once the lesson was over Mark would drive back to the flat and sit outside in the car, listening intently and politely as his instructor described his errors and weaknesses and what required Mark's urgent attention. He resolved to get a car and after three hours of learning to drive he was taken by Paul, accompanied by June, to his friend's used car lot where Mark, unabused by any knowledge of what constituted a good or bad car purchase, laid down a hundred pounds on a five year old Mini, plus five pounds on insurance.

He stood back with pride, admiring the Mini's faultless dark blue finish and light grey interior, taping an 'L' plate to the vehicle's radiator grill, and one to the rear bumper.

June, with a full driver's licence, sat alongside Mark as they made their way back from Cricklewood. It was painfully slow, his lack of road knowledge equalled by his worrying hesitancy with the three pedals at his feet, the car stalling with a juddering halt as he failed to let out the clutch at the critical moment while changing gear. And June's legs, wonderfully on show as her mini skirt sat high on her thighs, did little to aid his concentration.

Despite his unpromising display June agreed to accompany him for an hour after his driving lessons and was much heartened by his rapidly improving proficiency. He was very appreciative but silently wished it had been Lynda who had made the offer. Sadly for him, she did not get home every evening until ten, tired and hungry although very pleased Mark had not only booked driving lessons but had been exceptionally positive and had bought a car. She handed him fifty pounds, courtesy of her father, a contribution to the cost of the car, as promised, the gift pleasing him, he willfully misreading it as confirmation of her commitment to their relationship.

On Saturday morning they drove to the John Barnes department store in Swiss Cottage where Lynda bought two very simple black dresses, low cut, 'for work' she explained, sitting at a roulette wheel, or sliding cards from a Blackjack table shoe. He sat and watched as she tried them on, enjoying the display of her breasts. Until he realised the show would not be for him, but instead for the punters, the men who'd ogle her, get a hard on. "It's what Nicola told me to do. Get some dresses for the men. As she said, *I display, they play!*"

He liked the phrase but not the thought men would stand before her, looking across the roulette table, mesmerised by her tits, some doubtless fondling their genitals, leering at her as they bought and placed their chips.

On another floor they found the hosiery department where Lynda looked for black tights but found nothing other than stockings and theatrical fishnets tights. "I'll have to get fishnets. I'll be shortening the dresses. Can't wear stockings."

Over a ham salad lunch in the store's restaurant Mark attempted to mine information from Lynda on her day away from London while he dilly-dallied with June, he taking care not to reveal what June had already told him. "We drove up to look at some of the clubs. They weren't open but they let us in to look at the set-up, the layout. And I met some of the croups, saw one of the caravans they stay in."

"Where did you go? Great Yarmouth?"

"Yes, we did a tour. Yarmouth, Fakenham, Hunstanton, Caister, Stilton. And I called on my parents. We had tea there."

"We?"

"Baz's partner, Apollo."

"Right." Mark hesitated. "Where does he fit in?"

"Don't really know. Guess he and Baz run the gambling side of things at these clubs. Don't really want to know, just as long as they pay me!"

Mark looked at her, not entirely sure whether she was telling the truth or being disingenuous.

"How will they pay you?"

"Cash. I have to do my own tax and stamp. May use my dad's accountant for all that."

"So, will you be coming home at the weekends?"

She looked at him, sighing with wearied boredom. "I don't know Mark. It's unlikely while the clubs are busy with holidaymakers." She paused. "But it doesn't have to be weekends. I might be home during the week. All depends on how busy the clubs are. If it's slow then they'll send me home, expect me to wait for when it gets busy."

"So, you could be home for a few days, maybe longer." He smiled. "That's good news."

"No, it's not Mark. I don't get paid if I don't work!"

He slumped back. "Right." But then he brightened. "So, if you don't work you'll look for a permanent job in London?"

"Could be. Might try for a croup at one of the London clubs, Blaise's or the Cromwell..."

"But not secretarial work?"

"Good God no! Anything but that again!"

Mark frowned with the fear Lynda would leave London and never return. Or, worse, return one day in the not-so-distant future but make no attempt to look him up, make no fresh contact, show no signs of wanting to see him. Forgotten, rejected. He felt the despair inside him. It pained him. She really didn't care that much about him. And he couldn't come to terms with it, nor accept it.

"So, if it all goes to plan you'll be working as a croupier in a few weeks' time."

"I've got to put my notice in. So, more like mid-August." "Then we've got to make the most of what's left of our time together..."

"We're seeing *Funny Girl* tonight. Let's go on somewhere afterwards."

"Annie's Room. We can hear some good jazz."

"Where's that?"

"Drury Lane. Just opened by Annie Ross, you know, the Lambert, Hendricks and Ross singing group?"

"Not sure..."

"I've got Annie Ross's *Handful of Songs* LP in my collection. You must listen to it. Great music!"

"I will..."

"And next Saturday we can go to the *Talk of the Town*. Never been there. We can get a meal and watch the cabaret."

"Prefer to go to *Raymond's Revue Bar*!"

"You serious?"

"Sure! Let's go there! Much prefer watching the strippers than a collection of second league television acts!"

He laughed, stretched a hand across the table to squeeze one of Lynda's. "That's why I love you so much! You're independent, got your brain, a free spirit!" He immediately knew it sounded patronising but hoped she would accept it as something akin to a compliment. She did. Of course she did. She knew Mark would never ridicule or humiliate her. With his love came respect. Indeed, she knew all too well, respect was a cornerstone of his love for her. But she felt no guilt in not being in love with him. She had no respect for Mark's desire to imprison them in marriage at such a young age.

It was almost nine. Mark woke before Lynda. He always did, weekday, Saturday or Sunday. He wouldn't dare complain for there was nothing to complain about. He looked down at her, in the red baby doll he'd got her in March for her birthday, a few weeks beyond the first three months of their relationship. He lightly kissed her bare shoulder and she murmured something indecipherable but remained asleep. He looked at her as a young husband would admiringly look at his young wife. And sighed. They weren't married and would, he admitted, never be admiring husband and baby doll wife. Then that song from *Funny Girl* entered and hi-jacked his head *Don't tell me not to live, just sit and putter, life's candy and the sun's a ball of butter. Don't bring around a cloud to rain on my parade. Don't tell me not to fly I've simply got to. If someone takes a spill, it's me and not you. Who told you you're allowed to rain on my parade!*

He told himself, with some of that admiration for her, that it was Lynda's song, not Fanny Brice's. Last night, in the theatre, it was Barbra Streisand playing Fanny Brice but, for Mark, it wasn't a song describing the personality of an Edwardian female American entertainer, it was a song with a few clever lines that perfectly described his girlfriend: her enterprise, desire for freedom, her energy and ambition.

He also enjoyed taking Lynda to *Beotys* Greek restaurant, thankfully a short walk from the theatre. He'd had lunch there a few times, tucking into their famed moussaka, and harboured a desire to take Lynda to share his pleasure with their authentic Greek food. She appeared to appreciate it.

In the kitchen he made himself a coffee, taking care to be as silent as possible, sitting at the table, staring into the dark brown liquid made from a very fine powder over which he poured hot water. What, he wondered, was the dust-like powder made from. Coffee beans? Unlikely. It tasted utterly synthetic, clearly developed in some Frankenstein's laboratory. If only he could afford to buy real ground coffee, made from real beans.

He took his mug upstairs, into the bathroom and showered. As he left, bath towel wrapped around his hips, June slipped from her room, walking towards the bathroom, slowly, deftly, waif-like, smiling at him, both exchanging looks but saying nothing until he finally whispered a '*good morning*'. She stopped, placed a hand on his arm, leant into his face, spoke *sotto voce*. "Come back Mark. Let me suck you off." For a fraction of a second he felt like saying 'OK'. Instead he gave June a wearisome look. "Nice try but I've got my girlfriend waiting in bed for me." She grimaced and disappeared into the bathroom.

Mark dressed and went out to get his paper. As always on an early Sunday morning, the pavements along either side of Kilburn High Road were deserted, no other pedestrians in sight, everything closed save for the paper shop, the only apparent road traffic a 16 bus, and the occasional car. He bought an *Observer* and *Sunday Times* and back in the flat spread himself out on the settee, tuned into Radio London and waited for Lynda to wake. Mark told himself he would suggest they use the Sunday for drive up the Edgware Road and into the Hertfordshire countryside. He would drive while Lynda would make sure he didn't pile into other road users.

But Lynda had other plans. Over a breakfast of eggs and bacon he'd cooked, plus toast and coffee, Mark set out his wish to drive in the Mini to the countryside, spend the day in the bucolic sunshine. Lynda sighed, clearly uncomfortable at pricking his balloon. "I've got to learn how to play blackjack, and I was going to ask you to help me."

He spluttered with incredulousness. "What?!" He gave her a fierce look. "Lynda, you've got every night this week to learn how to play bloody blackjack! Today's a Sunday, we should be together sharing it, going somewhere, especially now we've got the car!"

She retreated. "OK, OK! We'll go out but can we not get back too late so I can do some boning up?"

"Sure. Bring whatever it is you have with you. We can do a tutorial while we lie in the shade of a tree by a babbling brook."

"Babbling brook? Where exactly are we going?"

"Drive up the Edgware Road, see where it takes us. Find a pub with a garden, get something to eat."

The day was not a success. While Mark drove, keen to converse, Lynda buried her face in the sheets of blackjack rules, reluctant to engage in any verbal exchanges and when he attempted to stroke her thigh, she unceremoniously pushed his hand away, admonishing him in an unnerving imitation of Joyce Grenfell censuring nursery schoolboy George: "Don't do that, please. I'm trying to concentrate."

He meandered off the Edgware Road into Elstree, drove past the film studios, and found a pub opposite a village green and pond. They sat in the pub garden, in the warm sun, ate bland cheese and ham sandwiches, emptied bags of Smith's crisps, drank revoltingly bad British lager instead of wine the pub did not sell. And Lynda could only discuss the rules of blackjack, repeatedly reading the rules, asking Mark to quiz her. He humoured her for thirty minutes before his frustration tetchily surfaced. "This is not a relaxing day out, Lynda! Can you stuff those bloody rules away and let us enjoy things!" She gave him a pained expression, theatrically folded the rules and slipped them into her bag. "OK, Mark, what are we going to do?"

"Let's go and find somewhere to have sex."

She supplied another pained expression. "You must be joking. I have no intention of having sex in public."

"Don't worry. I wasn't serious." He gave her a broad smile. "Let's get back in the car and just drive. Enjoy the countryside." He paused. "And I need to get better at driving."

"No, Mark!" She sounded exasperated. "Let's get back to civilisation. We'll go and see a film. Let's see *What's New Pussycat*. I want to see that. It's on somewhere in the West End."

"Odeon, Leicester Square."

"OK. Let's get back. And don't kill us."

The drive back was undertaken in almost total silence. The car didn't have a radio and, with Lynda buried in her sheets, he increasingly began to miss listening to Radio London's Sunday afternoon Top 40 hit records show, even Alan Freeman's *Pick of the Pops* programme. In what was his effective solitude Mark ruminated, annoyed that Lynda had ruined what promised to be a successful afternoon, and frustrated at his own pathological failure to influence, if not control, events.

* * * *

Monday night Lynda arrived home from croupier training earlier than normal and let no time pass before informing Mark they'd have one week left before she took up her new job, somewhere a hundred miles north-east of London. "British Railways said I can go on Friday," Lynda generously explained, Mark's face draining of life and energy, leaving it lined with fear and disappointment. "They owe me more than two weeks' holiday time so they've knocked that off my notice."

"So, when do you actually leave here, Chatsworth Road?"

"Sunday next week..."

"So our last full day is next Saturday."

"Yes. I'm being picked up on Sunday, around lunchtime."

"Who by?"

"Does it matter Mark?" She was defensive. "Probably Nicola..."

"Where to?"

"Not sure yet, probably Great Yarmouth or Huntstanton. I'll know this week sometime."

"So you won't be training every evening this week, you'll be here?"

"No, I won't. I've been asked to train some other girls..."

"Every evening?"

"Yes. I get paid for it, five pounds a time!"

"Great for you, Lynda. Not much good for us!"

"Don't start Mark. Don't be so bloody negative..."

"Don't rain on my parade..."

"Yes, don't be so down on what I do! You should be proud of me! I've just learnt how to play roulette and blackjack, and I'm so good I can now teach others to play them!"

He closed his eyes, partially to avoid her unhappiness, and to also hide his lack of a positive embrace, churlishness, mask his obvious self-pitying.

"OK. So, it's Saturday night, Sunday morning for us. Better make it memorable then."

"Raymond's Revue Bar!"

"You really mean it? Not too naff?"

"Of course it is but it'll be fun to see some strippers. We can then cross it off our list!"

* * * *

The experience was indeed naff and they both quickly slipped from Raymond's Revue Bar into the Soho night, both hungry after the shockingly bad food produced for their consumption during the hour or so they persevered as half a dozen naked women and men pranced around the stage. "We've never been to an Indian restaurant, have we?"

"No. Why?"

"Let's go to *Veeraswamy*'s, not far from here. Great Indian restaurant!"

He led them across Regent Street, remembered correctly the corner where the restaurant was located and enjoyed a leisurely meal. "Better than the ones in Southall!" declared Mark. "This must be the authentic way of cooking Indian food. I've been here for business lunches a few times, never been disappointed."

Afterwards, they walked back into Soho, keen to enjoy what was left of the early hours of the morning before clubs closed. "It's a choice of listening to jazz at Ronnie Scott's or dancing to R and B at the Marquee."

"Marquee!" She squeezed his arm and they strode towards Wardour Street where they spent two hours dancing to Zoot Money's Big Roll Band, packed on the dance floor like sardines, in oven heat temperatures. At four the club finally closed its doors and they found their way back to where Mark had parked the car, Goslett Yard, the dead-end, unlit alleyway that led to Freddie Mills' club.

In the car they kissed, lightly at first, then with increasing passion and when Mark unzipped his slacks, Lynda required no coaxing, easing his iron hardness free, dropping her head, her mouth closing over the enlarged head of his erection. Her mouth was warm, sensuous, exciting, lips and teeth masturbating him with a growing intensity. Within ten minutes he climaxed, letting out a low moan as his sperm left him, entered her, spurting onto tongue and throat. Back at the flat they sped to their room, undressed and continued their lovemaking in their bed with a fierce intensity, both recognising this would almost certainly be the last time for weeks, maybe a month, they'd be able to indulge in any form of intimacy, torrid or otherwise. They crashed into sleep and remained lost to the world, curled in each other's arms until mid-day, when the phone on the landing rang, followed by a knock on the bedroom door. "Lynda, it's for you. Someone called Nicola."

Mark cooked them what he knew would be their last Sunday breakfast together for many weeks, Lynda reassuring him that she'd continue to pay rent, that she'd be back as often as she could, mid-week if not weekends, and doubted the whole adventure would last beyond the end of summer. At least he knew she'd be in Hunstanton that night, even if he didn't quite know where it was, other than "north of King's Lynn" according to Lynda.

He helped her pack, digging out of drawers her underwear, stockings, tights, handkerchiefs, jewellery, plus tampons, toothpaste, mouthwash, birth control pills, every item representing erasure of part of their life together, their all-too short relationship. And when Nicola arrived mid-afternoon, he took the suitcase and walked like a condemned man to the car.

He lifted the case into the car boot, Lynda pecking him quickly on the cheek, sliding onto the grey leather of the front passenger seat, her denim mini-skirt, revealing attractive thighs, sending a final jet of excitement along his spine. He pushed shut the door. "Don't worry, Mark! I'll look after her! She'll be back in one piece!" Nicola beamed a large smile, her voice mocking him. The car shot off, he waved energetically, his eyes welled, and June walked from the house, slipped her arm in his as he stood, motionless, hypnotised by the fast-fading image of Nicola's Austin Cambridge.

"It's like that old film, isn't it?" June had glee in her voice. "The one with that woman leaning out of the carriage window, the man on the platform, saying goodbye, all teary..."

"You mean *Brief Encounter*. And it's nothing like that. She was a bored married woman in a dead marriage, passing up an affair with another man."

"Sounds like you and Lynda."

He turned, gave her a stern look. "You trying to annoy me?"

She squeezed his arm. "No, darling, just trying to be helpful." She moved around to face him, placed a hand on his neck, stroking him. "Come upstairs, Mark. I've got some really groovy weed. We can have a lovely smoke, then you can do me! Can't say fairer than that!"

He remained silent, wanting to fight the temptation but, once again, his head housed an overwhelming negative attitude towards Lynda, a desire to 'get even'. He placed both his hands on June's hips, lent forward, kissed her lightly on the lips. "OK. You win."

After sex they showered, dressed and walked arm in arm along Kilburn High Road, en route to the State cinema where they saw *Rattle of a Simple Man*, some three years after he'd seen it as a play in the West End. As they left, discussing the film and its story of the naive football fan in London for the cup game and the tart with a heart, Mark quickly became aware that, unlike Lynda, June had little or no facility to intellectually dissect a film, compare notes on direction, storytelling, performance of the actors. His heart sank and inside his head he called out for Lynda and her cerebral power. They were soul mates and now she was gone. He hated the world for ganging up on him.

But, stiff upper lip, he masked his despair and walked back, arm in arm with June, abandoning any hope of sensible debate on the film, instead engaging in conversation about their musical tastes. Yet, even here, there was a chasm as he found it difficult to comprehend someone who hadn't heard anything of Ray Charles' work other than *Hit the Road Jack.*

Back at the flat she pulled him to her room and, annoyed with life, he willingly joined her in bed, un-made from their mid-afternoon tryst, her underwear and tights littering the floor. For him the sex was perfunctory and while June fell asleep almost immediately after he climaxed, Mark remained awake, eyes fixed on the ceiling rose, lit haltingly by the moonlight that danced into the room as curtains waved in the night breeze. And his mind was consumed by wondering where exactly Lynda was 'north of King's Lynn' and what she was doing. He couldn't cope with the idea that she was now making new friends, people he'd never meet. She was beginning a new chapter in her life and it didn't include him. She was easing him from her immediate life. He had no phone number for her. No address. No idea how long she'd be in Hunstanton before moving on to Great Yarmouth, or wherever she was sent. She wouldn't tell him. He was yesterday's paper, *I'm her Yesterday's Man, Well, my friends that's what I am.*

Mark eventually slid off the bed, careful not to wake June, and made his way to his room, his and Lynda's room. He flicked on the bedside light, opened the wardrobe and looked forlornly at the dresses and coats that his girlfriend, the woman he so desperately loved, had left behind. And he cried, a slow, low bass-note sobbing, falling onto the bed, burying his head in the bedcovers.

* * * *

The post card arrived on Thursday, from Hunstanton, not addressed to Mark, just '89 Chatsworth Road, London NW2' with a short message *Hello everyone. Having lovely time. Great Yarmouth tomorrow! Best wishes, Lynda.* Mark stared at it, annoyed it conveyed nothing else, nothing about what club she was working in, the people she was working with, and no address, no phone number.

They passed the card round, each in turn absorbing the colour photograph of a fun fair with the hint of sea in the background, each wondering where Hunstanton was and whether they should all jump in a car and go there for the weekend. Mark liked the idea but was careful not to sound too keen, not wanting to look as though he wasn't coping with Lynda's absence. "I'll ask Paul where Hunstanton is, see if we can get there and back in a day." Kay was enthusiastic. "Maybe we can stay there overnight, in some B&B, if it's too far."

Mark chimed in. "It's about three hours by car. I checked it at work with our UK map. You have to go up the A1 then turn off at Huntingdon for King's Lynn. Or, we can all go by train."

"We could go this weekend, Saturday, stay there, back Sunday..."

"She might not be there, might be in Great Yarmouth." Mark found it hard to be enthusiastic. He wanted to see Lynda but not as a gang of Enid Blyton-type *Five go to Hunstanton* jolly japesters.

"Can you find out if she's there?"

"I can ring the number she gave me when she was training."

"Do it now, see if she'll be there!"

He went upstairs to the phone and dug out Baz's business card Lynda had given him.

The voice was female, Cockney accent, told him to hold on. He complied and ten seconds later a breezy 'Hello' broke the silence. It was Nicola. "Hello, Nicola, it's Mark. Just wondering where Lynda was this weekend. We're thinking of coming up to see her."

"She'll be at the Sandringham Hotel, Hunstanton, in the casino." She paused. "But you cannot talk to her when she's working. The croupiers have to concentrate..."

"No, we won't. We'll probably play. We'll probably see her during the day, go for a meal. Then we'll drive back to London. It'll be a day by the seaside."

"OK. I'll tell her you're coming up."

"It'll be all of us, not just me." He hesitated. "Can you ask her to call me?"

* * * *

Kay was the only other one with a full driver's licence but refused to accompany Mark in his car, not wishing to be apart from her boyfriend as he drove the others. So, in the back of Paul's Mini sat Mark, June and Anna, squeezed onto a seat designed for two adults. And the journey north felt like it would never end, the A1 either snaked before them in open country with narrow sweeping bends, or ground to a halt, evaporating in tiny, cramped towns enjoying market day.

They departed Chatsworth Road at ten vowing to drive non-stop, aiming to arrive in Hunstanton at one. But after two hours they recognised a break was necessary and north of Huntingdon they pulled into a village pub, pleasantly surprised to see it had functioning lavatories. A glass each of a local brew, lacklustre sandwiches, and they were on the road again, this time Mark driving, with Paul alongside him.

The road to Hunstanton followed the railway line and at the station Mark turned into the Hotel Sandringham's car park. He exited the car with a noisy display of stiffness, pulled the girls from the back of the car, and surveyed the fading glory of the hotel's facade. Inside there was no Lynda, just the dining room with, at its far end, the roped off casino, resplendent with green baize tables, a poor man's *Casino Royale* thought Mark. And with no 007, not shaken, nor stirred.

"She's not here, no idea where she is. They've never heard of her."

"Let's go the beach, get a bucket and spade, make sandcastles!" June waved her arms, attempting to capture the sky and sun.

"You go to the beach, I'll walk around, see if I can find her." Mark moved off, not waiting for a reply.

"OK, find us on the beach!"

Mark walked through the fun fair, along the sea front, optimistic eyes darting everywhere, frustrated that a place so small, although busy with holidaymakers, could hide anyone, doubling back towards the hotel, finally looking out across the beach to discover Lynda sitting with the others. They'd found her while he wandered. He cursed his bad luck.

"Hello there!" He was genuinely happy to see her but disappointed she didn't get up to greet him. He fell to the sand as close as he could get to her, the others not moving to make way. Then he saw it as he spoke in his bright, positive voice. "How's things? Everything OK?" His voice trailed away as his eyes landed on, hypnotised by the love bite on her neck. He gulped with shock, unable to say anything else, a massive chasm in his gut opening up, his heart broken as the penny dropped: she'd only been away a week and she'd already had sex with someone, and she had no shame, no attempt to cover up the dark brown bite, on unfettered display for everyone to see.

As she spoke, told him everything was fine, and she was enjoying herself, he wanted to move away. He didn't want be in front of the others with his so-called girlfriend blatantly displaying the sign of torrid sex, so large and powerful on her neck. He felt like being aggressive, rude, but stifled it, sinking his pride, but dis-engaging from conversation with her, allowing the others to occupy her. In his silence he attempted to understand what was happening to his relationship with her, and the fact was as plain as a pikestaff : it was

168

over, there could be no turning back. She had humiliated him in front of the others, not by accident but by design. A cunning, manipulative bitch, whore, he told himself. How could she? How could she behave like some slag from a kitchen sink film, like Vera in *The Servant*?

In his stunned silence June ran two fingertips across his hand, a conspiratorial smile on her hips. He pulled his hand away, darting a fierce, 'not now' look at her. In his suppressed anger he knew he had to retain his concentration, keep his head clear for any analysis that might be required, any questions he could ask that would provide him an insight on Lynda's situation, information that would make valid his decision to cut her loose, let go, finally face the fact she was a lost cause.

The only question Mark could raise was to elicit from Lynda where she was living while in Hunstanton. "In a caravan. There are four of us, so it's cramped, same when I was in Great Yarmouth." She was cheery, bright, lively, completely unaware of Mark's darkness, answering his question as though everything was normal, unchanged. He fell back into silence letting the others converse with her, while Anna dug her camera from her bag and took photographs.

And they remained on the sand for an hour, soaking up the sun before Lynda told them she'd had to leave, to the casino, she was helping train a new girl. "We'll see you tonight, probably play some roulette. Let us win!" Paul beamed as Lynda brushed sand off her shorts. "Are you staying here tonight?" Paul looked at Mark. "Are we?"

"Where? Bit late to book a room..."

"Unless you can afford the hotel, the only places are B and Bs and they'll all be gone. This place hasn't much in the way of rooms, it's more caravan parks." Lynda smiled, waved and walked off. "Might see you tonight then!"

"We'll drive back tonight. I'll drive." Mark was decided, firm.

Paul agreed. "OK. I'll share the driving with you."

169

"Is that it? We're going back tonight?" Anna looked pained.

"If the hotel is our only choice then it's going to be very expensive." Paul was equally firm. "I'd much prefer to get back to London, even if we don't arrive until the early hours."

"It's the seaside. Let's get some fish and chips!" June jumped up, pulling on Mark's hand. "Come on, let's go!"

They walked slowly off the beach and towards the helter skelter and carousel, the scurrying, squealing children, their parents, the elderly couples, ruddy-faced farm workers, promenading, the short parade of shops and cafes, the ice cream parlour, the pink-coloured rock with *Hunstanton* through it, the buckets and spades, fish nets on bamboo sticks, sun hats, beach shoes. And fish and chips. They sat at the table in the window, ordered cod and chips, brown bread, vinegar, salt, a pot of tea for four. "This is the life, eh?!" exclaimed a happy Paul. "Just like when I was ten or twelve, at the seaside with my parents and brother."

"The English way," observed Mark. "When we were kids we'd go to places like Weymouth and Paignton. My dad worked for the railway and he got free travel, privilege tickets, for him and the family so each summer we'd go off to Devon..."

"Just Devon?"

"Yes, think so. Can't remember anywhere else, certainly not eastern England. He worked all his life for the Great Western Railway so Devon was the natural place to go for summer hols." But as he spoke he felt the awful anguish in his bones, in the pit of his stomach, the harrowing realisation that he had worn his heart on his sleeve, devoid of any deviousness, all to no affect, and was now emotionally crippled by the disloyalty of the girl he loved so much. He wanted to sit in a dark room and cry and cry. Instead he had to play act with his Chatsworth Road flat mates *all the world's a stage, and all the men and women merely players, they have their exits and their entrances*.

Sleep on the beach followed before they made their way to the bar of the Sandringham, first occupying the toilets in an attempt to wash, clean themselves of the Hunstanton sand, the girls applying make-up to reduce the sight of wind-induced blush on cheeks.

The casino opened at eight and a crowd of about thirty people, mainly men, were already waiting, prepared to gamble away their holiday pay. Mark and the others trailed in from the bar. Right at the front was Lynda, sitting at a roulette wheel. Cascading away behind her were four other tables, two each for roulette and blackjack. And, Mark noticed, standing in the background, dressed in dinner suit, white shirt and black bow tie was Apollo.

Lynda was dressed, as he expected, in a low cut dress, revealing an expanse of cleavage and as he approached he could see that she had applied some cosmetic paste over the love bite, cleverly hidden from sight to all but those who'd seen it unadorned. She made no sign of recognition as he stood in front of the table with Paul and Kay. They bought chips, placed them on numbered squares, some black, some red, and, in a voice clear with authority, Lynda said 'no more bets'. She spun the wheel, flicked the white ball against the spin of the wheel, and it eventually landed. 'Black twenty-nine'.

Mark gave it five minutes and eventually walked away, deeper into the room, stopping at a blackjack table, impressed with the quick, smooth exit of the cards from the shoe, deposited in front of seated gamblers. And at the end of the room he caught up with June and Anna, both deeply hypnotised by a roulette wheel. "How much have you lost?" They both gave him the smile of the victor. "Nothing! We're quids in! We've won about fifteen pounds!"

"Be careful. They don't like people winning. They'll throw you off the premises!"

It was nine when Paul suggested they start their journey back to London. They all agreed and Mark was relieved. He left the casino without any attempt to say 'goodbye' to Lynda, not that she would have acknowledged any such nicety he told himself. The petrol tank was replenished at King's Lynn and Mark drove south to the A1 along a narrow unlit road that dissected the fields, he searching for directional signs as they slipped into Huntingdon. In the back the three girls discussed their gambling successes but soon fell asleep. As eventually did Paul. And Mark was all alone. Just him, the head lamp-lit road, some ten feet in front of the car, and his thoughts, his private anguish, the emotion of being so classically tricked, double-crossed, betrayed.

They all awoke as Mark traversed the roads between the A1 and Edgware Road. "Edgware! Nearly home! And quarter of a tank left!"

"What time is it?" Mark raised his wrist.

"Just gone midnight."

Paul was apologetic. "Sorry old chum, really out of it. You should have woken me."

At Chatsworth Road Mark made for the kitchen. "Need a coffee after that drive!" "I'll join you, if you don't mind." June gave him a sympathetic look, he returned a knowing smile. She stood alongside him as he stared blankly at the rumbling kettle, slid an arm around his waist. "Think that love bite said it all Mark." He sighed, gave out a world-weary laugh. "Think you're right." And they went upstairs to her room. At the door June kissed him on the cheek. "You're not too tired?" He smiled wanly, said nothing but followed her into the bedroom, and closed the door.

* * * *

Mark woke with his arm wrapped around June's waist. He instinctively squeezed the naked flesh, instantly remembering it wasn't Lynda lying alongside him, pulling back his arm in a silent horror, as if discovering it was hugging a predatory reptile, not a slim, attractive, compliant female. June stirred and he froze, only moving again when he felt sure she'd fallen securely back to sleep. He slid slowly from the bed, aware he was naked, putting his shirt on, gathering up the remainder of his clothes. Just as his hand gripped the door handle, June woke, voice sleepy, "Mark, where you going?" He stared at the door for a second then turned. "Get a shower, get my paper."

Her voice went fully awake from sleepy, the tone incredulous. "Mark, for fuck's sake, it's Sunday morning!" She looked at her alarm clock. "It's seven Mark, come back to bed, come back and do me! An early morning fuck, how's that? Can't turn that down, can you?"

He walked back to the bedside, falling onto the edge, June's breasts inches away from his hands. He wanted to stroke them, gently squeeze both nipples but didn't. Instead he smiled, and spoke in a voice anyone else might reserve for someone of limited education. "I'm going to shower, dress, get my paper and when I get back I'll make us some breakfast." She smiled, ran a hand down his cheek. "We need to talk, Mark, when you get back."

"Do we? About what?" He knew he was being obtuse. He knew full well what June wanted to talk about. "I'll make us that breakfast when I get back. What paper would you like?"

She fell back onto the pillow, her voice exasperated. "Don't read papers, Mark."

"OK, then I'll get you the *News of the World*."

"Don't wake me, please."

When he got back it was almost eight and June was sitting at the kitchen table, hands wrapped around a mug of coffee, body wrapped in a towelling robe Mark noted required a wash. "Egg and bacon?"

She affirmed, shaking her head. "If you're making it."

"I am. Egg, bacon and toast."

"So, what are you going to do, Mark?"

He didn't want to discuss him and Lynda. He wanted to get on with cracking open eggs without breaking yokes, slide in the pan rashers of streaky bacon, dig out slices of bread, ready for the toaster. "June, I don't know. Can't see anything left of me and Lynda. Looks like it's all over. But, you never know, she might come back to Chatsworth Road, and stay."

"She won't, Mark. She's paid this month's rent but she won't pay next month's. She'll tell us she's leaving for good..."

"Her clothes are still here." He wanted to turn to face June but the spitting eggs and bacon, rapidly converting to an edible state, demanded his full attention.

"She'll come back for those." June paused. "Or get you to drive all the way up there with them. You're so soft you'd even do it!"

"I might well if it meant a chance of saving our relationship."

"Plain as the nose on your face, Mark, it's over. Get it into your head, stop torturing yourself!"

He eased the eggs from pan to plate, adding the rashers of bacon and pushed one across the table towards June. "Thanks, Mark. That looks very eatable."

"Edible."

"What?"

"The word is edible, not eatable."

"Thanks for that, Mark. Sure the world will be much improved for that."

He changed the subject. "What are your plans today?"

"No plans. Why?"

"I don't want to stay in, and I don't want to wander around on my own..."

"Then we'll do something together. Hampstead Heath?"

"I was thinking of a walk along the river, Houses of Parliament to Tower Bridge."

"OK, sounds good. Let's go after this. I'll shower, get dressed." She paused. "What would you like me to wear?"

He liked being asked, almost as if his opinion was appreciated. "Knickers. Wouldn't want you to be arrested for indecency…"

"And as well as knickers? A skirt, or jeans?"

"Skirt. Short one, mini."

"OK." She lifted her fork to her mouth but suspended the implement mid-air. "Before I shower Mark, come with me to my room and do me. Please."

He shook his head slowly, in disbelief. "You never give up June, do you?"

"No, I'm a nympho, Mark. Don't say 'no', you'll enjoy it."

He smiled. "How's the breakfast?"

"Scrumptious! Don't change the subject."

* * * *

They caught a 16 bus to Victoria Street and walked towards the Abbey and Parliament Square, June's arm tucked inside his, her face a continual beaming smile. Mark admitted to himself he was glad she was so at ease, happy, and contented, reminding him, with some comfort, of happy times with Lynda, flashes of good episodes shooting through his consciousness. Tourists coagulated Parliament Square, Mark and June fighting their way to the riverside, stopping only to take photographs of themselves with Big Ben towering in the background.

He took immense personal delight in acting like a tourist guide, pointing out buildings and monuments along the Thames embankment that he believed had some historical importance, and she made a significant effort not to tell herself she wasn't a Japanese tourist, not to be too offended by his, albeit natural, patronising and didactic tone.

175

In the early afternoon sun and heat they walked past the Mermaid Theatre, and, tucked away down an alleyway near Mansion House station, found a greasy spoon where they ate cheese and ham sandwiches, drank milky tea served in workers' thick-rimmed ceramic mugs sporting the heraldic arms of the Corporation of the City of London. "So, what do you plan, Mark?" Her question was clearly simple but, for him, intensely complex. "I don't know, June. What do you suggest?"

"I suggest you and me, Mark."

"The queen is dead, long live the queen."

"What?"

"You mean taking over where Lynda left off?"

"Sort of Mark. You need to get her out of your head. It's over, she's not coming back, get used to it and look to the future..."

"And that future is us?"

"I think it is Mark. I think we could be very good together." She slid her hand over his, squeezing lightly. "I know I'm not as smart and clever as Lynda, bit of a bimbo, but I'm fun to be with..."

"Don't denigrate yourself June." He was uncomfortable at what he perceived as her selling herself. "I'm not looking for brains, just a very pleasant relationship." It was a lie. Mark wanted a girlfriend who matched him in IQ and intellectual wherewithal, he completely oblivious to the arrogance at the core of his view of himself. June, however, wasn't so blinded and, in her head, her modest powers of perception laid him bare. But she bit her tongue.

"I think we're right for each other, we could have a lot of fun together, no strings if you want, nothing too heavy, just being together, having fun..."

"I thought you were into women, men were just a bit of joke, things you played with, taking the piss out of them..."

"No, Mark! I'm not a dyke like that. It's the other way round, men first, women next. They're the playthings!"

"So, you'd drop the dyke thing?"

She hesitated. "No, Mark, not really. But it wouldn't get in the way of us. It wouldn't upset us. You wouldn't notice it."

He laughed. "What, no threesomes?"

"If you want." She joined in his laughter. "There's a change in relationships, Mark. Don't think you're with it. That hetero thing is a bit old hat. Men are going to have to get used to it. Women are not going to be slaves much longer. Sex isn't just men and women. It's women and women, men and men..."

"My boss is queer." He halted, realising it sounded like a confession.

"And you and he..." she paused. "Did it?"

"Long time ago. When I first started working for him. When I was seventeen..."

"Sweet seventeen, never been fucked..."

"Not quite. I lost my virginity when I was fourteen. One day in the school summer holidays, helping this woman deliver bread for the Co-op. On the way back to the bakery in West Drayton, she pulled over in some country lane, unzipped me, wanking me, then unzipped her jeans, got me on top of her, and in I went!"

"Jesus!"

"Yes, it was quite an experience. Remember her being fat, in black jeans with green stitching, bought from Woolworth's!"

"Did you enjoy it?"

"Yes, I did! Couldn't tell anyone of course, had to keep it to myself."

"What about her?"

"Sadly, it had a bad affect. She didn't ask me to help her deliver bread again."

"Guilt! You were underage."

"Yep, that must have been it."

"And your boss? Is that over? Or is he still fucking you?"

177

He heaved his shoulders. "No, he isn't! That's all way in the past!"

"Now, it's you who sound guilty!"

"I'm not! Just glad I got it out of my system when I was seventeen."

"Thoroughly hetero. With a closed mind!"

"I'm not into men, June. You might be into women as well as men, that's your kink. I'm into women. Period."

She laughed. "Women with periods."

"So, what do we do when Lynda returns?"

"She won't. She won't pay any more rent. It'll then be down to you. Can you afford it?"

"How do you know she won't come back?"

"Pretty sure. She'll make a lot of money as a croupier, won't want to come back to a dreary typist's job in London."

"She's got clothes here."

"As I said, she'll probably get you take them to her in Hunstanton, or wherever she's living."

"I won't be doing that June."

"If you're my boyfriend, you won't be allowed to do it!"

"Boyfriend's a bit strong according to your definition. You mean 'easy lay'..."

"Maybe. What I mean is that we could be a very groovy couple, Mark. There's a lot happening in London right now and we've got to be a part of it, join in, get hip, start grooving!"

"What do you mean? More parties?"

"We've got to get connected. Get involved, start making some waves. Do some happenings at Chatsworth Road, make it a groovy place to go to, lots of action, music, fun people, no boundaries..."

"Kilburn isn't Bloomsbury."

"What? What's Bloomsbury got to do with it?"

"It was a place where lots of artists and intellectuals gathered. Long time ago."

"Right. Well, we'll make Kilburn a place they'll want to be seen in, especially Chatsworth Road."

"What about the others? They may not like the flat becoming an arts centre."

"It'll be a groovy place to be. They'll love it! If they don't they can always leave!"

"And how's all this going to happen? You work full time, I work full time. We need to work to pay the bills. We can't swan around on no money."

"We'll find a way."

He made no further comment but quietly wondered exactly what she was hoping to achieve and how she would do it.

Back on the street they walked hand in hand, almost absent-mindedly drifting down Stew Lane, an alleyway that brought them out by the river, alongside a tall, very elderly timber-frame wharf. It threw a massive shadow which lowered the temperature and darkened the alleyway, and as they stood gazing at the tall chimney that rose from the redbrick power station on the opposite bank of the river, June ran her hand over the front of his jeans, giggling quietly to herself as she slowly brought his penis up hard. They kissed and in the shadows he unzipped his flies, she pulled her knickers down, and both engaged in vertical sex.

Mark said nothing but the experience took him back to Newman Passage, the beginning of his relationship with Lynda and their first penetrative sex. He laughed with June as they dressed themselves but as they walked back to the sunlight, hand in hand, Mark bit his lip, memories of the girl he loved all too easily consuming him, his heart heavy with suppressed pain and anger.

CHAPTER NINE

Mark stood back and watched himself drift into a relationship with June. Initially, he would return to his room after sex but within a few weeks he abandoned the pretence that he was *single*. At first, the others in the flat said nothing but as he would regularly materialise from June's room it was Kay who posed the first question.

Superficially, she wanted to know what was going to happen to the room he and Lynda had occupied. Had he heard from her? Was she coming back? No, he hadn't heard from her and if she continued the silence when the rent was due he'd pay it, then perhaps discuss what was to happen to the room. Kay also wanted to know whether the dalliances with June indicated a serious relationship or just naked lust. Again, his answer was foggy, marginally resenting Kay's curiosity, viewing it as an intrusion.

Yet in his head there was a growing confusion. Lynda had not said a word about what she'd be doing. What if she did return? Walk through the front door without any prior notice, find him in bed with June? What would he do? Be tough and say '*it's over Lynda. It's me and June now*.' Or, collapse, implode, and behave as if nothing had happened, glad to have her back, assume their relationship would re-start where it had stopped. It was, he told himself, academic. There was little chance of Lynda returning to work and live in London.

In bed with June she quietly set about his conversion from what she viewed as the buttoned-downed, intense and repressed business executive into a gentler, more relaxed individual, free of the angst of marriage, mortgage, and money. In her bedside drawer, in a white jewellery box, replete with a spinning musical ballerina, she maintained a regularly topped-up stash of cannabis. He didn't ask where she acquired the weed, didn't offer money to buy fresh stock, but willingly smoked the joints she rolled as a precursor to sex. And after, she'd roll another and as they smoked, she gently encouraged him to open his mind, abandon the precepts he harboured that governed his outlook on everything in life. He knew that would be difficult. "Dump all those principles my parents taught me?"

"No. Don't think I mean that." She fondled his penis and testicles as she spoke. "I mean you, me, become prisoners when we get on the treadmill of mortgage, house, kids, car, holidays. It's what the system wants us to do. Get snared like a fox in a trap, no way out. It's like a drug addict with a monkey on his back..."

"And what about working? The system wants us to work, nine to five, day in, day out." He paused. "If we didn't work we couldn't afford to pay rent, buy food..."

"Yeah, Mark, we have to work but we don't have to be in the pack. We can lead, set the programme, call the shots, use our brains to get out of the herd, stop being used, get up and out, lead the pack."

"So, how do we do all that?"

"I don't know, Mark but I think we should start with Mouse..."

"The fashion bloke?"

"Yes, the guy who runs *Little Red Rooster*. He's fashion Mark, and that's where it's at, with music, art, theatre..."

"So, how's he going to help us?"

"We're going to help him Mark."

"How?"

"You're in PR Mark. We're going to get Mouse noticed, get some fame going."

"My PR is technical, not fashion."

"Then, Mark, make the effort to get yourself fully *au fait* with fashion PR. Can't be that different, surely? It's all about press contacts, gimmicks, PR stunts, selling..."

Mark didn't enjoy being told to be imaginative by a non-PR person when his job's very *raison d'etre* was being imaginative with one-dimensional products and services.

"And I think I can help Mouse with some money." She halted. "Haven't worked it out in my head but think Apollo might like to put some money into Mouse's outfit. If I talk to him nicely."

"What does this Apollo guy do? What's his connection with our landlord and the gambling?"

"He's partners with Baz on the gambling but he's got money from his other businesses. Think he might put some of it into *Little Red Rooster*."

"He's Maltese. Is his money in Malta?"

"Don't know but he has money. He's Maltese mafia."

"Is he? Can't see him getting involved in groovy fashion.""I can. He'll see it as a way of cleaning up his money."

"So, we're going to see Mouse?"

"Yep. I'll call him. Try to see him this weekend."

"At his?"

"Yes, not here. Don't want the others to know, just yet." She paused, ran her hand through his hair. "And time to get rid of that hair style, Mark. That is so un-cool, like you're in the army, it's so short!"

"Rubbish! It's the Mod look!"

"That is so un-cool Mark! You're not a spotty-faced teenager now, not a Mod, you're fully grown. Well, almost..."

"You're not tuned into *Ready Steady Go* then?"

"No, why?"

"That's where all the Mods hang out. And they're not spotty-faced teenagers."

"Whatever, Mark. Just grow your hair, get it like Brian Jones. You've got to look like a rock and roll star, look the part, get the buzz! Get cool Mark!"

He told himself he rather enjoyed being told what to do, as long as the telling was pleasant, not a loud, aggressive voice, bent on humiliating him.

And he was privately pleased that he had a new girlfriend who was taking an interest in him, willing him on his conversion from buttoned-downed, repressed white collar worker to cultural revolutionary. He wanted it but couldn't believe it would happen. He was twenty-two and couldn't visualise his throwing away the rule book he'd used for all those years and writing a new one. But even with June's belief in him, her energy, and vision for them both, he still could not excise Lynda from somewhere deep within his consciousness. And he cursed himself for it.

* * * *

He slipped his arm around her waist, kissed her lightly on the forehead. "We're a team!"

"Yes, Mark, we're a team!" He wasn't falling in love with her, he told himself. But he was much enamoured, impressed by her mental application, her energy, her desire to achieve and succeed. He wasn't falling in love with her but he was much impressed by her. The hair was blonde, not Lynda's auburn, slimmer than Lynda, smaller breasts, the legs too Twiggy skinny but still exciting, attractive, provocative. And she enjoyed sex far more obviously than Lynda. Could he make the transition she wanted of him? From intense, smart-suited, buttoned-down executive to hip, cool, groovy creature with an open mind, a fearlessness, a rejection of marriage and mortgage? He genuinely wanted to impress her. She had set him a target and he told himself not to fail.

Mouse was far too flaky to be a successful business partner, Mark told himself. Which made a form of sense since flaky was a drug term he recalled from the article on pot in *Playboy*. Mouse wasn't always high but he was fragile. He gave off a very cool, anarchic vibe that defied concentration, organization, setting deadlines, or any hint that he understood the principles of budgetry control. Mark lived with such disciplines on a daily basis, working for a PR agency that demanded its employees work tirelessly to ensure it enjoyed a substantial income delivering a massive margin of net profit. And working for clients peopled by executives whose paranoiac fear of losing their jobs was etched around their darkened eyes.

They sat upstairs in the muddle of tailor's dummies, fabric swaths, giant-sized scissors, measuring tapes, and garments in all stages of completion hanging from hooks. For lunch Mouse and Suzie produced a large wedge of Cheddar cheese, two sticks of bread, and a bottle of red wine. They all hacked at the cheese as June tentatively sought to ascertain the success of *Little Red Rooster* and its place in London's *cool* firmament. Mouse's response was, Mark told himself, *waffle.* And it obliged June to move to her main point, explaining, haltingly, she wanted to be part of the London groove and saw *Little Red Rooster* as the way in. Mouse enjoyed the implied compliment, only too pleased to believe it to be true. "OK, I agree *Rooster* is groovy, lots of cool people coming to ask us to make clothes for them." He paused. "So, you want to design clothes for us?"

June laughed. "I wish!" She gave Mark a darting look. "No, we were wondering if you could do with some extra money, expand, get more people interested in your designs, sell more..."

"Never say 'no' to money but..." Mouse hesitated. "We're not a factory, not a Dorothy Perkins or C and A, Peter Robinson, we make bespoke things. Exclusive things, dresses for people like Sandie

Shaw, Marianne Faithful for when they go on TV, or turn up for a film premiere..."

"You could still do all that but you could also design a range of clothes for dolly birds and sell them through the big retailers..."

"Using the name *Little Red Rooster*, or *Red*, or *Rooster*." Mark interjected, his voice upbeat, optimistic. "Mini dresses and skirts first..."

Mouse looked interested. "OK, so how's it going to work?"

"Can you find out how much it will cost, selling in a few of the Oxford Street stores?" June pulled from her handbag a sheaf of papers, stapled together. "I've put this together. Some ideas. Do three designs for skirts and dresses, small, medium, large..."

"Sizes ten to sixteen?"

"Yes, ten, twelve, fourteen, sixteen. Cost them, six of each. Make and delivery to the major stores on Oxford Street..."

"Or mail order. Like they do in the States. You know, that Sears catalogue."

"Or in *Nova*, or the teen magazines."

"Yeah, advertise directly. That way you avoid the big stores' buying cycles. If you rely on them you'll be waiting 'til February before they stock..."

"And we'll launch with a happening at the Roundhouse." Mark again interjected, again in an upbeat voice. "Great music, great dope, get some big names there."

"You can do that?" Mouse was doubtful.

"Yeah, should be easy with my PR contacts." Mark was positive.

"So, who's going to pay for all this?"

"A friend of mine has some money to invest." June hesitated, hoping it didn't sound too trite, too pat. "If you can estimate the costs, close as you can get, I think he'll want to invest, think he'll like being part of groovy London."

"Does he know anything about fashion, especially the really cool stuff?"

"No, but that's where you and *Little Red Rooster* come in..."

"If he puts money in he'll want to start to interfering, telling us how to do our jobs, how to run my business..."

"No, he won't. I'll make sure he won't."

"OK, I'll talk to Nick and Toby, put some figures together. And some sort of timescale, so he knows how long it might take."

June beamed and lent forward, kissed Mouse on the cheek. "Thanks Mouse! That's groovy!"

Mouse dug from a pocket his tobacco tin, waved it in the air. "Let's fly a kite to the highest height!"

* * * *

Mark felt very guilty in walking past his barber's, hoping he was too busy to look out, watch Mark stride along the pavement, head down, eyes fixed on the cracks, ears closed to the energetic scissors clacking away inside. Equally Mark didn't want him to see his hair growing longer, less kempt, flying in different directions, at the mercy of the breeze. And he felt very uneasy at wearing flared trousers. Very few other men were wearing them and he felt very self-conscious, an outcast. They flapped at his feet as if they were too short, a hand-me-down from an elder brother or father. The wide lapels on the jacket were not an issue, nor the broad, flowery tie which enabled him to produce a fist-sized full Windsor knot. However, the floral voile shirt had to remain on the hanger back at Chatsworth Road, definitely something for the weekends.

His hair, June told him, would have to grow a little longer then she'd organize a perm for him. He laughed at the suggestion but was told very firmly there was nothing exclusively female about a perm.

She wanted his hair looking *cool, groovy* and wasn't going to be put off by his ersatz horror.

And on their way back from the meeting with Mouse June articulated her desire to quickly organize a party at the Chatsworth Road house with the express aim of getting Mouse's hip customers and friends there and ingratiating her and Mark, launching them into Mouse's world of *movers and shakers*.

Mark didn't like the suggestion but said it anyway. "We should move to a hip area, like Chelsea or Hampstead. Kilburn is run-down, poor, dirty."

"I can't afford to pay the rent you have to if you want to live in Chelsea or Hampstead. I'd end up with a bedsit, basement, shitty, doomy, I'd be suicidal in no time."

"We could share the rent. We'd get a better flat than a basement bedsit."

"We need to stay in Chatsworth Road for the time being. If we make some money then we can move. But not just yet."

Mark made no further comment but juggled with '...*if we make some money...*' He couldn't think of how any money would be made by them getting Mouse to design and make a range of skirts and dresses for sale at cheap prices in Oxford Street shops. And that assumed June could convince Apollo to invest whatever sum Mouse produced.

* * * *

The southern end of Soho was not a convenient destination for lunch but Mark chose a Friday, traditionally a *running down to the weekend* day, and hoped against hope that no-one in the office would notice his absence, or one of his more tiresome clients – the Dulux paranoiacs at Slough - would spitefully decide to make an urgent call.

He marched down Baker Street, across Oxford Street into Soho, weaved his way through the quarter's labyrinthine collection of roads, alleyways, secret passages and cul-de-sacs, all in deep shadow as their tall Victorian buildings swept skywards, rooftops converging to mask the sun. Then he found the *Coach and Horses*, strode in and immediately saw Glenn at the bar, alone on a stool, but in conversation with the suited barman. "Hello!" He beamed, Glenn looked surprised, then smiled, shook his hand. "Drink?" Mark nodded, impressed Glenn recognised him. "I'll have a pint of whatever you recommend." "Draught Directors." He slid onto a stool. "Have you ordered food?"

"Yes. It's fish and chips day. Suggest you get that." He paused. "Then order the lemon pudding. Recommend it."

"Fish and chips?" The barman gave him an inane grimace. But before Mark could answer he continued. "Quickly or they'll all be gone!"

"Yes, fish and chips! And lemon pudding!"

"That's Norman. London's rudest landlord."

"Right. But that wasn't that rude. He does it for effect?"

"He's only rude to the regulars. They love it."

Mark glimpsed the editor of *Private Eye*, sitting at the other end of the bar, at a table. "And that's the *Private Eye* mob? Richard Ingrams and Willie Rushton..."

"Yep. They all eat here at lunchtime, every day. And once a month they have the *Private Eye* lunch, upstairs. Great fun watching all the politicians come in, go upstairs..."

"Lot more entertaining than our office pub."

"So, what brings you to this neck of the woods?"

Mark hesitated, sipped his beer. "Well, you remember my girlfriend, from the party..."

"Yep, good-looking girl..."

"Lynda. Well, we split up, sad to say. But I've sort of fallen in with one of the other girls in the flat, June. She's got lots of ideas about wanting to become a mover and a shaker in the London hip scene..."

"London hip scene?" Glenn's voice was both incredulous and mocking.

"Well, you know what I mean. She wants to be part of it, not looking in but centre stage of things."

"What, you think I can help? I'm just a poor boy from Worksop. What the fuck do I know about what's hip and what's shit in London?"

"Just a hunch. You've been living in London for a few years, you probably know more hip people than I'll ever meet..."

"Maybe." He paused. "You know Ken Russell?"

"You mean the film director?"

"Yep, the film director. He's just finished making a film on Elgar and we know some of the production people. They live in the flat above ours. There's a party there tomorrow, a sort of celebration now the filming is finished. Turn up, any time after closing time. Just you and your girlfriend. Bring a bottle of decent wine."

"OK, will do." Mark felt triumphant, a goal successfully reached. "Better have your address then."

Glenn looked up. "Norman, have you got one of your address books for my friend here?"

"Course I have! Got 'undreds of the buggers!" He pulled a box out from under the bar, and gave Mark a small, palm-sized book, the red-coloured cover of which declared *With the compliments of Norman Balon, London's Rudest Landlord The Coach and Horses Greek Street Soho London W1.* Glenn wrote his address and phone number under 'H'. "We shall probably be drinking first in the Holly Bush, then go to the party. Better not get to the party before I do..."

"Then June and I will meet up with you at the Holly Bush. Not a pub I know. Where is it?"

"Hampstead, off Heath Street, just past the tube station..."

They ate their meal in near silence, entertained by Norman's regular piercing of the air with a defaming epithet that greeted every customer who reached the bar, clearly confusing those who, like Mark, were *London's Rudest Landlord* novices.

Mark was impressed with Glenn's insouciance, his apparent carelessness about life that made him envious, the contrast with his own, worrying intensity, the fear and the doubt instilled in him at age ten by his mother, his subsequent lack of self-confidence, the baggage that drove his desire for safe anchorage in marriage, a desire that appeared not to drive any others he currently knew, a desire he so desperately wanted to throw overboard. And a fault in his make-up that, he told himself, had frightened Lynda, driven her away.

* * * *

Mark got to Chatsworth Road at six-thirty, in time to wave goodbye to Kay and Paul, driving off to Barnstaple for the weekend. "We're staying at the Narracott Hotel, number's on the fridge if you want us. And Anna's also away. She's at her parents for the weekend. See you Sunday!"

He smiled them away, wondering why he didn't know the flat would be empty at the weekend, assuming June had been told but not passed the news on. Upstairs, he got out of his suit, showered, dug out a short-sleeved shirt and pulled on his Levis. Only then did he wonder where June was, deciding that they might eat out along Kilburn High Road then go to the State to the late showing of *Darling*.

Mark turned on the television and tuned into *Ready Steady Go*. Then he sat for an hour at the kitchen table, reading his *Guardian*, drinking coffee, checking his watch every few minutes before June eventually returned, noisily inebriated. He felt ill at ease, unsure whether to play along with her, or turn censorious. "You're in a good mood." The comment was lame and embarrassingly obvious. "I'll make you a coffee. Black."

"Don't bother. Come upstairs, fuck me!"

He felt like saying *'no, you're drunk'* but didn't. He wanted to avoid annoying her, avoid ruining the evening. "Let's go out, have a meal, then go to see *Darling*."

"Later! Don't be a wet blanket!" She grabbed his hand and pulled him out of his chair. He followed her up the stairs, into her bedroom which he now knew intimately well. She undressed with passion, he undressed with no enthusiasm but on the bed she excited him and it dawned on him they'd had no sex in the week since the meeting with Mouse. As he climaxed they kissed with a marked passion, then she fell away and into sleep. "I'm going to wake you up in an hour's time. Then we're going out to eat, see a movie!" She made no sound.

He cursed, got up and dressed, went back downstairs, the television still blaring out, recognising *Perry Mason*, wondering how long the BBC could go on running repeats of American soap operas. He turned off the television, dug out his Ray Charles double LP anthology and played it loud, made a coffee, flicked through *Mayfair*, the new girly magazine he'd seen on sale on his way back from the Coach and Horses, deciding it was intellectually threadbare, a very poor copy of *Playboy* magazine, hiding it away in the fold of his *Guardian*.

Then, with hands idle and mind undistracted, he began to think of Lynda. At first it was a few strands of memories from the first time they met, almost a year ago at Princeton College, sitting in the cafeteria during those first September weeks of term, sharing a tea in half-time break, the two of them mildly jousting, he keen not to be too didactic, intrusive or nosey but interested enough to wonder if she had a boyfriend. But, like a damn being opened, the first handful of memories became a flood of recalled happier times, recollections of early dates at the cinema, meals at Warwickshire House, then, as winter finally began to loosen its grip, evening walks in the mild air of early Spring, their first attempt at sexual intercourse upright in Newman Passage, the joy of it, the laughs, the kisses, the mess.

The memories flowed too quickly, began to suffocate him. He felt claustrophobic, beads of sweat around his neck. He got up, told himself he needed air, needed to walk, needed to be distracted. He ran upstairs, grabbed his jacket and strode from the house. He walked along the high street, hoping to clear his head of Lynda and the roll-call of enjoyable memories but it was impossible, she was too much a part of him, and everywhere he looked he saw her, every restaurant window, every pub, every convenience shop, he imagined her, saw her in his head with him, arms linked, laughing, chatting, joking, eyes bright, mouth welcoming, in love with him. Or, he told himself, looking as though she was in love with him. *'Playacting'* he murmured, the word re-introducing him to reality, like a cold shower, his frenzy over like a car hitting a wall, he stopping in his tracks, looking around and deciding that he'd been weak and foolish to allow memories of Lynda to abduct him.

Back in the flat he shook June back into consciousness, pulling her from the bed, telling her to shower and dress. And half an hour later they were walking along Chatsworth Road, arm in arm, en route to a restaurant with the late show at the State to follow. He said nothing about his Lynda agony pains but proudly told her they were off to a *'trendy arty party'* on Saturday evening. June was impressed, her glee manifesting itself in her swinging around a lamp-post. "So, who's is it? Julie Christie? Michael Caine?"

"Ken Russell, the film director."

"Ken who? Never heard of him!"

"He's made a number of films for the BBC, on composers."

"What, you mean Lennon and McCartney?"

"No, I mean classical music composers."

"Mark, that sounds like a very boring party. Lots of boring people sitting around listening to boring classical music!"

"I don't think it's going to be one of those parties. I have a sneaking suspicion it's going to be very cool, hip bash..."

"Who told you about it?"

"A guy I know through work. Glenn. He was at that party Mouse had a few months ago but he's been at a few meetings at one of my clients. Quite a coincidence..."

"What's he got to do with this guy?"

"The people who made the film live in the flat above his, in Hampstead."

"OK, Mark, we'll go. But if it turns out to be a lot of boring people sitting around listening to Beethoven, I'm off!"

"We have to meet up with Glenn before. At the Holly Bush pub."

"I know that one very well." She paused, then laughed. "Picked up quite a few men there!"

"Really?" He was intrigued but felt no feeling of shock or disgust as he most certainly would have experienced if it had been Lynda making the boast. "You might bump into some of your conquests."

* * * *

Mark woke with a start and quickly realised he was in his car, at the wheel and feeling the cold. He looked at his wrist watch. It was nearly seven and behind him he saw in the mirror the sun rising in a clear blue sky. He turned, expecting to see June on the back seat, prostrate with sleep. She wasn't there and he wondered whether the party was still going strong and she was still there.

He opened the door and walked back towards the redbrick mansion block only to realise he didn't have the flat number. Glenn had that and didn't pass it on. They'd met him in the pub, and followed him to the party, he opening the front door to the block, all of them travelling in the lift to the third floor, Mark not registering the flat number. He turned back to the car and drove to Chatsworth Road, stopping en route to buy an *Observer*. The flat revealed no sign of June but he wasn't disconcerted. His feelings for June were stunted, under-developed. Had it been Lynda he'd be in a rage of possession-driven jealousy. But it was June and he had long decided he was ambivalent, if not uncaring.

He showered and cooked himself eggs and bacon, flicking through the paper as he ate but, slowly at first, however with an increasing intensity, he began to recall the party. The images were confusing, clashing with each other but he clearly remembered the music, an eclectic mix of Stax and Atlantic soul and British rhythm and blues with some early sixties rock thrown in for good measure. And he remembered the people throwing the party, with some fondness. They were bohemians, artists, giving off the appearance of being carefree, dressed in clothes from the costume department, maybe a performance of *Twelfth Night.*

Mark admired their apparent freedom, wondering if they were as unburdened by life as their spirited autonomy implied. He smiled at the thought of whether they looked at him and asked themselves was he happy, contented, at ease with himself and life, wondering if they had some sixth sense that would inform them he was a restless, troubled soul, desperately in love with a girl who had abandoned him, leaving him lost in self-pity and worthlessness. But like that clown in *The Greatest Show on Earth* he was hiding behind a permanent, artificial face of fun.

No surprise then, he told himself, he willingly immersed himself at the party in the drugs on offer. The weed, the mescaline, as well as the alcohol. And the sex, so easily facilitated by the drugs, no questions asked, maximum involvement, minimum commitment.

The contrast with the working class moral code of the early sixties could not be more vivid, Mark told himself, his head in some turmoil, wondering where it take him, knowing he had to relax, get hip, but unsure whether he could make the transformation, as June insisted he should.

How did he get to the car? What time did he leave the party, and why? Mark roamed his head for a memory of something that would trigger an avalanche of recollections but all he could summon was his meeting Jason, a disc jockey on Radio Caroline, and Penny his wife. He smiled as he remembered Jason's self-promotion, boasting, all done in a loud, larger-than-life fashion as if he was in front of the microphone, speaking to thousands, revealing a deep-seated fear that, in reality, no-one was listening. But Mark was and he enjoyed Jason's company, understanding and appreciating his desire not to be dull, grey and predictably British.

There, Mark told himself, was someone who had made the transformation. *Hip, cool*, phony perhaps, but decidedly different, a threat to convention and the rule book. A revolutionary. And he wondered if he'd ever bump into him again, tap into that spirit, that energy, that courage, that fun fair barker confidence, that self-believe. "Not working in a PR agency with grey, one-dimensional clients, all staffed by corporate marionettes, all frightened of their own shadows. Just like me." He glumly told himself.

Dope was the answer. The very second he thought it, his head flooded with guilt and recriminations. His stolidly working class parents, steeped in their Methodist socialism, abhorred excessive consumption of alcohol. He didn't know their views on marijuana or mescaline, or French blues, but could guess what they were with some accuracy. The guilt raged in his head but he vowed to fight the demons and get acquainted with *pot, hash, blow, hemp, weed, tea*, and dig out the *Playboy* article and get *hip* with the scene. And the party at Chatsworth Road June wanted for Mouse's circle of friends had to be quickly organised while the summer bloomed with unbroken days of sun and heat.

Upstairs Mark stretched out on his bed and read a few pages of his paper before falling asleep. He'd bought a clapped-out Dansette auto-changer record player from an antiques shop off Portobello Road and, careful not to expect too much of it, slipped his Frank Sinatra *I Remember Tommy* LP on the turntable. He got to the third track and fell asleep. When he awoke it was the insistent ringing of the phone outside his room that brought him back to consciousness. His watch told him it was past eleven and he'd been asleep for two hours. He grabbed the receiver and shoved it on his ear, fully expecting the caller to be June telling him what time she'd be home. Or Anna or Kay, checking up, making sure he hadn't burnt the house down.

Instead, it was Lynda. The very second he heard her voice a shiver of delight and excitement ran down his spine. "Darling, hi, it's me!" He blurted it out, mangling the words, his voice hoarse with elation. Lynda was calm and collected. "Hello. How are you? Didn't expect you to answer."

"I miss you, Lynda. When are you coming back?"

She was marginally exasperated. "I'm not coming back, Mark. There's no point..."

"There's us, Lynda! The two of us, together, back as we were when we first met! What's wrong with us? What's wrong with me?"

She ignored his pleas. "London's not for me, Mark. I'm not cut out for office work..."

"Well, do something else! London's an amazing place, thousands of opportunities to do whatever you want to do! What are you going to do if you don't come back?"

"Don't know, Mark, but I don't have to decide anything while I'm a croup..."

"Is that really what you want to do in life?"

"Don't know but right now I'm enjoying things, better than sitting at a typewriter all day, every day!"

"I thought we had something really good, Lynda. I can't work out why you didn't want it. Can't work out what went wrong..."

"Nothing went wrong Mark. I just didn't want a serious relationship. I thought I did but changed my mind..."

"Yes, I know, I frightened you with that talk of marriage but I told you I agreed with you, we were both too young for that, I have no interest in getting married." Mark was talking with some speed, trying to get out what he wanted to say before Lynda interrupted him, cut him short or, worse, hang up on him. "But I am in love with you. I have no interest in denying that..."

"Mark, you've got to get me out of your head. Move on, find someone else. I'm not coming back. And that's why I rang. Please tell the others I'm not paying any more rent..."

"Oh, Lynda, that's terrible!" It's all he could summon, fully aware it was a limp response but he was crestfallen, pole-axed, crippled, and he fell against the wall, his knees weak, and he began to cry, trying hard to hide sobs in his throat, equally aware it sounded schoolboy juvenile when he had to be strong.

She appeared not to hear his throat. "And I'm going to get my aunt to collect my clothes. She's going to call you..."

"I can bring them up to you!" His voice was suddenly bright, optimistic. "No problem, just tell me what day would be best. I can take the time off!"

Lynda's voice was once again heavy with tedium. "No, Mark, I don't want my clothes here, I haven't got the space. My aunt has and she says she can hold them for now. She will call you. Her name is Frankie, short for Frances. She's an air hostess for BEA so not exactly sure when she'll call. I'd appreciate it if you could help by being able to be there when she can get round to the flat..."

"Where does she live? In London?"

"Yes, Primrose Hill."

"I can always drop them round..."

"Whatever you want, just make sure you don't miss anything. I've got bra and knickers in the drawers, and stockings. Dresses and coats, and my mac, all in the wardrobe..."

"And jewellery, handbags, shoes, your LPs..."

"Better if Frankie comes round and you give her the suitcase and she puts everything in. But I don't want the portable typewriter. You can have that. I'll sell it to you. Ten pounds..."

"OK. Ten pounds. Can I see you? Come up?"

"No, Mark, that won't help."

"Why not? All I'm asking is to see you, not try to change your mind. I know it's too late for that. Just to see you, for old time's sake."

Lynda hesitated, audibly sighing. "OK. I'm definitely in Caister next Saturday, at the Great Yarmouth Social Club. I start work at three so could see you for a few hours at twelve."

Mark was elated. "That's great news Lynda. I'll come up by train, let you know what time I arrive..."

"There's no station here. You'll have to go to Great Yarmouth, then get a cab. It's only a few miles to here." She paused. "I'll see you at twelve at the Ship Inn, on the Caister sea front. Don't be late, I won't be able to hang around."

"OK. What's your number?"

"I don't have one. I can't give you this one, it's a private number, can't give it out. If you can't make it, then ring Nicola in London. She'll pass on the message."

"I won't mess up. I'll be there."

"OK. In which case, can you bring with you my LPs?"

"Sure, will do."

"OK. See you on Saturday. Bye then." She hung up before Mark could wish her 'goodbye' in response. He looked at the receiver for a few seconds, wondering what Lynda meant by '*it's a private number*'. But decided not to dwell on it, thankful that he was going to see her, be able to make one last attempt to change her mind, understand why she abandoned him, and whether she was now involved with another male.

He guessed that the train to Yarmouth would go from Liverpool Street station and rang directory enquiries for their number. He learnt there was a Saturday train, direct to Yarmouth, leaving at nine a.m. delivering him at eleven-thirty, and left for Liverpool Street to buy a ticket.

Back at Chatsworth Road he found Kay and Paul lounging on the settee. "Hi! Good weekend?" They both swung their bodies round and sat upright. "Yes, very enjoyable. What about you?"

"June and I went to a party on Saturday. I got high as a kite on dope and some magic mushrooms, woke up this morning at seven in my car, completely detached!"

"Sounds like a great party. Who's was it?"

"Something to do with a film director called Ken Russell. He's just made a film on Elgar for the BBC and this was some sort of celebration. It was a groovy scene!"

"Sounds very groovy. If he holds another party, you'll let us know?"

"Have you seen June?"

"No, not yet. She's not here."

"OK. I've got some news." Mark sat in one of the armchairs, picked up the *Sunday Times* from the coffee table and, with eyes half on the headlines, continued. "Lynda rang. She's definitely not coming back. So, the rent on the room is all down to me."

"That's a shame. I really liked her. Did she say why?" Paul looked genuinely interested.

"Said she wasn't cut out for working in an office at a typewriter. Wanted freedom..."

"But you were very close weren't you? Didn't you want to get married?"

"I did. But that's another story, all over now. Got to face it, I've been dumped!"

"Bad luck. She didn't have to work as a typist. She could have done something else, so many opportunities in London right now. She was no slouch, very hip, cool chick, could have done a lot in London."

"Yep, you're right." Mark paused. "Well, I get to see her next Saturday. She's working in Caister and I arranged to go up there, talk to her. So, maybe, I'll find out more about what's going on in her head."

"Where's Caister?"

"Great Yarmouth way. I'm getting a train to Yarmouth, then cabbing it Caister, just a few miles."

"We could drive you up there. You could see Lynda and we can sit on the beach at Yarmouth with our buckets and spades."

"No, I've now got my train ticket. Thanks, but I think this is something I've got to do on my own."

"So, where did June get to? Wasn't she with you?"

"We certainly started the evening together but then I blew my mind with this mescaline and I was out of it completely. I must have left the party, got into my car then passed out. Woke up this morning, freezing to death!"

"We've got a party next Saturday, South Ken way. If you're back in time, come with us. We'll probably go first to Parsons in Fulham Road for some spaghetti, then to the Denmark for a pint or two."

"Thanks, sounds good. I should be back by six if I get the three o'clock train from Yarmouth..."

"Well, if not, we'll be at the Denmark till kicking out time."

"Sounds good." Mark got up. "Lynda's aunt is going to call to arrange to collect her clothes. If I'm not around could you please take her number and I'll call her back. Her name is Frankie, short for Frances."

"Sure thing! We're out this evening, seeing *What's New Pussycat*. Do you want to come with us?"

"Yeah, love to!"

* * * *

During the walk back from the State along Kilburn High Street they all agreed. *What's New Pussycat?* was pure confection, Hollywood entertainment, nothing to be serious about, a *French farce*. "But," qualified Mark, "*Topkapi* was fun, farcical. But it had a well-developed plot, almost believable. And it was well made, good acting."

"But it didn't have Tom Jones singing."

"No, just Melina Mercouri singing a Greek folk song."

"So, what have you done with June?" Paul was clearly bored with the possibility Mark might begin intellectualising about various movies. "Haven't seen her in ages."

"She was at the party with me last night. Can't remember when I saw her last..."

"She must have had a better offer." Paul laughed.

"She's probably back at the flat wondering where we are."

June was on the settee, in front of the television watching *The Avengers*. "Where've you been?"

Paul quickly responded. "Flicks! *What's New Pussycat?*

"Good?"

"Yeah, it was OK. Rubbishy escapism."

June got up. "Just what you need on a Sunday night."

Mark showed concern. "Where did you get to last night?"

"I met someone you know..."

"Really? Who?"

"Nigel Bishop. You know him?"

"Vaguely..." Mark furrowed his brow as he plumbed his memory banks. "Works at Atlas with Glenn?"

"Yeah, think so." She hesitated. "Come upstairs, I'll tell you more."

He looked at her, wondering what demanded the secrecy. Upstairs, she fell onto the bed, beaming widely. "We've got the bread for the clothing range."

Mark repeated his furrowed brow face. "Bread?"

"Yes, Mark, bread. It's the hip word for money. We don't say *money*, we say *bread*."

"Do we?"

"Nigel Bishop's dad is in the rag trade..."

"Is he?"

"In South Africa..."

"Nigel's South African?"

"Guess so. Doesn't sound like it. Doesn't have that awful Afrikaans accent, does he?"

"Nope." Mark paused. "How do we get the money from South Africa to here?"

"Not sure. Nigel has to speak to his dad but it looks good. His old man wants to get tuned into groovy London. Nigel thinks this will sway him to go for Mouse's range of groovy clothes..."

"How much money?"

"Bread. Don't know. Mouse hasn't got back, so I've left a message for him on his answer machine."

"So, we're meeting Mouse?"

Yeah, with Nigel. Got to move this quickly or we'll lose out all round." June halted, opened her bedside cabinet, pulled out the white jewellery box with its spinning ballerina. "Roll us a *jay*." Mark fell onto the bed, opened the box and pulled out a pack of Rizla papers, sticking two together, pulling strings of intertwined tobacco and

202

cannabis into the paper. He rolled and sealed it into a fat tube, offering it to June to light. She did, inhaled deeply, held the cannabis in her lungs, lifted the joint above her head and closed her eyes, whispering her appreciation. "Jesus, that's so fucking good!"

Mark took the joint from her fingers, inhaled on it and instantly felt the tetrahydrocannabinol enter his blood stream, lifting him into a welcoming, unthreatening soporific hinterland. June repossessed the joint and as she inhaled patted the bed, inviting him to lie alongside her. Mark obliged and as she handed him back the remains of the joint she unbuckled his belt, unzipped his flies and gently extracted his penis, taking its head in her mouth, his body immediately enjoying a bullet of electricity along his spine, his flaccid penis simultaneously lengthening and thickening, June responding by sinking more of the erection in her mouth, until it touched her throat.

She then broke off and fell back alongside Mark, whispering "Take my nicks off Mark and fuck me." He kissed her, tongue deep inside her mouth, a hand sliding along her thigh, fingers pulling the flimsy nylon of her knickers away, over knees, down to ankles. She parted her legs as he lifted himself across her, lowering his hips, guiding his erection to her vagina, entering her with consummate ease, eliciting a soft, breathless *'oh, yes!'* from her.

He moved his hips to and fro in a slow, gentle motion, she linking hands around his neck, his eyes locked with hers. "Nigel's got a big cock. We fucked all night long at his. Lynda likes big cocks doesn't she? When you swopped with Paul and Kay, Paul's so big she was away in nirvana..."

"Was she?" Mark was interested in anything Lynda but not hearing about her sexual exploits with Paul while he was making love to June. But it excited him and he increased the intensity of his lovemaking, quickly climaxing, ejaculating with a loud growling *'yes!'* He fell forward, kissed her, collapsing alongside her. "So, you had a great time with Nigel. Can you tell me what happened to me? I found myself in my car at seven in the morning, freezing to death."

"You pulled some dolly bird, called Terry. Said she was a singer. You both got high on some *shrooms*, fucked each other's brains out."

"Don't remember that at all!"

"Don't think twice baby, it's all right!"

"I won't be here next Saturday. I'm going up to see Lynda." He looked shame-faced at the statement, aware that it exposed his core weaknesses, and fully expected the verbal assault from June. She didn't disappoint. "Oh, Mark! You really are a prat! What the fuck are you doing wasting your time with her? She's not interested in you! She's dumped you, moved on! Stop being a right Charley and move on yourself!"

He felt very uncomfortable, embarrassed. "Yes, you're right but I just have to see her one last time..."

"I thought we were on the same wavelength Mark. I want you to become hip, groovy, cool. I want to get your hair to grow, get you in hip clothes, get you looking really hip. But all you want is to be fucking suburban! I just don't get it! How can you be so fucking un-cool?!"

"I'm just seeing her one last time, that's all. I know she's not coming back. I know we're finished. Just need to say a last 'goodbye'."

"I'm not going to waste my time with you, Mark. If you don't sort yourself out, I really don't want to spend my precious time with you..."

He got off the bed. "OK, understood." And walked to his own bedroom.

* * * *

"I'm meeting Mouse and Nigel this evening, at Mouse's. Do you want to come?"

Mark told himself the invitation was an afterthought, June didn't want him there, her tone of voice informing him she'd abandoned all hope in him ever being hip and cool. But he knew he had to be positive, not provincial. "Sure! I want to be there!"

Mark went straight from work and in the twenty minutes it took to arrive at *Little Red Rooster* in Portobello Road from Baker Street he grew increasingly concerned at what his role would be in June's plans to be a *mover and shaker* in London's fashion world. Yes, he had an understanding of marketing, and an outstanding ability to forge productive relationships with journalists, albeit technical, not fashion. He could certainly organize a press launch, write news releases, get photography done. And he could appreciate the usefulness of the fame, if any, that might accrue from a successful launch of Mouse's range of *dolly bird* clothes.

"I can make dresses for a pound each, if I order two hundred at a time." Mouse looked confident, bright. "I've got a factory in South Wales and another in Leicester, rock bottom labour costs. Then I've got to add transport costs, getting the gear from the factory to somewhere we can store them."

"You mean a distribution centre, a warehouse?" Mark enjoyed his contribution, his amplification of Mouse's remarks.

"So, that's factory costs, transport costs, warehousing costs..."

"Unless I can get a deal with a retailer and then all the gear goes straight to them from the factory and they distribute to their shops."

"What's your profit on this?"

"If we can sell each dress at five pounds each and not pay for the transport and warehousing then it's four pounds a dress..." Mouse was confident.

"And that, guys, is just the beginning." June beamed with equal confidence. "If we're successful with this then Mouse will get other retailers asking him to design ranges. It'll become very big business."

"So, we make dresses then sell them?" Nigel was enthusiastic.

Mouse laughed. "No! I have to do some designs, get some samples made up, then try to get some orders."

"Couldn't we make them, two or three hundred, and sell them ourselves?"

"No, Nigel. For starters we need somewhere to store them and I can tell you there's no-one in the rag trade I'd trust. We'd have to find our own place to store them, where they won't be stolen."

"What if you made a few hundred, boxed them up and sent them to my dad in South Africa?"

"Suppose I could." Mouse paused. "What will he do with them?"

"Sell them! He's got enough contacts in places like Cape Town and Jo'burg. And in Salisbury. They'd sell like hot cakes!"

There was a silence as Mouse, June and Mark attempted to understand Nigel's suggestion. Mark was first to breach the pressing quiet. "We're talking about really trendy mini dresses. I'm not even sure they'd sell in the UK, let alone *Suid-Afrika*." He affected an Afrikaans accent. It fell flat, ignored by Nigel. "You'd be surprised. The young girls are really hot for trendy fashions and they all read about what's happening in London." Mark felt like commenting on *'young girls'* meaning white young girls, not young black girls in apartheid townships. But he bit his tongue.

"I'm really only interested in making dresses for the UK, Nigel." Mouse was firm. "We could look at the market in South Africa later, once we got going here..."

"My dad has enough money to help you make dresses here for the UK and pay for dresses to be made in South Africa. Really cheap *goffels* who work for next to nothing." Mark said nothing but assumed *goffels* was derogatory slang for African women. Inside him, he loathed everything about *Suid-Afrika* Afrikaaners, their white supremacy, their Sharpeville politics. But he liked Nigel. He was handsome, tall, erudite, well-dressed, and despite his living in Britain had yet to learn that apartheid was vile but, one day, would catch up with liberal morals. Until that day, Mark knew he had to allow Nigel some licence.

"OK, Nigel. I will get some samples made. Dresses and skirts, get them to my people in South Wales, make sure I've got my costs correct." He paused. "I will also get samples to you, Nigel, for your dad to have a look-see, get some costs confirmed. The designs are mine, so no pinching!"

"Sure. No pinching!" Nigel laughed. "My dad will be a lot cheaper than your factories in Wales."

"We'll see." Mouse looked confident. "Let's go to the boozer. It's Friday night!"

* * * *

Mark flicked through the LPs that sat on the floor of the living room, alongside the Festival of Britain period radio-gram, with its four spindly legs at each corner. He singled out Lynda's dozen LPs, admiring her taste as he did. *Ray Charles, Frank Sinatra, Dave Brubeck, Bob Dylan, Joan Baez, Peter, Paul and Mary.* He recalled they had only played the Ray Charles, a double LP compilation of the singer's 1950s hits. It had been a Sunday afternoon when others in the flat had trekked to Regent's Park for the sun, heat, paddling pool and 99 ice cream cones.

Alone, he and Lynda read the papers to the accompaniment of *Lonely Avenue, I Got a Woman, What'd I Say* until the music ran out and they went to the bedroom. There Lynda put on her tart wear and they spent an hour engaged in torrid sex before falling asleep for an hour, woken by the others returning. Anna and June cooked them all liver, bacon, and mashed potatoes before en masse they jumped a bus to the Marble Arch Odeon to see *Thunderball*.

Mark put the dozen LPs into a voluminous *Peter Robinson* bag, resplendent with coloured cord handles. Another memory as he held up the bag to test its durability, remembering the rust red dress he'd bought her for her birthday from the *Peter Robinson* store in the Strand, both of them taken with the dress's metallic affect.

At Liverpool Street he learnt he'd have to change trains at Norwich and on the relatively short journey from London he was only able to get to the foreign news pages of his *Guardian*, making redundant his James Bond *Goldfinger* Pan paperback, and copy of the latest *Private Eye*. The cab journey from Great Yarmouth station to Caister was less than ten minutes, on a road that gave him an enjoyable view of the beach and a calm North Sea, all bathed in sun, the cabbie depositing him at the Ship Inn ten minutes to mid-day.

Inside, the bar was heaving with red-faced men in short-sleeved shirts, holidaymakers who'd walked off the beach, leaving wives and children behind, the air thick with cigarette smoke. He couldn't see Lynda and had no desire to remain indoors. Outside, he paced up and down the pavement, eyes darting in all directions, hoping to see Lynda on the horizon, or suddenly turning a corner. Instead, a chrome-heavy Vauxhall Cresta pulled up and there she was, at the driving wheel. He smiled, pulled open the door, "Hi, there!" and slid in, kissing her on the cheek, dropping the *Peter Robinson* bag on the floor in front of him.

"How are you?" He immediately noticed she was wearing a shapeless summery floral-decorated dress he hadn't seen before.

"I'm fine, thanks." Lynda stared directly ahead, not at him, shoved the gear stick into first and pulled away.

"Your car?"

"Don't be silly! I can't afford to run a car like this."

He ached to ask her whose car it was but controlled his nosiness. "I take it we're not going into the Ship..."

"No, we're going back to my caravan. I have to work this afternoon so can't spend too much time with you. Sorry about that."

"When do you start?"

"Three. So, I'll have to say 'bye' to you at two."

"That early?"

"What time's your train back?"

"There's a three o'clock and a five o'clock back to Norwich, then I get the London train."

"Get the three o'clock, make sure you don't miss the London train." She paused. "There's a bloke in a caravan who runs a cab. He'll take you back to Yarmouth."

"You work every day?"

"Yes, most times I do an afternoon, then a break, then an evening. The seaside places are the busiest, the ones that make the most money."

"Hope you're making a lot of dough!"

"Not bad. The punters give me tips when they win. Very useful."

"So, what happens when the summer is over? Where will you go then?"

"Maybe the other clubs, like the ones at Fakenham and Wisbech. That's if I've got a job. No guarantees."

"You could always try to get a job as a croupier in London."

"Maybe." She stopped herself. "That's if I want to go on being a croup. I may not." She turned into the caravan park and pulled up outside a large white trailer, supported by a set of tyred wheels and a pile of bricks in each of four corners. "I share the caravan with another girl, Vicky. We've made shepherd's pie between us, so that's what we'll be eating. Hope it doesn't kill you."

"Sounds good!" Mark wasn't at all pleased. He'd hoped he and Lynda would be spending the time alone, not shared with a stranger.

He deduced Lynda had engineered Vicky's presence to ensure he didn't get too personal, or even attempt to seduce her. Vicky was tall, gangly, with short blond hair, in shorts that revealed long legs in perfect white, not a trace of tan.

Mark sat at the dining table, already set with knives, forks, and Worcestershire sauce. "I'll make some coffee." Lynda filled the kettle while Vicky checked the oven. "Not long now. Hope you like shepherd's pie." He sat at the table, alone, increasingly uncomfortable, increasingly depressed, wanting desperately to engage Lynda with a journey down their collective memory lane, recalling the day they first met at Princeton College, their first date, their first penetrative sex. Instead, he told himself he'd travelled all the way from London to the back of beyond and all he was going to get was a plate of cooked minced beef topped with mashed potato, and frustratingly one-dimensional small talk.

"Do you come from round here, Vicky?"

She turned, smiled. "No, I'm a Londoner. Tottenham. You?"

"West London, place called Hayes." He paused. "But I'm now living in a flat in Kilburn. We shared it, didn't we Lynda?"

"Yes, we did, Mark..."

"You were Lynda's boyfriend?"

"Yes. Not ashamed to say Lynda was the first girl I'd fallen in love with." Mark felt good as he paraded his heart on his sleeve, secretly hoping it might embarrass Lynda.

"Yes, but there's love and then there's love..."

"What do you mean?" Mark was confused.

"What I mean is that people need freedom. Not put in cages, like birds. People shouldn't try to control people..."

"Didn't know I was doing that." Mark was affronted, annoyed.

"You're in love and you don't think you're cornering someone..."

"Right. I certainly didn't plan that, didn't think I was doing that."

Lynda handed Mark his coffee. "So, can you live with freedom, Mark?"

"I don't know about that Lynda." He paused and fixed his stare directly at her. "What I do know is that I fell in love with you, but you didn't fall in love with me, and I was very naive, too honest, too immature about it all, and that worried you..."

"You wanted marriage, Mark, and I didn't. Not just yet. One day, but not now."

"So, you're going to continue with this." He waved his hand at the caravan's interior.

"Yes, until I get sacked or bored. Then I'll do something else. Car mechanics, learn to fly, design clothes..."

"Come back to London sometime?"

"Sure I will! One day."

They ate their shepherd's pie in almost total silence. Mark admitted he had failed to even launch the discussion with Lynda he'd planned. On the train back he churned over in his head how he should have played it, becoming increasingly annoyed with himself at his failure to achieve anything positive, admitting Lynda had outfoxed him by having Vicky in attendance. Sitting alone in the train's compartment he allowed his self-pity to grow and gently cried at the loss of the love of his life. But he brought it to a halt, cursing what he regarded as a weakness heavily coated in pathos, opened his *Private Eye* and was laughing within minutes, vowing to finally put his relationship with Lynda behind him and move on to fresh pastures.

But he couldn't. At Chatsworth Road there greeted him a message. Lynda's aunt had phoned. She was going to call round that evening to collect Lynda's clothes, asking to ensure someone would be in since she *'was on duty flying across Europe for the next few weeks'*. He rang her back and requested she came round immediately since he didn't want to miss going with the others to the party in

South Kensington. She obliged, was at Chatsworth Road in half an hour, and brusque at the front door, clearly unhappy at having to divert her precious time to collecting her niece's apparel detritus, the remnants of a failed relationship.

He led her to the bedroom where he'd opened drawers and the wardrobe, leaving Lynda's Samsonite suitcase opened on the bed. "I'll let you get on." She didn't reply but busied herself with clearing drawers, allowing him to absorb her blond hair, good looks and legs. She was slim, shapely legs in dark brown hose. He guessed her age as mid-forties, certainly possessing the aura of an airline stewardess. He installed himself at the kitchen table and found it impossible not to think of Lynda with her aunt in his bedroom packing away all evidence that the room was once occupied by her niece, his girlfriend.

"Can you help me?" It was Frankie's voice, at the top of the stairs. He strode up to the landing and took the suitcase from her. "I didn't know it would be so heavy." She was apologetic. Mark smiled. "It's Lynda's winter coats." Outside, she opened the boot of her Morris Minor. "How will you get it out of the boot?" Frankie stared at the suitcase and pondered. "Good question." She paused. "Could you help me? I'll drive you back here."

"Sure!"

"I've got a lift in my block. Just need to get it out of the car, to the lift, then into my flat."

"Only too pleased to help!" And he was. He wanted to ensure she had a good impression of him, countering any negative view of him Lynda might relay to her aunt.

As she sat at the driving wheel, her simple woollen dress rode up, revealing her stocking tops, Mark wondering if it was by design, or an accident. Mark said nothing, despite admiring her stockings and attractive legs. In the short drive to Primrose Hill he made no reference to Lynda, nor did her aunt, but he told himself she might constitute some form of link with Lynda, if only he could stay in touch with her. He admitted an assumption, that Frankie was close to her niece, and that they were in regular contact. But in searching his memory he had also to admit Lynda had barely mentioned her aunt.

He silently cursed but, with a hint of panic, as Frankie turned her car into Chatsworth Road, he blurted out the suggestion they meet for a drink sometime, fully expecting to be rebuffed with some crushing remark. Instead she replied positively. "Yes, I'd like that." She paused, he felt heartened. "I'm away most of the time, flying here and there, but give me a call. There's a lovely Turkish near me, wonderful food. You can take me to dinner there."

"Who's that?" June was at the top of the stairs, arms folded, holding her dressing gown closed.

"Frankie, Lynda's aunt."

"What you doing with her." She paused. "Don't tell me you're screwing her!"

Mark ignored the crudity. "She came to collect Lynda's clothes. Lynda's not coming back."

"Not surprised. Let's hope you get her out of your head, concentrate on getting cool and hip."

"You getting ready to go out?"

"No, only been in an hour or so, been very busy day."

"What you been doing?"

"London. We did the Marquee, great music, Bo Street Runners, Georgie Fame."

"Right, sounds good. Saw the Bo Street Runners a few years ago. They're good."

"Marquee's the place to be. Lot of cool people there, listening to the music, hanging out..."

"Who'd you meet?"

"Brian Jones, some guys from Cambridge in a group called Pink Floyd, and some guys from Kent in a group called Soft Machine." She paused. "I've invited them to a bash. Next Saturday, here..."

"You mean a party? Here?"

"Bash, Mark, bash." She gave him another of her *get cool Mark* looks. "Got to get connected Mark with all these cool people..."

"And they're going to travel to Kilburn?"

"Yeah, why not? It's not the end of the earth, Mark. It's only a few fucking miles from the West End!"

"Sure!" He felt embarrassed. He knew Kilburn was no less cool than Hampstead or Chelsea, just run-down, centre of Rachman housing, poor West Indians exploited by Whitey. "And if you're talking about getting connected then let's get plugged into some of the West Indian groups playing in Kilburn. Y'know, ska music outfits..."

"OK, sounds good. Let's do it!"

"And when will we have the *Red Rooster* launch party?"

"Mid-September. Got to give Mouse the time, sort out the money."

CHAPTER TEN

"I'm all for parties!" Paul was enthusiastic but June was concerned that his eagerness clouded his understanding. She wanted him and Kay, and Anna, to appreciate the party would be jointly hosted by her and Mouse, and would be all about launching the *Rockin' Red Rooster* range of dolly bird apparel. Paul was quizzical. "Well, I'm no expert at these things but don't you launch new clothes ranges in fashion houses, on cat walks? Never heard of them being launched in a house on a side street in Kilburn."

"That's why it makes it so cool. We're launching a clothes range for ordinary people, not millionaires..."

"So, what, we're going to have press people here, photographers, fashion writers?"

"Yep, and we're going to have some pop stars here too!"

"Really? Who?"

"Yes, they'll be here!" June laughed at her excruciatingly poor joke.

Paul maintained a straight face. "So, the Stones, Beatles, Kinks, Manfred Mann..."

"You'd be surprised!"

"So, how's this party going to work? Is it a party or a fashion show?"

"Both, Paul!" June beamed. "We'll have half a dozen girls in the minis, proving they look good, perfect for any dolly bird..."

"What design, what pattern, look? What's on them?" Kay sounded keen.

"Why, do you want to wear one?"

"Yes. As long as the design is OK. Not going to wear anything you'd find in Marks."

"Don't worry, Mouse is a great fashion designer. He wouldn't know how to do a bad design. He's going to be one of the country's top fashion designers. Just you watch!"

"So, we invite all our friends, as normal, and you invite the beautiful people?" Paul smiled broadly.

"Yes, spot on!"

"And when?"

"Well, guess we better avoid the new-fangled bank holiday weekend, people will be away. Guess Mouse will be able to make the sample dresses in time. I'll ask him..."

"I'm size twelve." Kay piped up, concern in her voice, revealing that she'd was worried June had already forgotten her.

"And I'm ten," added Anna.

"OK, see what I can do."

Mark edged June to one side. "What's happening with the money side of things? Is Nigel's dad putting any money in?"

"Yes, he's paying for the samples. Six for him in South Africa, six for us here in London. Mouse has to get colour photographs taken of girls wearing the gear, he needs to get them out to his contacts in the big shops."

"Expensive. I've got some photographers on my list, see if I can pull in some favours..."

"Yeah, and you'll need to work with Mouse in getting some publicity. I've got a business card from one of the two wankers I met at Mouse's. From the *Daily Express.* They took photographs of me and Lynda. Afraid they were only interested in our crotches but they could be useful. I'll dig the card out."

"And you said this guy Apollo might be interested in Mouse's stuff..."

"I want to keep him out of things for the time being."

"Why?"

"Just don't want him near Mouse's business right now. Not until it's really needed." June hesitated. "He's Maltese mafia. Don't really want him near Mouse..."

"You did originally."

"Yep, I did. Changed my mind."

"And he's a partner of Baz's, in the gambling."

"Yeah, and a lot else..."

"What else?"

"Drop it, Mark. He's got no place in our plans."

Mark fell quiet but became uncomfortable at the thought Lynda was working for a gangster, felt compelled to make contact with her, warn her. But quickly lost the urge as he realised that she was a *big girl* and could look after herself. He also told himself he was no longer responsible for her, despite deep down wanting to actively care for her.

* * * *

The late August sun was hot, welcome and brought alive the Saturday pavements of Kilburn High Road. Mark had walked the length from Chatsworth Road to the Gaumont State cinema many times, invariably with Lynda and occasionally the others. But he couldn't remember walking beyond, all the way until the shops ran out, where the high road became Maida Vale, shops giving way to residential property. He bought his *Guardian* from his normal paper shop, folded it under his arm and strode down one side of the road, heartened by the number of music and record shops peppering both sides. At Maida Vale, he crossed the road and walked back, finally entering the Kilburn Record Centre, the largest of the half dozen or so music shops the high street supported.

Mark dived into one of the numerous display racks, each full of either single records or LPs, slowly flicking through the contents, jammed in, making it difficult to pull anything from the densely packed displays. He appreciated the music. It was Bobby Darin from his *That's All* LP, one of two Mark owned by the singer, in which he successfully apes Frank Sinatra. But it most definitely wasn't ska. It wasn't rock, or rhythm and blues, or jazz, and Mark wondered whether the Kilburn Record Centre wasn't quite what its name implied. But he found the courage to ask at the counter. He hadn't rehearsed it but felt good as he asked the middle-aged man behind the counter where he might find ska music being played live, pub or club in the area, Mark convinced he wouldn't receive a useful answer. But he was wrong. "The only place I know is the Shakespeare pub. They have gigs there for the groups who record at Island records..."

"Island records?"

"Yep. They're a West Indian label, based next door to the Shakespeare. They only record West Indian music, like ska. I sell a few every week, not much, but it's catching on..."

"*My Boy Lollipop*?"

"Yeah, that was a big hit. Not much since."

"Thanks for that. Where's the Shakespeare?"

"Cambridge Road, off Kilburn Park Road."

"OK, guess that's not too far from here?"

"No, about ten minutes. Walk down the high road, turn into Kilburn Park Road, then Cambridge. Can't miss it..."

"OK. While I'm here do you have a Gerry Mulligan LP from the fifties. Think it was called *Nights at the Roundtable...*"

"We've got a few Gerry Mulligan LPs. That might be one of them. Don't recognise it."

Mark found no Mulligan LPs he didn't already own but took a fancy to an import LP by Herbie Mann, *Nirvana*. He'd heard Mann on the radio and was intrigued by his jazz flute. Mark eased two pound notes from his wallet. "Let me know how you get on with the ska thing." Mark smiled. "Will do!"

Outside the sun was markedly hotter than the twenty minutes earlier before he had entered the Kilburn Record Centre. He browsed through the racks that sat in front of the shop window, picking out single records he'd bought just five years before, from *Quarter to Three* to *Watch Your Step*, remembering how they got him, and everyone else, up dancing at the Blue Moon Club on a Sunday evening or at Burton's Uxbridge on a Saturday.

Ten minutes later he was at the Shakespeare and although he didn't want a drink he went in and ordered half a pint of bitter, fearing a request for a glass of red wine would mark him out as a *nancy boy* in what was a rougher part of Kilburn, decidedly more *Notting Hill* than the Chatsworth Road end of the borough. "Do you have music here? Ska music?" The young student-aged male behind the bar gave him a look of some suspicion, and Mark immediately thought he must look like a nosey policeman. He quickly back-peddled an explanation. "It's just me and my girlfriend like the music, we've heard on the radio, and we'd like to actually see someone play it."

"Radio? Who's played it on the radio?"

Mark went red-faced and lied. "It was that guy on Caroline, Jumbo Jimmy Gordon."

"We have some live ska here on a Friday night, eight 'til closing time."

"Thanks." Mark took his glass of beer and went outside, sat at one of the tables, soaking in the sun's hot rays, enjoying the chatting, friendly white and black men who trouped into the pub, he assuming they were the musicians and recording technicians from across the road, from Island records. And as he downed the last of his beer the barman appeared. "If you're really interested in Jamaican music, there's a lot of it tonight. It's a sort of private party, at a house. It's what a lot of the West Indian guys do. They perform at people's houses. They can't get bookings at pubs and dance halls so they play in people's houses..."

"But it's private."

"Well, sort of. Not much different from any other party. If you're interested, come down here tonight with your girlfriend and after closing time we'll go along, see if I can get you in."

"Where is it?"

"Elgin Avenue. Harrow Road end."

"Do I need my car?"

"That would be handy."

"OK. See you here this evening. What's your name?"

"Rob. Rob Bell."

"OK, Rob. I'm Mark, girlfriend is June."

Mark returned to the house to an angry Anna and Kay. He had left the house without cleaning it, despite his name being top of the rota pinned to the message board. "OK, you do it next Saturday." Kay scratched out a name and wrote Mark's over it. "Don't forget this time!" Mark felt a growing humiliation, felt like he was a ten year old boy again, being reprimanded by his mother. "I'll mow the lawn." Kay refused to relent. "Can you and June do some shopping? We need bread, milk, eggs, all the usual stuff. Take money from the kitty, the list is on the board." Chastened, he went upstairs to find June, still in bed. "Get up, shower, dress, we've got to do the weekly shopping..."

"Didn't think it was my turn."

"It is now. And while we shop I can tell you all about ska music, and a private party tonight..."

"Sounds good. Give me ten minutes."

* * * *

The heat of the day had left its legacy in the air of the evening and June and Mark stood outside the Shakespeare pub amongst a group of a dozen or more other drinkers, June opting to wear her 1950s style black velvet 'pedal pusher' toreador pants. By the time Rob was able to free himself from his bar duties June and Mark were alone outside, looking decidedly suspicious. They climbed into the Mini and Rob successfully directed Mark, and they pulled up outside the terraced house in Elgin Avenue within five minutes. Rob immediately looked apprehensive. "I hope this works. If they don't like the look of you they'll tell you to take a hike." He paused. "Should have told you not to dress like cops."

Mark was incredulous. "We look like cops? I don't think so Rob. We look like mods."

"OK. Don't say anything. I'll do the talking."

Rob led the way, rang the doorbell, smartly answered by a heavily-set West Indian male who opened the door the width of his body, ran his eyes up and down Mark, then June before engaging Rob. "Can I help?" Rob sounded nervous. "We're invited to the party, by Sonny Roberts. I work at the Shakespeare pub, cross the road from Island records. Sonny mentioned the party, thought it'd be OK to come along." The West Indian looked unconvinced. "I see you at the Shakespeare. You OK, but not your friends. They got trouble in mind." Rob affected a sadness in his voice. "No, they're clean. They just like ska music. They can't seem to find any place to hear to it. I told them there'd be a lot of it at this party. They just like ska." The West Indian said nothing but swung the door open. "OK, let me check your pockets." He shot hands inside Rob's jacket pockets, then Mark's, indicating to June to open her handbag. He then nodded them through.

Mark felt like commenting but bit his tongue, deciding to leave his remarks 'til later, rapidly becoming fascinated by the music that got closer as they all proceeded along the hall towards a room from where a group of young West Indians were spilling, each of them craning their necks to see the music's performers. "Sounds good, doesn't it?" asked Mark, turning to June. "Sure does, want to dance to it."

"The room's packed, can't see anything. Certainly no space to dance." But as he moved himself to secure a better view he became aware of a small group of boys, all white, jumping in the air, as if on pogo sticks, in time to the music. He'd never seen anything like it before, pulling an incredulous face, before registering that each of the boys was not just white but shaven-headed. Must be a cult he told himself, hoping June has seen the same vision, wanting to comment on it, but careful not to say anything, wary that he might easily offend those around him. But before he could say anything a shoulder barged him to one side. "Sorry, mate." And the shoulder and body moved into the crowd, slicing through the phalanx, Mark's jaw fell open, stunned at the clothes he wore, braces, Levi's rolled up the calf, and boots that followed the jeans up the shin. He turned to June who gave him an equally strained look of incredulous disbelief, before breaking into a smile. "Different!"

The music stopped and June pushed forward, Mark quickly following in her slipstream, reaching the front, a tall black male giving her a wide smile. June returned the smile. "Who's that playing?" His smile remained fixed. "Who's that asking?" June gave him her *'do me a favour face'*. "I'm only asking because we like ska but we don't see any of it being played anywhere. It's like it's banned."

"Could be. No-one digs it but us rude boys. Pubs only play whitey's music, not Jamaica's music from the sun..."

"So you have to play it in people's houses?"

222

"That's about it. For the time being. It will get big, catch on..."

"So, who's this group?"

"They called Glass Bucket Boys. From the island, got here a few months back. They the authentic thing."

"I'm helping a friend launch a clothes range. Might be good to have some ska music there to help it go..."

"So you fashion model?"

June laughed. "No, not me, just helping a friend to get his name known. He's a great fashion designer but nobody knows his name."

"Where's this all happening then? Carnaby Street?"

"No! That place is a joke, full of tourists! Wrong image for my friend's clothes..."

"King's Road?"

"That's better but not there. It'll be where I live, a house. We'll have a house party to launch the clothes, and this band and the music could be just right for the launch."

"You ask the lead singer. His name Senator Michael. He'll fix it for you."

"Thanks." June turned to Mark. "What do you think? It could work, no-one's heard this ska music, it's different..."

"Yeah, guess so." Mark paused, his voice carrying a hint of doubt. "It's just the music. Sounds like you'd use it if you were launching some clothes for a Caribbean holiday, not groovy, gear London."

June ignored the comment. "Mouse will love it! I'll talk to the singer and see where they're next on, get Mouse to see them."

Senator Michael was, Mark observed, very thin, early twenties and spoke with a heavy Jamaican accent. Both Mark and June had to concentrate to understand, especially when he slipped into patios but it was clear he was interested, stating he would personally want thirty pounds as payment, and ten pounds each for the three musicians in the group. June smiled. "Shouldn't be a problem..." while Mark silently allowed a sharp intake of breath. Sixty pounds was a lot of money, he assuming June's sangfroid owed everything to the comfort of knowing the deep pockets of Nigel's father would find the required readies. "If you're for serious call me at Island records. They'll pass on the message."

"I'm serious!" June sounded affronted. "I'll call as soon as we've decided on a date." Senator Michael smiled, a lack of belief all over his face, and walked away. "Don't think he believed you." Mark wanted to be serious but couldn't avoid being flippant. "He probably thinks you're a copper." June was less than impressed. "I don't look like a bloody copper!" She hesitated, then prodded him in the chest. "You do! It was you who scared him off..."

"OK. Let's go. We've seen enough."

Outside, they got into the car. June brightened. "Let's go to Mouse's!"

"He's not expecting us June. Might not be convenient."

"Fuck that. Just drive there. He'll be glad to see us."

"If he's not there let's go the Cromwellian..."

"You've been there?"

"No, just read about it. Or we could try Blaise's."

"No, let's go to the Crom. I know Tony Mitchell, he runs the place. He'll get us in."

"Did you see those guys tonight with the shaven heads, boots, jeans halfway up their legs, braces. What's that all about?"

"Don't know but they didn't look too friendly. Wouldn't like to meet one of them late at night..."

"And dancing, jumping up in the air. Like a kids party!"

"Didn't see anyone smoking any weed. Thought these West Indians lived on the stuff."

"That's probably an exaggeration. One they've encouraged."

"Not sure if I could ever trust any one of them. They all look on edge, suspicious..."

"D'you blame them? They've been screwed for centuries by Whitey. Got every right to mistrust us, specially since Rachman and the Notting Hill riots..."

"Don't think I could ever go with one of them."

"You mean there's one group of men you haven't screwed?"

"Not funny Mark. I'm not a slut. I just like sex."

"Jean Harlow. Seat belts on, it's going to be a bumpy ride."

Mouse wasn't at home. Mark drove south to Kensington, found a parking space on Thurloe Square, and they both walked the short distance to the Cromwell Road and the Cromwellian club, June sliding her arm inside Mark's. At the door June did the talking, got them signed in as guests, and made their way to a bar where he got himself a whiskey, in a tall glass full to the brim with ice. June opted for a Cuba Libre. And they parted. Mark followed the music, slipped downstairs to the discotheque, while June went to one of the roulette wheels. Mark halted at the base of the stairs, held by the crowd of people unable to access the small dancing area. "Great music, shame to waste it." The girl was in front of him and it took Mark a second or two to realise she was addressing him. He laughed. "Yep, great shame. Wonder why the discotheque bit is so small."

"They're only interested in the gambling, don't make any money out of people dancing."

"Yeah, you're right." He paused. "You fancy pushing your way forward, I'll follow, we can dance then."

She smiled. "I'll try." And she eased her way onto the dance area, quickly followed by Mark, both immediately swinging into a soft gyration to *Respect*, then *The In Crowd*, and an unbroken run of records nakedly, unashamedly, designed for dancing. Until, after some twenty minutes, she called a halt, waved her hands, mouthed she'd had enough and before he could attempt to convince her to remain dancing, she was gone, slipping into the gloom, leaving him standing, abandoned, while others continued to dance around him.

He silently cursed, sought out his drink, and made his way up the stairs, wondering why she had so quickly left the dance floor, blaming himself for his poor dancing technique, maybe his flies were open, couldn't be bad breath, they weren't dancing that close.

He went looking for June, found her at a table, in the company of someone he'd seen on television, but couldn't quite place him, or begin to wonder his name. Others at the tables were more recognisable, from Eric Burdon and Simon Dee to Jeff Beck and Sandie Shaw. Mark finished his drink and left. Outside on the pavement he enjoyed the warm air, free of cigarette smoke, made his way to the car, weaved his way north through Kensington's labyrinthine road network until he found road signs that directed him to Kilburn.

It was three in the morning as Mark pulled to a halt in Chatsworth Road. Inside, he made himself a cup of Nescafé, a cheese sandwich, and sat in the kitchen, listening to a track from *The Atomic Mr Basie* on Radio London. He wondered if anyone else was home, or whether they were all still out, partying somewhere. And his empty head landed on Lynda. Where was she? Who was she with? Still working at three in the morning *Place Your Bets Please* or in bed, alone or otherwise? He emptied his mug, washed it out, and walked stiffly up the stairs, climbing into his bed, the clanging of a far off goods train floating in through the open window, easing him into a welcome sleep as he vowed to contact Frankie, telling himself she would know what Lynda was up to.

* * * *

"September 18th. Put it in your diary!"

Mark looked up. "You mean the *Red Rooster* launch? Here?"

"Yes, here. It's not a launch, Mark. It's a happening. The *Little Red Rooster Happening*!"

"June, you can't be serious about using this place for a 'happening'. It's a flat in a run-down part of London. They won't come, they'll be scared of being mugged!"

"We're doing it here because we're the opposite to the flashy, expensive fashion house that's out of ordinary people's reach. We're all about hip, cool, groovy London! Not fucking stuck-up London!"

"If it's a flop everyone's going to be really pissed off. They might turn nasty."

"It will be a massive hit, Mark. And if you don't believe in it, say so and you can piss off!"

"Thanks, June. I'm only saying. I've organised press launches where only a few people have turned up. It happens."

"This isn't your run-of-the-mill press launch. This is a *happening*!" She paused. "And anyway, Nigel tried to get the Roundhouse but it's booked. And they charge the earth for a booking, plus drinks. Then he tried the Countdown Club. No deal. All too expensive."

Mark allowed himself a smile. "Three weeks then. I need to photograph the clothes, get a press release written..."

"Get round to Mouse's, then! Chop, chop!"

Mark made his way to Portobello Road straight from work, arriving at seven, surprised to see the shop still open and full of people browsing the racks of *groovy* clothing. Mouse was busy, conversing with customers, young girls with slim figures and attendant legs, all dressed in shapeless sack-like dresses, all wanting *hip, cool gear* for parties, bopping at the *Speakeasy*, or on camera on Channel Three's *Ready, Steady Go!* Kingsway studios, in the building that Mark had discovered once housed the Second World War headquarters of the Royal Air Force.

He stood to one side of the shop, aware that he mustn't impede any sales prospect. The girl in the dark green dress smiled at him, as she ran her hand through the rack of dresses. He smiled back, taken with her red hair that hit her shoulders then bounced up in a perfectly formed wave that circled the nape of her neck. "I love your hair. Perfect Maureen O'Hara."

She smiled, a short laugh in her throat. "I'll take that as a compliment."

He was surprised she appeared not to know who Maureen O'Hara was. "She's a film star, Irish I think, with really deep red hair. Real, too!"

"Mine is!"

"And you got ragged at school."

"Sure did!"

"So did I!" He paused. "I had really red hair when I was a kid ten years ago. Then it went blond..."

"I wouldn't say 'blond', more like fair."

"Your name isn't Lynda is it?"

"No, it isn't. Why, do I look like a 'Lynda'?"

"Sort of. My ex was a Lynda. You remind me of her."

"Really? You don't know me..."

"It's your look, your air of confidence."

She laughed at the compliment that sounded too like a threadbare chat-up line. "So, what are you doing here? Buying a dress for your ex?"

"No. Wish I could but she's long gone..."

"So what are you doing here? Chatting up girls?"

"No. A few of us are launching a new clothes line for girls, dresses, and Mouse is designing them..."

"Mouse?"

"Yeah, that's him over there. He and a few of his friends run this place. He's the designer..."

"When is the launch?"

"Soon. You'll see it in all the papers."

"Oh, you're not going to invite me to the launch?"

228

"Could do. Have you got a card?"

She opened her bag and pulled one out. He read it, *Jacqueline Cane, Personnel Department, North Thames Gas Board.* "Jacqueline..."

"Jackie."

"OK, I'll give you a call." He paused. "I'm Mark. Let me give you my card." He dug out his wallet and extracted a card. She surveyed it. "You're in PR."

"Yeah. Luckily, I work for one of the major PR agencies. Lots of opportunities."

"Sounds glamorous. Not like boring old personnel."

He laughed. "What are you doing now, this evening?"

"Nothing. Why?"

"Just thought you might like to go for a drink, or a meal?"

She shrugged her shoulders in a take it or leave it fashion. "OK..."

"I just need to speak to Mouse. Do you mind waiting? Won't be long."

"OK, I'll keep looking at these clothes. Too expensive for me."

"Thanks. I'll be as quick as I can."

Mark pulled Mouse to one side. "Just need to cover a few things, Mouse, on the launch. Got the date from June, September 18th, so now need to get photographs organised of the gear, get a media invitation list together, get writing a press release..." He trailed off as it dawned on him that Mouse wasn't paying attention, his mind on the group of four females on the other side of the shop. Then it dawned on Mark that two of them were Twiggy and Jean Shrimpton, all clearly interested in Mouse's designs. Mark pulled back. "OK, Mouse, you better go look after them. Just to say we need to photograph the gear soon as possible, we've only got a few weeks to the 18th."

Mouse slapped Mark on the shoulder. "Yeah, it's all cool. I've asked Hoppy Hopkins to do the photography..."

"Who?"

"Friend of mine. Great guy, great photographer. We'll do black and white and some colour." He sped away from Mark and joined the females, leaving him wondering if Mouse would deliver anything for the launch. He turned and joined Jackie. "I heard you. He sounds a bit flaky." Mark nodded. "Sure does." He paused, leant into Jackie and whispered. "That's Twiggy and Jean Shrimpton over there." She looked across his shoulder. "Thought I recognised them. What are they doing here?" He shrugged. "Guess they are going to model some of Mouse's gear..."

"What, the clothes you're launching?"

His eyes widened. "Could be!" He laughed, enthusiasm and motivation returning to bolster his spirit. "Let's go! Find somewhere to eat. If you like Chinese there's a great restaurant in Queensway, near Whiteley's."

"OK. Is it far from here?"

"No, we can walk it, about ten minutes." He took a gulp of air. "Do you live near a tube station?"

"Yes. Why?"

"Don't want to drag you too far from home. If you can get a tube home that helps..."

"I live near East Acton station, Central line."

"I live in Kilburn, Bakerloo line, near the tube station."

Over dinner Mark was careful not to drone on about Lynda. Jackie did ask and he responded with a brief summation but avoided any suggestion he was a broken-hearted victim of unrequited love. He was keen to find out about her personal situation, encouraged to learn she was single, also fresh from a collapsed relationship which she clearly did not regret. He discovered they shared Irish grandparents, agreeing her red hair was part of her Irish heritage, she refusing to believe he ever had red hair.

He carefully weaved anecdotes about himself into discussion that elicited information from her. Mark discovered she had been born into an authoritarian Catholic family from which she managed to finally escape, on reaching her twenty-first birthday, moving from the family home in Aylesbury to one bedsit after another, acquiring a boyfriend en route, doomed to a subsequent break-up, while also securing a reliable if one-dimensional job-for-life in the personnel department of a state-owned utility.

Her eyes were dark, skin a clichéd pure white, reminding him of painful summer sunburn, assuming she took precautions, always sitting in the shade, reading a book, alone, self-sufficient, independent, haughty. And the red hair, pure in its density, fiery in its promise.

They finished their meal with a final cup of jasmine tea and at the restaurant door he suggested he accompany her to Paddington station where she could take a Circle line train to Notting Hill, changing there to a Central line train for East Acton. At Paddington he remained with her, wanting to tell her she made him feel very relaxed, what good company she was, wanted to see her again. But he didn't. Instead, at Notting Hill station, he blurted out the closest he could get to saying how much he liked her. "Look, I'll see you home. Can't let you go home alone." She smiled. "OK." Then looked him full in the face. "How will you get home? Kilburn is the opposite direction." He looked across the busy road, then back to her. "I'll cab it, claim it back on expenses."

As they slipped down the staircase at East Acton station Jackie slid her arm inside his and he pressed it against his body as she guided them towards her flat. It was a large single room, on the top floor of a bland, anonymous 1920s house, containing a bed at one end and a kitchen area at the other end, a small dining table and two chairs, a floral patterned sofa. "The loo's on the landing, next to the bathroom."

He went over to the record player. "What shall I put on?" She joined him. "Nothing too loud." She bent down. "Here, put this one on." Mark bent low. "MJQ, *Fontessa*. Love them, love this record." He turned, their eyes met and he leaned forward and they kissed, lightly, before both brought themselves up, self-consciously parting. "Coffee?" He watched as she walked towards the kitchen area. "Yes please." And he placed the record on the turntable, swung the needle onto the disc, waited for the opening chords before walking over to where Jackie was preparing two mugs of Nescafé. He slid his arms around her waist and kissed her hair.

She turned and they kissed, gracefully at first, then with a growing abandonment. Mark was surprised as he felt a hand at his trouser zip and as a finger slowly pulled it open, Jackie slid to her knees, and, looking up whispered a calm "I'm having a period," easing his erected penis out, placing its tip in her mouth. Her warm tongue and saliva sent a shiver along his spine and he murmured his enjoyment, then moaned, gently placing his hands on her red hair, his excitement rising until after five minutes he finally climaxed, her mouth filling with his sperm. She gracefully rose and they kissed passionately before eventually breaking off. He looked at her and whispered. "Are you ready for a boyfriend?" She smiled. "Are you ready for a girlfriend?"

"Ready, willing, and able."

"Good! So, when shall we meet?"

"Wednesday evening? I could come straight from work. We could see a film in Ealing or Shepherd's Bush..."

"OK, you can stay the night if you want. But I got my period, so we can't..."

"Don't worry about that. It's not just sex, life's more than that."

"I get home about six-thirty. See you then?"

"Yes, probably a bit later, can't get away dead on five-thirty, clients screw up your private life."

"There's no phone here so if you can't make it you'll have to call me before I leave the office."

"Jackie, I'll be here, come hell or high water. If some client gets in the way, I'll still be here, as late as it takes."

"Don't make it too late!"

He kissed her, and hand in hand they both walked down the stairs to the front door. They kissed again, he broke off and bit into the flesh on her neck, she whimpered a moan before breaking away. "Hey! Go now, Mark! See you Wednesday!"

He made his way back to Chatsworth Road, wrapped in a bubble of elation. He knew nothing about Jackie, she knew nothing about him, but he recognised he was on the brink of infatuation. Or was it love? If it was love, why did he fall so easily? What was the chemical formula that had him fall in love with certain types of girl, all without any significant prompting? But if it was just infatuation, was it simply his way of shoving endless sheets of absorbent blotting paper into the seemingly deep void created by Lynda's abandoning him?

At Notting Hill station the elation bubble burst, and Mark cursed the route home to Kilburn by tube, a circuitous dog-leg of a journey that took him back into the west end, to Baker Street, only to get a train north out of the city. Three separate train journeys. He was angry at opting not to wave down a cab, and vowed to use his car on Wednesday evening, even if he stayed over as Jackie had suggested.

* * * *

Despite a note Sellotaped to June's bedroom door, Mark did not get to see her until Tuesday evening. He reported his abortive meeting with Mouse, emphasising his concern about the photography of the gear he was producing. "I couldn't get to speak to him properly. He had Twiggy and Jean Shrimpton there. He couldn't concentrate. Think he was also high..."

"Twiggy and Jean Shrimpton? What were they doing there?"

"I didn't get to ask. Maybe they're going to model our clothes."

"Groovy!"

"I asked him when the clothes would be ready for photographs and he said he was going to get them done, said a friend would be taking them."

"Well, that's OK then..."

"No June, it isn't. You can't rely on Mouse. He's not a business person, he's not someone who understands deadlines..."

"You worry too much! He'll deliver."

"We've got three weeks to go and if we don't have photographs for the press then it'll all be complete waste..."

"OK, calm down. I'll talk to him."

"Yeah, please. Go round there, don't call him on the phone. Speak to him face to face. Believe me, I've organised a few press launches in my time and you need to tie every detail down."

"You'll have to come with me, Mark. You're the launch whiz, Mouse will listen to you, won't listen to me telling him to get a move on."

"OK. But don't make it tomorrow evening. I'm out."

She gave him a sarcastic look. "Oh, don't say the wonderful Lynda is back..."

"No, not as far as I know..."

"And - please - don't tell me you're chasing her aunt. She's old enough to be your mother!"

"Hardly. She's only in her forties." He paused. "No, someone else..."

"...really! Who?!"

"Someone I met at Mouse's..."

"Male or female?"

"Female of course!" His voice conveyed a mock disgust.

"Don't pretend you're shocked Mark. I know your little secret."

234

The smile vanished from his face, replaced by an expression significantly more serious. "Secret? What secret?" And as he said the words he knew what June was going to say.

"Your affair with your boss, thirty years older than you!"

He gulped, felt his face going red. "My affair with my boss?"

"Yes, you know darn well. Nigel told me all about it..."

"Nigel?"

"Yes. He also got involved with this guy, Richard. Got to hear all about you. He isn't very discreet, is he?"

"Nigel?"

"No, dope, your boyfriend Richard."

"He's not my boyfriend..."

"I'm not criticising Mark. I'm bi so I'm not making any negative comment..."

"Then why mention it?"

"Don't know, should have kept my trap shut." She paused, squeezed his arm. "Sorry! So, who's the lucky girl?"

"A girl. Jackie. Just met her. She's rather special. Let's leave it at that!" He wanted to learn more about Nigel and Richard but had no intention of encouraging further discussion with June, risking having to reveal more about his relationship with Richard, a period that covered three years, expiring in the early Spring of 1964, after Richard had passed him on to two men in the antiques trade, one young and very handsome, one elderly, like Richard, but with a gut and a pug face. He had been careful not to hint at any relationship in his conversations with Lynda and by the time he first met her, six months later at night school, he regarded it as an aberration, fast-fading. But news that Nigel had engaged in some sexual encounter with Richard piqued his interest and he quietly wondered how he might learn more.

* * * *

235

Mark telephoned Jackie exactly at ten o'clock. He hadn't agreed with her that he would and when she answered her voice collapsed from a cheery *'hello'* to *"oh no, you're not going to cancel are you?"*

He allowed himself a quiet laugh. "No, of course not! I'm just calling to confirm you're still 'on' for tonight."

"Of course! Looking forward to it. Where are we going?"

"Let's go and see the Liz Taylor film, *The Sandpipers*. If you haven't already seen it."

"No, I haven't. Where's it on?"

"Ealing. At the Walpole cinema. You been there?"

"Might have..."

"*Shadow of Your Smile* is the song from the film..."

"Barbra Streisand..."

"Don't think it's a great movie but it does have Richard Burton as well as Liz...

"Saw them in *The VIPs* and that was absolute rubbish..."

"Yes, remember that. Hope this one's better." He paused. "I'll use my car tonight. Pick you up at seven. OK?"

"I'll be ready."

"We'll eat somewhere afterwards. Classy, like a Wimpy."

She laughed. "Sounds good!"

He affected a serious voice. "I'm really looking forward to seeing you, Jackie."

"I'm looking forward to seeing you Mark!"

For the remainder of the day he uncomplainingly fell into a haze, finding it difficult to concentrate on work, desperate for the end of the afternoon to arrive, when he could slip away, rush back to the car on Chatsworth Road and make his way to East Acton and Jackie. But, as fazed as he was, Mark kept up a good act of being involved in, and committed to, his various clients' commercial objectives, as well as the efficient administration of his employer's business. And when he knew he could slip away without precipitating the end of civilisation Mark was off, getting to the car within forty minutes, and to Jackie's an hour after leaving the office at 84 Baker Street.

They kissed lightly at the front door, but with an abandoned passion once inside her bedsit, she pulling him towards the bed. He assumed she was no longer experiencing a period and on the bed she pulled up her skirt while Mark removed her knickers. He entered her roughly, consumed by their mutual passion, and shoved in and out of her, bereft of any finesse. He was above her, their eyes fixed on each other, both smiling at each other's torridly generated excitement, their bodies in a fluid, rhythmic unison as his hips crashed to and fro, Mark eventually climaxing after five minutes, both collapsing in each other's arms, kissing wildly.

After the film, they walked hand in hand along the Broadway, both agreeing *The Sandpipers* was yet another calamitous film for Burton and Taylor. They found a quiet, discreet Chinese restaurant hidden away behind Bentall's department store, and tucked into sweet and sour beef and a glass each of red wine. He reported his and June's meeting the evening before with Mouse, admitting he was unsure of whether the *Red Rooster* clothes range would be ready for a launch, agreeing that the essence of a *'happening'* was something totally unplanned that erupts on the spot and, thus, he shouldn't be too concerned. "Do *'happenings'* happen in Kilburn?" she asked, laughing. "No, they don't!" He joined in her laughter. "Kilburn is a run-down backwater, full of poor whites and blacks. The only happening in Kilburn happens every night when the white cops arrest the blacks. Just because they're black."

"But June thinks that's what makes it different?"

"What, arresting blacks?"

"No, silly! Kilburn!"

"Yes. She says Kilburn gives *Red Rooster* bags of relevance and credibility, the right place to launch a range of clothes for the ordinary girl..."

"At a house party?"

"Yes, she wants what the Americans call a 'bash', a riot of a party. Just the right atmosphere she says to get everyone who matters to the party and in a relaxed frame of mind."

"And you're organising it?"

"Not sure if that's the right word. I'm meant to be getting the gear photographed, writing a press release, and inviting the press..."

"...that's what you do isn't it?"

"Yes, except I don't know he fashion press too well. Don't know it all."

"But you work with people who do. Right?"

"Yeah. Except I can't involve them. I'll have to do it secretly. Can't do work for anyone, especially not a commercial outfit, for free, even in my own time. So, I'll have to copy press lists when no-one is looking. Not easy."

Back at the East Acton flat they went to bed, made love and fell asleep. In the morning he drove to work, found a free parking meter in Montague Square and, with two hours before he risked feeding the meter again, launched his working day with arranging a client visit to Dulux at Slough.

* * * *

Like Doctor Frankenstein connecting his monster to the power, Mark discovered his relationship with Jackie had reconnected him to some divine, supernatural power, the result of which was his newfound self-confidence, bordering on arrogance, the brightness in his voice, his positive demeanour, and his ability to talk back to his boss, albeit with tongue in cheek. Entering its third week, the relationship with Jackie displayed all the signs of being solid and dependable, promising some longevity although he refused to discuss with himself whether she would eventually, inevitably, lose interest. Stay positive *forming, storming, norming, performing.*

He silently repeated to himself the business management litany that he decided applied to his relationship with Jackie. And he felt no compulsion to contact Frankie, ask her out to dinner and attempt to learn how Lynda was faring. He confidently told himself that Lynda's spirit, for so long a living being inside him, was now exorcised. But he mustn't frighten Jackie. No talk of living together, let alone marriage. Let the relationship grow naturally, unforced, untainted by his arrogance, his assumptions about the intellect of the people he met, and keep locked away any airing of his didactic, patronising tone of voice.

And the relationship grew without him applying any undue pressure, very much as it was in his early Warwickshire House days with Lynda. They alternated evenings when they met, opting for Monday, Wednesday and Friday, plus the weekend, but he was careful not to assume Jackie was always free on their nominated evenings. But when she was they'd share their time watching the passing parades along King's and Portobello roads, avoiding Carnaby Street, visiting the occasional club, partying, aware that the autumn was beginning to shorten the days, introducing a chill to late evening air, and that the launch of *Red Rooster* had arrived.

With some trepidation he broached with Jackie his desire to have her dress for the launch in something *groovy, hip, cool.* He expected resentment at the implication she wasn't already garbed in *cool, groovy* clothes. And her disdain at being regarded a chattel. But Jackie was perfectly happy and they toured the shops along King's Road, eventually purchasing a simple floral mini dress from a boutique at the kink in the King's Road, near Roy Brooks' office at World's End.

In bed, Mark found Jackie less adventurous than Lynda, willing to be led but not launch any initiatives, a passivity that marginally irritated him given that in all other aspects she appeared independent and self-sufficient. Perhaps, he told himself, she was maintaining a silence to ensure she didn't do anything that might upset him, or not fully confident with him. Or, he shuddered, she didn't like him enough to throw herself into wild sessions of wanton sex.

On the day of the party he suggested she stay out of the way and arrive mid-evening, explaining that he and June would be heavily committed to bringing together the launch, especially organising Mouse, his models, and the *hip, groovy Red Rooster* gear. Mark had confessed he'd got only negative reaction from the national newspapers, fashion magazines and writers but got a warm response from *Nova,* and *Queen* and the plethora of teen magazines, *Jackie, Boyfriend, Fabulous, Marilyn, Mirabelle, Romeo, Roxy, and Valentine.* And a few of the music rags had also shown some interest. If they all turned up it would be a coup. He'd mailed them all the press release and photographs so their promise to attend the party was taken with a pinch of salt but their interest buoyed his confidence.

Without any discussion June decided to abandon using the ska music group in which they had invested a Saturday evening hovering outside the Shakespeare, waiting to be secreted into the house party in Maida Vale to see them perform. Leaving it until a few hours before the party was due to begin before informing him, Mark regarded her action as high-handed but bit his tongue, intrigued at her alternative choice, a psychedelic band with the name of The Smoke, a group of four musicians whom, she enthused, came with a light show. They were, June said, part of Mouse's group of friends. "Not called *tiger in the smoke*?"

"What?" June looked anxious.

"*Tiger in the Smoke.* It was a cops and robbers film, about five years ago. *The Smoke* is criminal slang for London."

"No, Mark. Just called The Smoke."

"Let's hope they're good!

"They're knockout!" She opened her handbag, took out her purse. "This is for you. From Mouse. Make sure you're in the groove at the launch." In her palm were two small pills. He recognised one as a French Blue, the other mescaline, identical to the one that gave him the trip on Primrose Hill. "If that's mesco, then I'll have another, if you have it. I want to take Jackie on a trip, it'll be her first."

She dug a pill from her purse, handed it to her. "Give me back the French blue."

He was superfluous when Mouse and his *Little Red Rooster* partners, Nick and Toby, arrived with six girls dressed in the *Red Rooster* range of mini length *hip groovy gear.* They buzzed around June in excited conversation and he could only watch, expecting to be summoned but was quietly pleased when they continued without him, showing no signs of requiring his contribution. Instead he found a role when The Smoke arrived, guitars, amplifiers and drum cases spilling from their arms. He took them to the end of the living room from where he and June had decided they should perform.

And with Anna, Kay and Paul he watched with admiration as the group expertly set up, surprised at their acceptance of the small performance area they'd been given, plugging in the little black box that projected a series of moving, changing coloured shapes on the wall and ceiling, some blobs travelling faster than others, while some metamorphosed into images resembling snakes and worms, or bacteria under a microscope, each shape chasing the other before merging and reforming. For Mark it was *déjà vu*. It was his mescaline trip on Primrose Hill.

Before meeting Lynda the number of parties he had attended was less than the fingers of one hand. But in the brief six months they'd been together he'd gone from famine to feast, each party a lesson, learning about hip, cool London, and the hip, cool people loosening the city's sclerotic, rigid body, energizing it, transforming it from rooted *rigor mortis* to sudden, garish life, juvenile japes, freedom, promise and optimism. He understood perfectly why June wanted to launch *Red Rooster* in a flat in Kilburn. It was one of London's poorest areas, a long history of Irish immigration. Now black immigrants from the West Indies. It pretended to be nothing else but impoverished, ignored, raw, basic, the opposite end of the galaxy to Chelsea's King's Road, Kensington's Biba, and the West End's Carnaby Street.

In the first wave of guests materialised Jackie. He broke into a broad smile. She looked stunning, his breath taken away by not just the floral mini dress he'd bought her on King's Road, but the white knee length boots she paired with the dress, boots he'd never seen her wear before. He kissed her lightly on the lips. "You look so sexy in those boots. They go so well with the dress. You look a million dollars, like someone on *Ready, Steady Go!*" She smiled. "Glad you approve!" She squeezed his hand, folding her arm around his. "Where are your flat mates? Which one is June? And Mouse?"

He pointed at the group surrounding the models in the *Red Rooster* gear. "They're busy talking to the fashion people from the magazines."

"You managed to get some here?"

"Yeah. Half a dozen have turned up. *Nova, Jackie, Mirabelle*, a few others."

"Good for you, darling!"

He enjoyed the compliment, kissed her. "Be interesting to see if any music people turn up. A lot of them know Mouse. So, who knows?"

"And Twiggy and Jean Shrimpton!"

Soon after pub closing time the second wave arrived, filling the living room, people spilling into the garden but in the crush he didn't recognise any well-known pop stars or musicians. No Brian Jones, Donovan, Sandie Shaw, or Cilla Black, but suspected there were a few musicians in the throng, all waiting for their *Big Break*. Doubtless, Mark told himself, they were the source of the exotic aromas that began to fill the space above everyone's heads, wondering if June would delve into her stash to roll a joint or two, or opt for a tab of amphetamine, or some mescaline. He fingered the two pills in the back pocket of his Levis, excited by the thought of taking Jackie with him on their first trip together, wondering the best time to embark. He had no idea when the band would end their stint but assumed they'd not go beyond one a.m. The party would then begin to thin, Mark told himself, sure to reveal June, Mouse, his girlfriend, Suzie, plus others, all sitting in a circle somewhere, floating free, worshipping at the high alter of pot. If they were huddled in a darkly-lit corner, that would be the ideal setting for his and Jackie's own magic carpet ride.

Mark was quietly pleased that Jackie remained with him during the party. It contrasted with Lynda who, at parties, for effect and to unnerve him, fire his jealousy, would abandon him, behaving as if single, not in a relationship. He decided that, on balance, he much preferred Jackie's loyalty even if it revealed a lack of strident individuality or independence. He told himself that if they were faults he preferred them to Lynda's unfaithfulness. What worried him though, deep in his brain like one of those little worms he found when shelling his father's garden peas for Sunday lunch, as a kid in the mid-1950s, was his head's refusal to forget Lynda. She kept returning to his consciousness, getting in the way, like telephone engineers sitting in a hole in the pavement, disturbing a clear course ahead, forcing him to go round the obstruction.

But he couldn't wait for June and Mouse to gather in a corner and took Jackie's hand. "Let's go upstairs." She didn't move. "What about the party darling? You can't leave it..."

"We'll come back later...it's June's party anyway. Her and Mouse..." He continued to walk, she followed and inside his

243

bedroom, her back against the door, they kissed, lightly at first, then with a growing passion. She said nothing as his hands pulled her knickers down but unzipped him, a hand deftly entering his Levis, bringing out his erection, stroking it as they kissed. He broke away, slipped a hand inside his back pocket. "Let's have some really great sex darling. Go on a very sexy trip." Fingers found and pulled the two white tablets from his back pocket. He rolled them into his palm. Jackie looked at them. "What are they? Bennies?"

"No. Mescaline. You'll have a dream like trip and you'll be very randy, make sure you have some great sex, we'll have some great sex..."

"What's mescaline? Sounds like something Aztec."

"Could be. They give you this fantastic magic carpet ride. Magical colours, shapes, birds, dragons, all sorts..."

"Mark, don't like the idea of that. I mean, what if you get ill? I won't be able to help, I'll be just as out of things as you. What if I get ill? You wouldn't be able to do anything about me, you'd be completely high, totally out of it!"

Mark was dumbfounded, and began to get annoyed. He had not expected Jackie, his girlfriend, to deny his request. OK, he told himself , they'd hadn't been in a relationship for much more than a month but he had told himself Jackie was enamoured of him, if not besotted. But she wasn't. There was no unquestioning of his desire to be *cool, hip, groovy*. Instead, he decided, she was being very suburban, very provincial.

"I don't mind bennies, Mark. Or French blues. They're speed, used to take those in my *Ricky Tick* days, when I was thirteen. You can have some really great sex on speed!"

He broke away. "I know that Jackie, but I don't have any speed, just mescaline..."

"OK, let's go back downstairs, clear the party out, then have a joint with June and Mouse and your flatmates, then back here. How's that?"

Mark smiled, kissed her lightly, opened the door. But as he walked onto the landing, he heard a loud voice, muscular, rich in testosteronic menace. He couldn't make out what was being said but instantly knew the voice belonged to a police officer. He walked back into the room, Jackie right behind him. "What's up?"

He whispered. "It's the police. It's a raid."

"Shit! Stuff those pills away somewhere..."

"One of my suits, in a pocket."

"They may not come up here."

"Have you got any drugs on you?"

"None. Have you got anything else here?"

"No, but June has a stash in her bedside drawer." He motioned her silence with a finger at his lips as he attempted to listen through the shut door. He abandoned that and went to the bedroom window. Below him was the front garden and Chatsworth Road, and he stood behind the curtain and waited for either more police to arrive, or those in the living room to finally leave. He breathed a sigh of immense relief as he witnessed two uniforms leave the house and climb into their Morris Minor *Panda* patrol car, and drive away.

He turned. "They've gone, let's go downstairs."

In the living room there were a few small groups standing around, motionless, talking to each other in conspiratorial huddles in an arid atmosphere, free of any music from any source. He walked across to June, seeing immediately that she had been crying. She was standing in a tight circle with Mouse, his girlfriend, and business partners. He put an arm around her shoulder. "What happened?" She didn't answer but Mouse did. "They said they'd got a complaint about noise but I think they were fishing for drugs." He paused, looked at June. "Luckily, they didn't find any. They didn't look too hard, think it was a warning. Hold another party and they'll search everyone and everything."

"They didn't bother going upstairs, checking bedrooms."

"No. Not sure, think they need a search warrant for that." Mark knew there was nothing he could add without sounding lightweight but he ploughed ahead. "How did the launch go? Get to talk to all the magazines?"

Mouse shrugged his shoulders. "Think so. We'll have to see if they use anything."

"They might call you on Monday for more info."

"Can I help clear up?" It was Jackie, clearly marginalised by any conversations to do with police raids and fashion magazines. "Where d'you keep the black bags?"

* * * *

For the fashion magazine journalists who remained late at the party Mark fully expected the police raid would make their reports hum with excitement, delivering to the *Red Rooster* launch a *groovy hipness* that money couldn't acquire. Indeed, at the party, the people from *Nova* magazine wondered if the police raid was all part of the *happening*, whether it was real or the men in uniform were costumed out of work actors. Mark checked every daily newspaper every morning for anything about the launch. Checking the papers for client references or anything connected with their business was a 'standing order' every morning when he arrived at the office. Only this time, for a few weeks, he closely perused the fashion pages. Only the *Daily Sketch* ran a small paragraph of no useful effect. Mark quietly hoped the teen and women's interest magazines would 'do the business' as his office colleagues would say of anyone expected to produce success for a client.

Every bone in his body wanted to lobby Jackie to abandon her bedsit in East Acton and share a bed and room with him in Chatsworth Road, Kilburn. But every time he felt such warm feelings wash over him he went for a metaphorical cold shower. She had made no noises to encourage him to consider her moving in, itself a fact that worried him, if only in the margins. If she was so enamoured of him, he told himself, why hadn't she suggested they live together? It was an irritant that he was able to push back into the shadows given his history of cloying togetherness with Lynda.

There were other ways of being together, he informed himself. And suggested to Jackie a weekend away, 'somewhere warm', informing her that his Aunt Joan and her husband, a German, Kurt, owned a small hotel on Jersey, overlooking the sea at a place called L'Etacq. They compared calendars and agreed early October for a long weekend on the island as all the holiday brochures reported mild, sunny weather in weeks forty-one and two. Mark suggested they take the train to Weymouth, then boat to St Helier. He confirmed with his aunt who would meet them at the port, and a few days later he had all the necessary tickets, overnight sailing, he and Jackie would have to sleep on couchettes. And another four days they were boarding the mid-evening boat train at Waterloo.

"Joan's my father's youngest sister. He had two, he's the eldest I think, then came Wyn, then Joan. Think she was born in 1920. I used to fantasise about her when I was a kid in the fifties. She was so slim and sexy in her seamed stockings and high heels!"

Jackie pulled a face. "My gawd! The family that lays together stays together!"

"Don't say anything but Joan was in a very juicy divorce case, made the *News of the Screws*..."

"*News of the Screws*?"

"*News of the World*! Like now, in the fifties it didn't have any news in it, just jam-packed full of juicy divorce reports. And that included Joan's divorce from her first husband. All sorts came out in the court, from notes in shoes left at the local menders to the Duke of Edinburgh fancying her when he visited his hairdresser's in St James's. Joan was the receptionist there at the time..."

"When was all this?"

"Mid-fifties sometime. My dad had to go to court, act as a character witness for her. But my mum stopped him going so they had to subpoena him!"

"So, Kurt was the man she left her first husband for?"

"Oh, no! Kurt only came along a few years ago. No idea where the met but they got married and at some point got this hotel in Jersey."

"And I assume you don't want me to mention any of the divorce?"

"Good God no!" Mark laughed. "It's one of the family skeletons!"

Neither Mark nor Jackie had slept well, but cleaned themselves up and waited on the upper deck as the ship entered St Helier. He hadn't seen his aunt in over five years since the Christmas when she was a guest in his parents' house. When he recognised her on the dockside, he waved. He saw no aging in her face, she remained slim, dressed in white summer slacks that fitted tight around her slender backside. Beneath the hem of the slacks he spied yellow high-heeled sandals. Kurt, however, was rotund, red-faced, immensely jovial and friendly, and with full disembarkation, he wildly shook Mark and Jackie's hand. The car journey was less than fifteen minutes and Joan dominated its duration along winding country roads with an excited, urgent list of all the places on Jersey they could visit. "Too much for one weekend, aunt! We go back on Monday!"

"I'm Joan. Call me Joan! And Kurt is Kurt!"

"Sure thing. Joan."

"Now we're out of season we have more time and we normally go the casino on a Saturday evening. We know the owners, and we have a meal there. Very good food, then we watch the cabaret show. Then we do some gambling. Not too much. Haven't got much to lose!"

"Any discotheques in Jersey?"

Joan displayed her community pride. "Yes! We have at least one, in St Helier, called the Dungeon. We could go there after the cabaret show. It's open to three a.m. We know the owners."

The hotel was a modern, two-storey structure with a grey slate Mansard roof, built on a cliff top, some hundred feet above a bay. Their bedroom, on the top floor via a staircase, was large and well-appointed, dominated by a double-bed. Mark walked around the room, into the bathroom. "Looks like they've given us the honeymoon suite." They unpacked their grips, hung up clothes, put them away in drawers. Jackie peered out the window across to the cliff edge. "Looks like it's going to stay sunny and warm, if not hot. I'd like to do some sunbathing." Mark pulled a face. "Don't you want to go on a tour of the island? That's what Joan and Kurt would like to do. They're very proud of the island, want to show it off."

"Can't we do that tomorrow? I'm sure Joan and Kurt won't mind, after all we're here on a break and there's no sun like this back in London." Jackie put on a floral bikini that Mark took an instant dislike to. It was not only large but looked like something she'd acquired at the jumble sale. Or, more likely a bikini she'd been wearing since teenage years. If they ever went away again to somewhere in the sun he vowed to buy her beforehand a few bikinis that were fashionably scantier and stark plain.

They both walked down the hundred wooden, not too secure steps from the cliff top to the beach. Joan and Kurt had given them a large beach blanket and they promised to be back for the lunch Kurt was cooking them all. Jackie had brought *Buddwing* to read and behind sun glasses laid herself out on the blanket, restarting where she had last left the story. Mark, in his fashionably scanty swimming briefs, placed himself alongside Jackie, opened his copy of *The Spy Who Came in From the Cold* bought in Soho as an import from America, courtesy of Transworld Publications, importers of his *Playboy* and *Billboard* magazines.

"Have you read this?" Jackie waved the *Buddwing* paperback at him.

"No, I haven't. It's a sex novel isn't it?"

"No, it isn't. It has lots of sex but it's about a guy who's lost his memory, doesn't know who he is. Tries to find out..."

"Sounds interesting..."

"Except it's really about America trying to find out who it is, not this one man."

"Right. So, it's a metaphor, this guy losing his memory, searching for who he really is."

"Is that what 'metaphor' means?"

"Believe so. Maybe I mean 'analogy'. Not sure."

"Have you been to America?"

"Not yet. I did think of trying to get a PR job in New York, wrote to the American Institute of Public Relations and they told me I needed a sponsor to get a job in the US."

"How do you get that?"

"With difficulty!" He paused. "But I have an aunt who lives in Orlando, Florida..."

"Another aunt! Why aren't we on a beach in Florida instead of Jersey?"

He laughed. "But when I wrote to my aunt she never replied, so guessed she had no interest in sponsoring me, or getting involved in any ideas I had for working in the States." He ran a finger across the flat of her stomach. "But we could go to New York for Christmas and New Year's Eve. They know how to celebrate it there."

"Think my parents expect me to spend it with them. I always have, ever since I was born!"

"Same with my parents but that's no reason for not changing it..."

"Except it's all about families at Christmas..."

"But change is all around us now. We shouldn't be hidebound by old conventions. This is the mid-sixties, not the mid-fifties."

"You're more forward-thinking than me. I'm very conventional, bit like my parents." She paused. "But I like being with you, someone who dares to think differently." She laughed. "You know, I didn't have a mini-dress until you got me a few. Never been to King's Road before!"

"But you did get to Portobello Road."

"Only because I read something about it and finally made an effort to see it, after work, too bored to go home to a bedsit, sit all alone..."

"Glad you did! We'd never have met if you hadn't gone to Portobello, walked into *Little Red Rooster*." He leant across and they kissed. "Have you thought about moving in with me, Jackie?"

"Yes I have, Mark. But it's too soon. Think we should leave it a bit longer. Maybe after Christmas?"

"You like me, but not that much."

"I like you lot, Mark. But we've only known each other a month or so. I haven't even told my parents about you. They don't know I've got a boyfriend, let alone moving in with him!"

He shrugged his shoulders. "Do they need to know about us before you move in?"

"I think so, Mark. You don't know my parents, they're very old fashioned, living together without being married is 'living in sin'! They'd be up in arms, create a really awful scene."

"It's your life, Jackie, not theirs."

"Of course it is but they are very Victorian, set in their ways so if I'm going to talk to them about us living together, or going to New

York for Christmas I have to find a way of taking it step by step, no upsets, no feeling their sweet, innocent daughter has let them down..."

"I guess they don't know you're on the pill."

"Of course not! She fell silent for a few seconds. "But, then, you didn't ask if I was..."

"No, I didn't but most girls are, aren't they?"

"Maybe. But you assumed, you didn't ask..."

"Sorry, I automatically assumed when we had sex the first time you were on the pill. If you weren't then I assumed you'd say so and it'd be me who'd have to use a johnny. When my last girlfriend and I started to have sex she went on the pill straightaway. I didn't say anything, she didn't discuss it, she just did it."

"I was already on the pill when we met, from when I had my previous boyfriend. But after we broke up I could have come off but didn't. Thought we might get back together."

Mark sped away from the subject. "So, you're staying in East Acton. And you want to stay in Aylesbury for Christmas."

"Maybe. Don't know."

* * * *

In the third week of October, for the first time in six months, and after a weekend on his own while Jackie went home to her parents, Mark found himself waking up to a chill Monday in his bedroom. In the corner was a small, two-bar heater that was clearly insufficient for the large size of his room. He flicked it on as he slipped from his bed and headed towards the bathroom, returning from a hot shower to a room bristling with cold, the anaemic bars of the heater unsurprisingly producing no noticeable change in the room's temperature. He vowed to make it the basis for a fresh bid to convince Jackie to join him at Chatsworth Road, cuddling together through the winter to make not just a warm bed but hot sex.

The *happening* had become a fond memory, a rich vein mined for various conversations but June had to admit that the sparse coverage in the weekly teen magazines was not encouraging. Mark attempted being positive with promises that the monthly women's press would 'do the biz'. And Mouse lost interest, more concerned at retaining his *Little Red Rooster* boutique's name as a *cool, hip, groovy* designer amongst swinging London's movers and shakers, leaving June to work out with Nigel a future for *Red Rooster* clothes. During the evenings he was ensconced at Chatsworth Road with June, Mark enjoyed Nigel's company. He was erudite, witty and exceptionally good looking, a slender face framed in black, tightly curled hair, and Mark remained intrigued at his affair, if that what is was, with Richard, Mark's old boss.

It did not surprise him when, a week or so after the *happening* he bumped into Nigel after a client meeting. They joked and jousted and agreed to meet for a drink that evening. Although he spoke later to Jackie he didn't say a word about meeting Nigel. He felt very uncomfortable, as if he was being unfaithful, but could not mention Nigel to her, she would jump to a conclusion, make the wrong assumption, he told himself. But why did he want to meet Nigel? Was it just a drink, a catch-up, comparing notes on Richard, or more? The answer partly arrived with a phone call from Nigel, switching the venue for the drinks from the Sussex in Upper St Martin's Lane to the Grenadier in Knightsbridge, a well-known male homosexual haunt. Mark was positive, laughing, recalling his affair with Richard and the occasional evening spent there with him and his queer friends, before they all removed for sex to Richard's weekday flat in John Adam Street.

He did not feel tricked when he saw Nigel standing at the bar with Richard. It was so predictable he told himself but, what's more his head told him, he really wanted Richard's company. It had been some eighteen months since they had last met with no contact since apart from a Christmas card. Richard got him a *whiskey mac* and for Mark it was a surreal hour spent discussing their mutual sexual relationships. It was something of a relief when he suggested they get dinner, departing for the Strand Palace Hotel, from where they could walk to his flat, at the top of a vertiginous seven floor, late-Georgian terrace, on the corner of John Adam Street and Robert Street. And Mark enjoyed the sex, cursing silently that he had regressed all too easily from his absolute heterosexual state to his all too comfortable homosexual setting, fellating both Richard and Nigel, fully aware that he'd gossip to June at the earliest opportunity.

It was one in the morning and he sat sullenly in the cab he hailed on Villiers Street that took him back to Chatsworth Road, increasingly annoyed at what he'd done that evening, and why. He tried to tell himself it was his weakness, his lack of self-discipline, his poor morals. But it didn't wash. It was half the story. He tried hard not to admit it but his relationship with Jackie was not all-consuming, not all-diverting, nothing as complete or total as that with Lynda. No wonder when queer temptation came his way he cravenly acquiesced. He comforted himself with the thought, the concept, that had he still been with Lynda there'd be holes in his relationship, and anyway Lynda was sufficiently sophisticated and cultured to cope with any of his sexual indiscretions. After all, he told himself, she'd dallied with lesbianism while at Warwickshire House, and clearly enjoyed the sex with June, Mouse and his girlfriend. He just hoped Nigel would maintain some sophistication and not blab to June. He cursed his luck.

* * * *

Mark hadn't been in more than ten minutes, was still the first in the room he shared with two others - Sue with the irritating low self-esteem, and Terry, *Rockfist Rogan* in the unassuming Burton's suit – when the phone rang. Early! Bloody Dulux! "Hi, Bob!" The voice laughed and his jaw dropped. It was Lynda. "Who's Bob?"

"Hi, Lynda! A pleasant surprise. How are you?"

"I'm fine..."

"You in London?"

"Yes, staying with my aunt for a few days. You free today for lunch?"

"Sure thing! Let's go to the Greek we went to a few times. The Hellenic, the one near where I work. Best Greek in town!"

"Yeah, OK, I remember it. Run by a family."

"See you here in our reception at twelve-thirty. The address is on my business card."

"Sorry, Mark, don't have that with me."

"No excuses, Lynda. Should be the closest thing to your heart. It's eighty-four Baker Street. I'll be waiting in reception at twelve-thirty!"

She looked spectacular. The camel trouser suit was the one he'd bought her in March from Peter Robinson's in The Strand for her birthday. Her hair was swept back into a bun, forehead and face a gentle English summer brown, blue eye shadow was more vivid than he recalled, and the safe mid-red on her lips and finger nails would never have been his choice. But he approved of the vast expanse of tanned chest displayed with it hint of cleavage, a gilt halter chain around her neck.

"So, are you still crouping?"

"Yes, 'til the end of the end of October then I'll probably stop."

"Probably?"

"Well, all the summer cabaret clubs are closing and that only leaves one club up in Blackpool and I don't fancy working there all winter."

"So, you're coming to work in London?"

"No, don't want to work in London ever again." She paused, spread a large pearl of humous onto her pita bread, delicately lifting it to her mouth, closing teeth around it, chewing for a few seconds before continuing. "I'm thinking of taking a City and Guilds course in arts and crafts. I want to design and make furniture. My own company."

"Impressive. But City and Guilds is London, it's near where you used to work, Liverpool Street station. If you study there you'd have to live in London."

"Yes, some of my course would be in London, the rest of it in Peterborough. I'd drive down, stay with my aunt, then back home, live with my parents."

"Why furniture?"

"Why not? I know a few people who would pay to have their own furniture, their own design, and made by craftsmen. And women."

"And you need a City and Guilds for that?"

"Think so. Need to understand how to design, make things, sell things..."

"So there's no chance of us getting back together?"

"No, Mark. I just don't want any ties, any involvement, just want to concentrate on achieving something, anything but sitting at a typewriter, doing shorthand. Bored out of my brain!"

"What about PR? You could work in a PR agency, working for fashion or perfume accounts..."

"Really, Mark, I'm not a PR person! Not being rude but I want to make a better contribution than that!"

"Nothing wrong with PR Lynda. It all makes the world go round. If you start a business selling things then you'll want publicity. If you don't know how to go about it then you'll want an expert. That'll be a PR person!" Mark paused and looked directly in Lynda's eyes. "I was hoping we'd get back together Lynda, hoping your spell as a croupier was just a way of you working something out, then you'd come back to London, and we'd get back together, not the same as before, maybe do something different, maybe start a business..."

"No, Mark, it isn't going to happen. I'm moving on, life doesn't stand still, none of us do, that includes you..."

"...what's the betting if we hadn't met you'd still be a typist at British Railways..."

"I was a secretary Mark, a secretary..."

"But do you think you'd have left the job for blackjack and roulette?"

"Yes, Mark, I'm not stupid, I know when we met you took me out of myself, got me living again, knocked some life into me, got me out of the rut I was in..."

"I was your first boyfriend in a long time..."

"Yes, Mark, you were. Until you came along all I had was that creepy boss of mine, sex with him was revolting, can't believe I actually sucked him off in the office, and we actually went away twice for a dirty weekend. Can't believe his wife didn't know what was going on!"

"I had this concept in my head, for us. It was Chatsworth Road. The two of us together, making it together, making a life, being together, us against the world, like Sonny and Cher..."

"You're making me laugh Mark. We were never a 'concept,' we weren't one of Lionel Bart's musicals, Mark."

"You know what I mean..."

"Mark, we were just a boy and a girl. That's all!"

"Not for me Lynda. You were always a lot more, bags more. You still are. You were the first girl I ever fell in love with, first ever since leaving school in fifty-eight. Everything about you just yelled out to me. Your looks, your hair, great legs, your intellect, your sophistication. I'd never seen anything like it before..."

"You must have led a very sheltered life..."

"I'm serious Lynda. We met just over a year ago at Princeton College and we began by talking to each other in the tea breaks in the lessons, and we pretty soon discovered we were identical in so many things, liked so much the same things, books, music, films, theatre. And I really admired you for leaving home for London, your bravery, getting on and doing something with your life..."

"I wasn't that exceptional Mark. I was living in a hostel when we met, hardly anything to boast about..."

"That wasn't because you lacked imagination, just circumstances. But we put that way behind us and built a great relationship, really different, positive, and I really can't cope with having to admit we're over, finished. We can't be! We had something so good, so wonderful, we can't be through Lynda, all that destroyed, gone!"

"Mark, all you really wanted was marriage, and I wasn't interested. It wasn't what I wanted, now or then. I'm only twenty-four! I don't want to get married for years yet. And you shouldn't either. You're even younger than me. You shouldn't be thinking about marriage, you should be thinking about seeing the world. Look at young people today, they're not marrying like their parents did, they're travelling the world, India, Australia, Canada, Africa, you name it..."

"I'm not talking about marriage Lynda. I dumped that ages ago, and you know it. I'm talking about a partnership..."

"Same difference, Mark. I don't want to be tied down, my view of our relationship is different to yours. I didn't fall in love with you, Mark. We had a very enjoyable relationship, a great time together but it wasn't hearts and flowers for me like it was for you. Sorry, it just wasn't..."

"So, that's it, end of Mark and Lynda. Rest in peace." Mark was deflated but, silently, vowed never to give up on her and their relationship. He swore it would rebirth one day.

"When I start this City and Guilds thing I will call you and we can meet every now and again for a drink or meal. As friends. We can be good friends can't we?"

Mark smiled wanly. "Sure! Of course!"

"Do you need the Mini, the car?"

"Why, you want it?"

"Well, I need to get up and down the A1 when I start my City and Guilds course..."

"Can't do it by train?"

"Not that easily. Better to have a car, especially in my first year, not so necessary in my second year when I don't have to come to London every week..."

"And you want the Mini?"

"Well, my dad did give fifty pounds towards it. If you aren't using it..."

"I do, work, going to parties..."

"You can use cabs, can't you?"

"Maybe..."

"Well, if you want to keep it can you give me back the fifty pounds? I can put it towards my own car."

"So, that's what our relationship has come down to? Fifty pounds?"

"Don't be silly, Mark. My dad gave us the money before things changed..."

"Yes, when you told him and your mum that we were the real thing, that you'd finally found the man who meant something more to you than a one-night stand..."

"OK, Mark, yes I did tell them I thought we were in a serious relationship, not likely to go off the rails. Yes, I got it wrong." She paused. "Now, can I have the fifty pounds back, Mark? Please."

"No! You can have the car. I need to get a bigger one, thinking of an Austin Eleven Hundred. You can give me back the fifty pounds I put in to buy the Mini."

"OK. So, can we do that this afternoon? Can we go back to Chatsworth Road to get the car?"

"See if I can get the afternoon off. I've got no meetings. Might be able to work it if my colleagues can cover for me."

"Well, I could make it worth your while." She paused, a smile curling her lips. "Would you like some sex?"

"Where, at Frankie's?"

"No, stupid! At yours, Chatsworth Road." She laughed. "Just sex, Mark, no strings. OK?"

"Do you have a boyfriend?"

"I do. Not serious of course. And you, got a girlfriend?"

"Yes, I do. But we don't live together."

On the bed he rolled them a joint as she took his erect penis in her mouth, gurgling her appreciation as she brought him off, his semen filling her mouth. She fell into his shoulder as they smoked the weed. The sex that followed the interval was muscular, robust, with both in a ravenous devouring of the other, bodies crashing against each other, as if seeking a prize for all-consuming carnality, suffused with a basic, inelegant animalism. Lynda brought her legs up around the small of Mark's back and lifted herself perpendicular, kissing him with a physical passion, her tongue inside his mouth, withdrawing to whisper encouragement. "You're so big Mark. I can feel you right up inside me," pounding her body against his in emphasis. And he responded by sinking his teeth into her neck. He had promised himself he would balance the books, leave his florid shadow on her neck, in the identical position to the bite she paraded that day he visited her in Hunstanton.

Mark knew, more than sensed, Lynda was appreciably more wanton than during their relationship, their time together. She was clearly more abandoned than he remembered, revealing herself totally in tune with his desires, she pressing her neck into his teeth, willing him on to leave a deep, livid bite, she emitting a low undulating moan of growing ecstasy as his teeth obliged.

Mark suspended his pelvic thrusts as he finally climaxed inside her, Lynda responding with an energized, passionate kiss, her hands behind his head, pressing his mouth onto hers before they fell in unison onto the pillows, both breaking out in a juvenile laughter, he realising for the first time both their bodies were wet with rivulets of perspiration.

Outside he stood by the car as she climbed in, desperate to say something that would have her halting her progress, stopping, getting out and telling him, *'yes, Mark, you're right, you're the only man for me, and I'm coming back to live with you...'* Instead, feeling completely hopeless, all he could do was lean into the window as she fired up the engine. "Lynda, you do know we're unfinished business, don't you?"

She smiled. "Yes, Mark. I know we are."

THE END